Fakin' It

by

Diana Rubino

Fakin' It

Cover Art by *Tina Lynn*

The Wild Rose Press
PO Box 708
Adams Basin, NY 14410-0706
Visit us at www.thewildrosepress.com

Publishing History
First Faery Rose Edition, 2010
Print ISBN 1-60154-710-2
Previously released: Domhan books, 2001
Too Much For Words

Published in the United States of America

"Now tell me what's so urgent. I hope this leaded coffee you're pumping me with will keep me awake." He drummed his fingers on the cup.

"Felix, don't be shocked, now." She sat across from him. "We've been through a lot together, haven't we?" She clasped her palms together. They were starting to sweat. A lot.

"I can see this is going to be an all-nighter. Let me guess. You've been selling these books like hot dogs at a Yankee game, so I know you can't be having financial problems."

"No, it's not financial."

He lifted a brow. "You're being stalked by a jealous ex? Or a wacko fan?"

"No, none of my exes care enough to be jealous, and fans don't get wacko until you run out of freebies at signings." She took a sip of milk.

"You got me. What can it possibly be?" He gulped his latte.

"It's about...I don't even know what to call him. Your creation."

"What about him?"

She drew in a deep breath and blurted it out, "I want him."

Praise for *FAKIN' IT*

"*FAKIN' IT* is what science fiction novelist Judi Somers gets when she begs Felix, her old school chum turned brilliant scientist, to translate her fictional hero into a lifelike android.

"On paper, Race Parsec is an interplanetary swashbuckling hero, the man against whom she measures all other men. But for Felix, who's been in love with Judi for years, creating her perfect mate is pure agony. But Felix gets even when he delivers the man of Judi's dreams—or is he?

"With nods to several SF writers, Diana Rubino's narrative is a funny, entertaining peek at what happens when one woman actually gets what she asked for. This is a refreshing departure from Ms. Rubino's historical writing."

~Kelly Rae Cooper, Romantic Times (Top Pick, 4.5 stars)

Dedication

To Chris, my real hero.

Chapter One

The Three Steps Down Café
Bleecker Street, New York City

"Okay, how can I end this so they'll come begging for more?" With one last creative blast, Judi poised her fingers on her laptop keyboard and tapped out the grand finale of her tenth novel in the wildly popular series.

Race Parsec maneuvered the battle shuttle Venture through the conquered enemy's floating debris. Another victory—but to him, just another mission to save Earth. Entering Mother Earth's atmosphere, he radioed Starbase Central. "This is the Venture. I'll be coming in at seventeen-hundred hours, more or less." He then made a detour. On the way to base, he swung by and picked up a dozen roses and two steaks—it was his turn to cook dinner.
THE END

"Yes! The End!" After nineteen drafts and a two-week trek to Antarctica, Judi finally finished Barbarian Hordes of the Dark Nebula, number ten in the Race Parsec series. She scrolled up to the Prologue, where Race bade his ladylove farewell on the launching pad.

She mouthed the words from her monitor: "Finestra, my love for you transcends the vastness of space, however warped."

Judi closed her eyes and sighed. Oh, to live in her made-up world, where heroes never cheated, and lovers never grew apart, no matter how many galaxies separated them. "If only love could transcend warped space in our universe."

She glanced over her rimless specs. No one paid attention to the muttering redhead in the newsboy cap. The literati here at Three Steps Down tapped on laptops, read from their Kindles, and chatted with others—or with themselves.

The Village Vanguard rated this place Number One for trendsetters in poetry, film noir, and flavored lattes. The whirring ceiling fans created a pillowy breeze. A young Usher wannabee sang off-key with no kicking bass or backup hotties, only snapping fingers.

Tonight she dressed more BoHo than usual in a flowered Foery of Scotland dress with a cascade of frills down the front, a bronze-buttoned military style coat, and Arturo Bandini boots. Although the new boots squeezed her toes like thumbscrews, the mix of wools and tweeds and dainty details gave her a kick. In this setting, she became the live version of her futuristic nom de plume, Juno Ursa.

Judi glanced at her watch. Race and the barbarian hordes took a few weeks over deadline to ride off into the setting suns, as Iris, her editor, climbed the walls.

You poor dear, Iris. At least find a man to climb.

Inhaling the sweet caramel aroma of coffee, she scanned the blackboard on the wall. Conversation Colombia boasted an extra shot of caffeine, to help deadline-weary writers sprint that last mile. Just as she narrowed her choice down to Bleecker Nutty Blend, her gaze landed on an academic type standing at the bar alone. His searching eyes and friendly smile told her he hoped someone, male or female, would give him the time of day. In his shirt buttoned-up dress shirt, black tailored blazer, and black khaki pants, he looked far too Upper West

Side, and probably knew it. Could that be—no! Feeling brazen, she snapped the laptop shut, cocked her newsboy cap back a fraction, and approached the bar. Reaching across him to grab a packet of As Sweet As Sugar, she attempted a casual bump.

She looked again.

"It is him!" she said to herself out loud.

She inched closer. It was him, all right, her childhood pal who'd stayed home on prom night to calculate the diameter of Pluto's third moon. The ally who helped her clean up after her wild parties. Those laser-green eyes sparkled even in this room's low glow.

"Felix!"

He scanned her from cap to boots. He didn't utter a word, but his dubious expression and cocked brow said it all: And who the hell are you?

She swept off the glasses and cap. "It's me, Judi!"

An instant smile gladdened his features as he gave her shoulders a quick squeeze. "Judi, I can't believe it! How've you been?"

Studying Felix, she saw that the last decade or so hadn't been too hard on him. His face had filled out a bit, he still sported a full head of blond hair, and the uptown duds hugged a set of six-pack abs.

"Hangin' tough, I guess."

"You look like a successful author." He gestured at her, up and down.

"Thanks, but authors don't usually dress like this. I usually live in sweats."

"Well, I'm sure dressed a little too M.I.T. for the occasion." He smoothed down his tailored blazer.

"They do admit the token scientist occasionally. It's not all posers."

They shared a tension-easing laugh.

"Is this one of your usual hangouts?" He glanced around and then zeroed back in on her.

"It's an occasional haunt. I don't hang out with writers. I don't know any poets, either. Dead or alive. But what are you doing down here? I'd expect to run into you at the Intergalactic Space Museum, but not anywhere subterranean."

Felix just wasn't the below-Fourteenth-Street type. The "hip" Village had never been his scene.

"I had dinner with some colleagues, and we came down here for coffee. They just left, but I thought I'd get one for the road. Where do you call home these days?"

"I own a loft on West Ninth and lease the one next door to a couple of sculptors. I've been living there since the divorce settlement." As she moved nearer him to close up the space, she inhaled a long-forgotten woodsy fragrance. The long-defunct Bengardino for Men! Only rare perfume stores had that—and not too often.

"Yeah, your dad told me. I ran into him and your stepmom about a year ago. I'm sorry about your divorce. Join the club."

"When did yours become final?" she asked.

"Oh, that was at least two years ago." His vagueness and dismissive tone told her he was well over it.

"Any significant other in your life right now?"

"Not anymore. We broke up about a month ago."

"Oh, I'm sorry." But from what she saw, he didn't seem sorry; he sure was getting on with his life at breakneck speed.

"I also see that your books still fly off the shelves," he said, changing the subject.

"As long as they want to read 'em, I'll write 'em." She fanned herself with her gloves. "Let's go outside and talk. It's getting too hot down here."

He cupped her elbow and guided her around the tables, up the brick steps, and into the evening air.

Once outside, they joined the flow of pedestrian

traffic.

From the corner of her eye, she caught him openly admiring her as he smacked into a guy walking twin poodles.

Regaining his pace, he said, "You sure look like a writer—sorry, author."

"Thanks. I go to Three Steps Down once in a while to work on drafts, eavesdrop on the literati, and see what the topic of the hour is." She slid her newsboy cap and specs into her satchel.

"And it is?"

"Chick lit is the big thing."

His blank look told her he didn't have a clue.

"Chick lit is cutting-edge fiction for twenty- and thirtysomethings," she explained.

"Oh." He let out an embarrassed laugh. "Is that what you're writing these days?"

"My editor is after me to. But I'd put a twist on it—paranormal chick lit. I think that would be a savvy move."

"You were always ahead of the herd, Judi. At the vanguard, I should say."

Happy as she was to see Felix, the timing could have been better. Why couldn't she be in sweats and barefoot like a normal writer? She hoped he didn't think she was putting on airs in her designer duds.

"We should meet up somewhere and do a Saturday or Sunday together," he offered. "We sure have a lot of catching up to do."

"I'd love that." She meant it. A sudden sadness washed over her. All these years they could've been in touch. She'd had more fun times hanging out with Felix than with her closest girlfriends. It was a shame they'd drifted apart like so many other school BFFs. "It's scary to think about how fast the time went."

He nodded. "Don't I know it. When we were kids, the Third Millennium seemed like a million years into the future."

"So—what've you been up to since the last century?" she asked. They turned the corner and strolled up MacDougal, lined with leafy trees and elegant brownstones behind iron gates. "Any breakthroughs?"

"A few. But none of them happened overnight. I teach physics at Columbia. In my off-campus life, I'm working on some cutting-edge projects." He spoke over beeping horns, the roar of a subway train coming up from a grate, and the scraping of inline skates over the sidewalk. "When I moved back from L.A., I started specializing in immunology. I'm doing a lot of experimenting to try to increase the body's resistance to disease and build up the immune system. The world needs that kind of thing. In a few generations, mankind will be desperate for self-preservation."

She shook her head in wonder. "A Nobel Prize is in your destiny, I know it."

"Somebody's gotta do it." He gave off a little shrug in that unpretentious style of his.

Will he ever flaunt just a little bit of ego? she wondered. Felix's ego was as anchored to terra firma as his feet. Each success just made him try harder next time instead of basking in it like her fictional hero did. Race had nothing to prove; action seemed to find him.

"You're too modest, Felix. You just might be the one to find a cure for cancer."

"That would put me in the running for immortality, wouldn't it?"

"And a Nobel Prize." She stepped around a garbage can on the sidewalk.

"Then I could swing in the hammock of success."

"You swinging in a hammock? Never!" But Race planned to spend his retirement planet-hopping in his red convertible sportship.

"Taken any breaks lately?" Judi knew his idea of a vacation was a week at the Space Travel Training Academy.

"During the holidays last year, I designed another game for Gamestar."

She shook her head in wonder. "You invent computer games on vacation time. Why don't fictional heroes ever do that? What's this one called?"

"Felix's Helix. It's a DNA game." As they waited to cross the street, he looked at her, his eyes twinkling.

"The game allows its users to manipulate DNA the way scientists have been doing in labs. Only if a player goofs, he can change things around and start all over. In the game, I re-created myself. I was immune to every disease known to man, had an Einstein genius level, and stood six-foot-two minus the shoes." He'd always been self-conscious about his height, not a hair over five-seven. "Enough about science and nature. Let's hear about the arts. What have you been up to?"

"Oh, about the same. Blowing it and starting over," she quipped. "Writing, writing, and more writing. I've got the tenth book in the series in here." She held up the laptop.

"Congratulations. Success sure is sweet, isn't it?"

The light changed. He took her hand, and they crossed Bleecker. She welcomed the warm shiver that fluttered through her. No one had touched her like this in so long.

"I'm having a blast, but I do make sacrifices," she said. "A love life, for instance." They turned onto Washington Square South. Looking over at him, she ventured, "Do you ever read my books, Felix?"

"Well..." He broke eye contact. "...that stuff just isn't my cup of chai, Judi. I go more for espionage

7

fiction."

"Ha! But I can pack an intergalactic battle, a smoldering love affair, and the return trip to Mother Earth into eighty-five thousand words. Let's see one of your spies do that."

"Sounds a bit too intense for me. I read light stuff to fall asleep at night."

Their eyes met again, and they shared a smile.

As they walked, Judi's feet screamed in agony. She took smaller steps.

"Anything wrong?"

"It's these boots. They aren't made for walkin'." She vowed inwardly never to buy footwear online again. Or bras. Certain apparel just needed to be tried on first.

"You want a lift? I'm parked in a lot on Fourth Street." He pulled a set of keys from his pocket.

"No, I can manage for a little while." Out of habit, she headed in the direction of her loft. Would inviting him in be too forward? she wondered. *Oh, go for it!* her frisky little voice told her. *It's not like he's a first date!* She smiled as they crossed West Ninth, knowing he wouldn't turn down her offer. "Would you like to see my loft—or my studio as I like to call it? I can take these vises off my feet, and we can have a drink."

"Sounds like a plan."

Anticipation put a little skip into her step, making the Bandinis less torturous. She had a sweet little surprise in store for him that made her smile all the way to her doorway. She disengaged the alarm, opened the four locks, and they entered the building. He followed her up the three flights of stairs, and she noticed he wasn't even winded.

Showing him around her cluttered but comfortable loft, she relived all her fondest memories of him. When they graduated college and went their separate ways, she didn't mope over him;

she started her a new life in the Village while he headed to grad school at Stanford. She loved Felix like family and always knew he'd make it big someday. So he'd never aspired to being one of the school jocks. But where were the jocks now?

The class "Best Looking" Mateo Garcia, served time for insurance fraud. Brian Ridley, the star quarterback, had a restraining order against him from his ex.

And "Campus King" Matthew DeGeorge pleaded guilty to an insider trading scam a week before the fifth reunion.

"So—your divorce is final?" She knew he'd married an archaeo-astronomer from Stanford and separated soon after. Her father and stepmother always dished out the Felix gossip.

"Yes," he replied without a trace of remorse.

"Mine will be eight years next week."

"Oh—I'm sorry. After those few times we talked on the phone, I didn't hear back from you, so I figured you were doing okay."

She remembered those endless phone sessions with him. Now a dark cloud of guilt hung over her head. She should have called him again after she got her life together.

"I'm sorry I didn't call you again, Felix. You really did help me out a lot, cheering me up. But the details were beamed all over the planet, on TV, and in the rag papers. Besides the emotional torture, having my personal business in the street was mortifying."

She cringed, even now, remembering the reporters' mikes in her face, the humiliating—and untrue—stories that Ryan, her ex, embezzled half her fortune and dumped her because of her alleged affair with some NBA star she'd never set eyes on— oh baby! What fiction! So, the good came with the bad. But thinking of how she'd hidden away for months, embarrassed to go out because she felt all eyes on her, an object of public ridicule, made her break out in goose bumps. Rubbing her arms rapidly, she chased them away.

"I know." He nodded. "The price of fame. But it was extra lousy of him to run off with your best friend."

Her chest tightened at the memory. She'd holed up in her loft, dodging the press whenever she did go out. But each time the paparazzi flashed a bulb in her face, another little piece of her died until she couldn't face the world at all for several months. Finally, she picked up the pieces and moved on, but not without a bruised heart and a battered soul.

She smiled wanly at Felix. "I realize Alyssa wasn't a friend to begin with. I tried to think of one damn thing I did to deserve it. Was I a lousy housekeeper, did I not satisfy him in bed, or were my family members driving him nuts? But it was none of those things. He had the hots for Alyssa and went for it." She focused on the floor, the pain of his betrayal returning. "It made me feel like two cents— what did she give him that I couldn't? I still don't know, but thank God I don't care anymore." Her voice quivered, and she swept at the tears she couldn't fight.

She turned to the poster of her latest cover displaying her tall, ripped, cosmos-black-haired hero, the antithesis of every flawed Earthling she'd ever dated.

"When they ducked out on me, I called him at all hours and begged him to come back. I finally kicked myself in the ass and got my life back." She paused for a deep breath and noted Felix's eyes wide with pity. "Don't look at me like that, I'm okay now. A few months later, out of desperate loneliness, I sat down and created Race, and as the series rode up the best seller charts, I began searching for a living Race because I'd fallen in love with the CGI version. Now, after seven years of gazing at him in cover art, I'm still searching for him in flesh and blood."

"I'm sorry, Judi. I knew Ryan wasn't worth it when you told me he ran off with your best friend. You're well rid of him. They deserve each other."

She nodded, knowing he was right. "I'm really sorry we lost touch, Felix."

"Well, with our parents keeping us up to date on each other and seeing your books in all the stores, I'm informed enough about you. The good stuff, that is."

She nodded. "When Dad told me you'd moved back here and were teaching at Columbia, I should have called you—or at least e-mailed."

He waved a dismissive hand. "Don't worry about it. We're here now. We may have grown up and apart, but we'll always be tight."

It was all in the smile they shared. As she showed him around her remodeled loft with her mixture of antique and eclectic furnishings and her small garden roof where she grew herbs, he nodded his approval. She led him over to the sofa and contemplated his profile. Small lines framed his eyes and mouth, etching character into his features.

She gazed down. "When do you have time to work out, with your crazy schedule?" She marveled at his physique, all muscle underneath the tailored threads, no longer the pudgy geek who wolfed burgers and fries for breakfast.

"I set up a weight room next to the lab at home, so if I want a workout at two a.m., I can hit the gym on my clock instead of on the health club's hours," he said.

"I've also taken up yoga—five minutes of centering helps me think when I'm trying to solve a problem instead of chanting into a bowl of rhodolytes."

"Will a beer disturb that harmonious balance?" Growing up, his idea of a stiff drink was a swig of root beer out of the bottle.

"No, a beer sounds great."

"You got it." She headed for the kitchen and got out two bottles of Gaelan's Red and two mugs. "Then I want to hear all about your scientific endeavors."

"Hey, remember the experiment we did with my chemistry set that almost blew my parents' house up? We called it Vesuvius?" Felix recalled, casually leafing through her *Astrophile* magazine and tossing it aside like he'd read it already.

"Sure do. The neighbors called 911. I bet the Westchester Fire Department never tried to douse a volcano before." They laughed as she poured their beers.

He shook his head in fond reminiscence. "Yeah, and the mess it made. We spent our whole vacation scraping plaster of Paris lava off the walls of my dad's study. I thought he'd blow his top and have a meltdown." Felix gazed straight ahead seemingly focused on nothing.

"What's wrong?" But sitting next to him, watching his smile fade, she felt it too.

"The time whizzed right by us, didn't it, Judi? Too damn fast. Time has always fascinated me. The scientific background, I guess." As he brought his gaze back to hers, his eyes bore the pain of regret.

"Sometimes I can't believe how old I am."

"We're not that old. We're still on the right side of forty."

"It's all relative. My students weren't alive when the Challenger exploded. I always wonder about the possibility of going back in time. To do it all right the next time around. Time travel. Wow, what a concept."

"And you think my books aren't realistic enough!" She took a sip. "You've done okay. You never give yourself enough credit."

"Well, there's always room for improvement. Thomas Edison said 'there's a better way to do it' and trying to accomplish just half of what he did can get frustrating."

"But you're not Thomas Edison. You're you. And I don't see much room for improvement." She squeezed his arm. With any other guy, this would've been flirting. But the idea of flirting with Felix was ludicrous. They so passed that ages ago.

"Thanks for the pep rally." He took a long draw of his beer.

"So tell me about your research."

He set the mug on the table, settled back, and played with his tie, coiled up in his jacket pocket. She never saw him actually wearing a tie. He always stuffed it into a pocket.

"I'm on contract with Oxytech, a new biotech company. They just raised several million dollars for all this design work. They have an affiliation with one of the major drug corporations, so they can deal with the FDA a lot more easily."

"I always knew it, Felix. I always knew you would make history."

"Well, I'm not making it yet." Praise always made him turn pink, and he opened the top button of his shirt, another of his familiar gestures that had faded from her mind until now. Race opened his shirt as a blatant sexual overture, but with Felix, it was a gesture of relaxation. Race, always "on stage," never relaxed.

"Anything else going on? I know there has to be."

"Actually, yes. I've been working on a project, but—" He stopped and stole a quick glance around.

"The place isn't bugged, Felix. My God, you do read too many espionage novels."

"Hey, truth is stranger than fiction."

They exchanged grins. He sat forward and hunched his shoulders, elbows on knees. She'd seen him this way a million times, another of his old habits, like drumming his fingers on any available surface. She also remembered him standing on his head to enable deeper thought, but for now he stayed right side up.

"Are you centering?" she asked cautiously, afraid to disrupt what might be some serious energy channeling.

"No, I do that cross-legged. It's just that I haven't told a soul about this project."

"Then you don't have to tell me if you can't. I don't want to breach national security."

He looked straight at her, his eyes dark and penetrating. "I've been dying to share this, Judi. This is the accomplishment of a lifetime for me. But until now I just didn't have the right person to tell."

"I'm honored you consider me the right person," she said sincerely, remembering all the dark secrets they'd shared in the past. Kid stuff, but secrets were important then, too. "It means a lot to me."

Nodding, he glanced at his empty mug, and she shot up to get him a refill. She returned with another bottle, tipped the mug, and poured.

"This is a very controversial issue, Judi. You've got to keep it under wraps."

"Felix, you know I'll always have your back. We're practically family." It hurt a little that he would doubt her, but her curiosity won out.

"I'm involved in an experiment that the general public may find immoral. Playing God, I guess you'd say."

"Well—what is it?" Despite the sip she'd just taken, her throat contracted. She'd always feared he'd get involved with some covert operation, in too deeply for his own safety. "What are you into now?" Her imagination soared.

"In grad school, I did some genetic engineering to prepare for my dissertation, but it wasn't cloning as such. With cloning, you inject a cell from the body of the subject to be cloned into an ovum after removing the nucleus. That's not what I'm doing."

She splayed her hands. "Then what are you doing? You always give the ten-thousand-foot view before the close up."

"I've been commissioned to create a being, Judi. Not a robot, mind you. An environmentally controlled being with human characteristics but without human faults. He's going to be perfect."

"P-perfect?" Her heart surged. That word did something to her.

"Well, not quite yet. My contract with Oxytech expires next month, but after I got my doctorate, I started doing some schematic design in my lab at home. I'm very close to my first prototype. It's been on my mind during most of my waking hours—and most of my sleeping ones, too. The—" He faltered, as if hesitant to share all his details— "outfit who commissioned me got wind of it through some faculty gossip and interviewed me about designing this being, the first of its kind."

"So, when will you start construction or production or whatever you call the process?"

"I don't know exactly. It'll take several months before I've ironed all the wrinkles out."

"Let me just ask you one question."

His eyes pierced her as if to say uh-oh. "What is it?"

"Why aren't you creating a perfect woman?"

He hesitated, and she knew she had him there. "Simple. The world has enough of those already."

She gave him a playful shove. "You always know just what to say."

"Never say always."

They caught up with the lesser details of each

other's lives, and when he glanced at his watch, he did a double take. "I've got an early start tomorrow, and I'm sure you do, too."

"Finally, someone who realizes I have a job."

He went to the bathroom, came back, and they parted with a warm, friendly embrace after exchanging e-mail addresses. She went to the window and watched him until he disappeared around the corner.

Felix. How great to see him after all these years.

Before forgetting, she turned her computer on and added him to her address book.

****

As Felix drove home, he tried to count all the times he'd wanted to call Judi after her divorce, ask her to jump on a plane, and come to L.A. for a spur-of-the-moment jaunt. Even when he moved back to New York, they may as well have remained a continent away; their lives became just too divergent. Now, with her living this close, he still never made that first call. Something always stopped him: her latest interview mentioning her frantic tour schedule or her folks telling him about her exploding career. So it never happened.

He wished he'd swept her scarf into his pocket—something simple and personal of hers. He still dreamed of her and scoured the bookstores to glimpse her jacket photo. He sought out women who resembled her in the remotest way, especially his last ex, Dr. Heather Adair, another Physics Department professor.

He enjoyed Dr. Adair's company but couldn't go on using her just because she reminded him of Judi. He had ended it barely a month ago.

He wanted to let Judi know how he'd felt about her all these years. *Don't get your hopes up.*

But his heart said, "Why not?"

Chapter Two

Too wound up to sit down, Judi paced her loft in circles and sipped a celebration Kahlua. She had two things to celebrate: finally finishing her tenth Race Parsec novel, and the joyful reunion with her old friend. She'd forgotten how easy it was to be with Felix, her biggest supporter through her ups and downs, and especially her divorce. If only she could find a man like him.

Her readers knew her as Juno Ursa with the out-of-this-world sex life, but she knew the truth. She'd been faking it. The wild nights out on the town. The jaunts to Italy with the Romantic Times crew, the research trips to Tahiti and China—all cover-ups for her broken heart. What she really wanted was a soul mate—to share her joys and her secrets. Why couldn't she find the perfect man, like Race—loving, attentive, never leaving the toilet seat up?

Race! Judi suddenly remembered her fidgety editor, probably plowing through a mountain of Crème de Framboise truffles waiting for her manuscript. "Iris!"

She grabbed the phone and pushed the button connecting her to Iris Allais, Editor-in-Chief of Infinity Spectrum Books. A winning team, she and Iris shared fantasies and facts alike for inspiration. They called each other at all hours to brainstorm. Like Iris, Judi came alive at night. What better time for an intergalactic odyssey, with the moon and stars to inspire the way? And to forget there was no man in her life other than Race—Mr. Perfection, created to her every spec and whim.

Iris answered after half a ring. "Judi! Where were you? I called you and texted you a hundred times."

"Working, but now I can finally announce that it's finished. It took longer than usual to put Race and Finestra to bed—no pun intended. I had to stop and catch my breath. You'd just hang up in disgust if anybody started panting into your phone."

"Au contraire," Iris said. "With caller ID, any panters call me, they're stuck with me. So when are you going to bequeath me the ninth product of your genius?"

"Tenth. But who's counting?"

"So this is a real milestone."

"More like another birthday. And after thirty, who counts? You want me to e-mail it to you now or to the office tomorrow?"

"Hey, I have a better idea." Iris's voice brightened. "Why don't you bring it over?"

"Now? It's kinda late, isn't it?" Seeing Felix again made her realize how much time had gone by, and she didn't feel up to a crit session. She just wanted to reflect—and prepare Race for his next quest.

"We can read your dialogue out loud, knock back some juleps...I just TiVo'd a hot movie, *My Sexiest Mistake*."

"I'd love to, Iris, but I'm flat worn out after finishing this one."

"All right, I'll cut you some slack. But if you change your mind before dawn, come by, and we can watch this flick. I'll fast forward to the climax, just for you."

"Eight inches worth?"

"Ciao, you pervert."

"Save some for me!" Judi added as the line clicked.

The real world soon vanished into the unreal as she jotted down ideas for a new storyline. By one a.m., she had a "drift" typed, a preliminary draft. She went to the bathroom, putting the seat back down after Felix. That brought a chuckle. Race would have put the seat down and cleaned up with a Pure & Fresh Sani-Wipe. As she returned to the computer, she wound Felix's necktie around her arm. He'd left it on her coffee table by "accident." She held it close and inhaled the spicy, woodsy scent of vintage Bengardino.

Her fingers tapped the keys. She listed everything about Race's latest alien enemies as clearly as if they were about to invade her loft and abduct her. Then she jotted down a few ways Race would confront and outmaneuver them. She knew him so well. He was an extension of her soul. She'd sent him to so many distant worlds to face disasters within a breath of his life, only to emerge unhurt, to brandish another gold medal on his silver metallic uniform and lead another victory parade.

She couldn't help but grin at the tag line her fan club had made up: "Race Parsec: The Intergalactic Crotch Rocket."

Raising her arms way above her head, she shook her hands to let the blood flow. Then, as her muse connected all the random wires of her mind, a revelation came, so fierce that she sprang out of her seat.

"I got it!" She clapped her hands to her head. "Felix!" She lunged for the phone, tripping over her feet. She grabbed her old address book, flipping the frayed pages until she found Felix Varlden's current phone number, written above his crossed-out L.A. number. Her stepmother had given her this number when he moved back to New York, urging, "Go on, call him, dear..." but Judi never did. This was her first call to him since his pep talks after her divorce, and it seemed strange—especially when she heard his sleepy hello. It sounded so—so bedroomy.

"Hi, Felix; it's me. Judi."

"Judi? Anything wrong?" He now sounded as alert as if the president had woken him.

"No, but you did leave something very valuable here. Besides your necktie, but I'm keeping that. And a ring on the table."

"I wasn't wearing a ring."

"A beer bottle ring."

"Oh. My bad. And what was valuable?" His tone sharpened with curiosity.

"A fabulous idea that I got after you left. I've got to talk to you about it."

"So what is it you wanted to tell me?" He kept his voice low.

"Felix, I have to talk to you immediately. I've come up with the most profound idea, and you're the only person who can help me."

"Can't it wait another six hours? I can call you from campus."

"Please, Felix, just come over now. Take a cab. I promise it won't take long."

"Judi, it's two o'clock."

"One-fifty-three is not two o'clock. And if you leave now instead of arguing with me, you'll be here by two-thirty."

Silence.

"Felix, please..." She hoped her plaintive tone would send him rushing to her aid like it did in the old days. "After all these years, I ask you one little thing—"

"One little thing? To come tearing-ass down to SoHo in the middle of the night?"

"Then I'll come over there."

"Stay put." The line went dead, and Judi's grin widened.

****

After wiping off the beer bottle ring he'd left on her table, Judi showered and answered the door looking like a writer—comfy sweats and no mascara.

She took Felix's jacket and slipped a mocha latte into his hand as he settled on the sofa. His bleary eyes brightened with the first sip, and he ran a hand through his uncombed hair. Any other guy showing up with unkempt hair would've slid down a notch on her scale, but with Felix it meant he'd hurried over. Knowing she was so much more important than a wet comb filled her heart with appreciation.

"Last time I rushed out of the house at two a.m. it was to tend a sick friend." He cocked a brow. "Now it happens again."

"I'm so sorry I disturbed you. But this is important."

"No big deal. I step out for midnight walks or do my yoga or Pilates at all hours."

You ain't seen nothin' yet, Judi thought, pouring herself a glass of soymilk.

"Now tell me what's so urgent. I hope this leaded coffee you're pumping me with will keep me awake." He drummed his fingers on the cup.

"Felix, don't be shocked, now." She sat across from him. "We've been through a lot together, haven't we?" She clasped her palms together. They were starting to sweat. A lot.

"I can see this is going to be an all-nighter. Let me guess. You've been selling these books like hot dogs at a Yankee game, so I know you can't be having financial problems."

"No, it's not financial."

He lifted a brow. "You're being stalked by a jealous ex? Or a wacko fan?"

"No, none of my exes care enough to be jealous, and fans don't get wacko until you run out of freebies at signings." She took a sip of milk.

"You got me. What can it possibly be?" He

gulped his latte.

"It's about...I don't even know what to call him. Your creation."

"What about him?"

She drew in a deep breath and blurted it out, "I want him."

Chapter Three

Judi expected Felix's reaction to be loud, unamused, or at worst, a simple, "I'm outta here." But he surprised her. His eyes widened, his jaw dropped, and she instantly knew he wanted to hear more. Aha! She gave a silent hoot of triumph. Once again his insatiable curiosity, the scourge of genius, got to him.

He swallowed his coffee and blinked in disbelief. "Run that by me again?"

"I want this creation of yours for myself, Felix."

"I know I'll be sorry I asked, but here goes: what the hell for?"

"To have and to hold. His 'n hers jammies. All without the civil union and the prenup. Ever since I created Race, I've fantasized about bringing him to life. Now it's feasible." Please say yes, she silently pleaded.

He tilted his head back and closed his eyes. "Judi, you've come up with some whacked out stuff in the past, but—"

"How can I make you understand?"

"You called me down here to tell me you want a relationship with a humanoid who doesn't even exist yet. I'm not designing him to be The Bachelor." He stood and headed for the window, hands in pockets, jingling his change.

"I'm pouring my heart out, and you're totally blowing me off."

Disappointment nagged at her. How could she make him understand her loneliness these last years? The pain of knowing the two people she'd

23

trusted most had betrayed her. The endless nights watching romances, writing romances, feeling dead inside. Trying to fathom the unfairness: the man who'd vowed to love her 'til death had ditched her for her best friend.

She swallowed a surge of tears as she felt another piece of her heart splinter.

"Sorry, but I feel like I just fell into the screenplay of *Frankenstein*. Or more accurately, the first draft of the screenplay." She followed him to the window as he peered out. Night sounds floated in through the thin glass—a horn blare, a barking dog, and the rumbling of a garbage can.

She turned him around, and their eyes locked. Their heights matched exactly.

"This is no whim, and I'll tell you why. It's because the man I want doesn't exist out there—or anywhere—except on the pages of my books and in my mind. Now it's finally feasible to...well, attain this dream I've always had of finding Mr. Right. You're designing the perfect creation, but he'll need a personality. You can make the prototype in the image of Race." She knew she was talking too fast, so she slowed down. "Of course he'll need someone to satisfy his needs, to take care of him, and to love him. I can take that on, help you to perfect him."

He leaned on the windowsill, palms flattened. "Judi, he won't need emotions. He won't have the capacity to feel love. He's only going to resemble a human. He won't be able to love. He'll have no feelings."

Spurts of adrenaline rocketed up her limbs and into her brain. She paced around and then halted beside him. "But you could give him emotions if you wanted to." She gestured toward her heart. "You're the creator."

He squeezed her shoulders before she could begin another clockwise lap. "That's not necessary. I told you he'd have a human body and face, but a heart's something he can do without."

Despair flooded her. "Felix, how could you have become so hard over the years? You were always so sensitive, so sentimental, and so mushy. Reading Elizabeth Barrett Browning, trying to write like Elizabeth Barrett Browning—I thought this being would be created in your image. And you're not giving him a heart? If you want another floor-scrubber, call Cheery Maids."

He shook his head slowly and deliberately. "He's hardly going to be me. That's not the object of this exercise, Judi. This isn't an ego-fulfillment wish here. The last thing he needs in this infinite vacuum of our universe is a heart. Or a stomach, or—any internal human organs. It's strictly a scientific project."

"So what's his point?" She searched his eyes for an answer. "I've never known you to do anything strictly for kicks. You're building this perfect robot to sit and look pretty?"

"He won't be a robot. And a heart is unnecessary. It's the brain I need to put most of the effort into."

"What are you saying, Felix?" At times she'd wondered—could he dream up an invention harmful to mankind?

He fanned his fingers through his hair. "I've told you this much already, so I may as well tell you the rest."

They sat back on the sofa, and he drained his coffee cup. She got up to refill it.

"Better yet, make it a double gin and tonic. Mix one for yourself while you're at it."

"I don't want to start drinking, Felix. Just tell me what you're up to. I'll take it much better if I'm sober. Same for you." But she mixed his gin and tonic on the potent side, splashing enough gin into the glass to make it at least a double.

As she handed him the glass, she looked into the sharp eyes darting around like wayward meteors. What was he up to? Would some G-men show up at the door after tailing him here? She'd always figured Felix would get involved in some top-secret drama.

He inched closer.

She inched back. "Give it up. I'll try not to cringe."

He tasted his drink and laced his fingers around the glass. "I'm doing this for the government."

Here it comes. "Whose?" Her breath halted.

"Ours, of course!"

She exhaled. But she hardly felt relieved. "I wouldn't put anything past you, Felix. All you geniuses, you're always going on secret missions and—"

"No, this is strictly in the interest of dear old Uncle Sam. ORBIT commissioned me to create this being. I've done some work for them on the space probes. The director himself approached me with this proposal. You know about ORBIT, don't you?"

"Outer Space Research something or other?"

"Organized Research Base for Interstellar Testing." He took a bigger sip this time and grimaced then licked his lips. "You went heavy on the sauce here. But I'm not complaining."

"What's his purpose? Espionage?"

"No. It's strictly for research," he said. "They're planning to send him to one of the planets orbiting Megasus."

"Megasus? The red dwarf that the Harvard astronomers just discovered?"

"Yeah. That's the one." He nodded, his eyes brightening. He raised his brows as if surprised she knew about it.

"Why are they going to send him out there?"

He paused to take a breath and hesitated before

speaking, as if wondering whether to divulge more details of this secret plan.

"Because Megasus has a planet in its solar system that's strikingly similar to Earth. The third planet from Megasus has an atmosphere like ours, contains oxygen, and the gravitational force is almost identical. The last probe brought back pictures and samples of its water and soil. So far they haven't discovered life there, but as that solar system's only habitable planet, that's where they're going to send my creation—to see if humans can stand the temperature, to seek evidence of biological life." His voice rose with excitement. "Infinity Seven is going to take him. We're going to send him there, Judi, my creation!" He clamped his hands so tightly around the glass that they whitened like marble. "The first being from Earth to travel to another planet."

She leaned toward him and squeezed his hand. "Oh, Felix, how fantastic. I'm so proud of you. But why didn't you want to tell me before? I'd never blab your business, you know that."

At that moment she realized how many years had flown by since they'd last sat together into the dark hours, marveling about the universe, how it all began, and their place in the grand scheme. Now they sat together, sharing dreams once again as if they'd only spoken yesterday. How good it felt to be with him, in his confidence again.

He twirled his glass. "I trust you. But ORBIT doesn't want anyone to know about this just yet. It's too controversial. This isn't Dolly the sheep. The fact that I'm creating a being that wasn't conceived by the miraculous union of sperm and egg is enough to generate a public uproar. Even in this day and age, experimenting with genetics and fetal tissue is still taboo in some segments of society.

"The government has been carefully regulating

27

and monitoring my progress, despite their almost nightly appearances on Let's Talk Polemics, denouncing it as unethical. And as far as the space mission, well, there's always a chance that life thrives on that planet, and it very well may be hostile life. And we, as a civilization, are going to remain anonymous until we reach a positive outcome to this project. There won't be any star maps with arrows pointing to Earth or messages in binary code or American flags to plunge into the soil or stenciled on the craft."

"Who else knows about this?"

"ORBIT and the highest officials in the Fed. If you breathe one word of this to anyone, they could very easily liquidate me."

"Liquidate?"

He nodded like it was no big deal.

"I'm afraid to ask, but—do you mind explaining that one? It sounds ominous."

"Only if I mess up. This is a very contentious project and the most costly in space-age history. It makes the missions to Mars look like junkets to Disney world. I told you because I trust you." He finished his drink.

Her heart warmed, knowing he still considered her his confidante. So it wasn't germ warfare but dangerous enough that Felix just had to get chosen. She wet her lips before continuing. "When is this supposed to take place?"

"There's no deadline yet, but they'd like to launch it within a year."

"Well, that gives you plenty of time." She got up to refresh his drink, but he shook his head.

"There's never enough time. It's not going to be easy, Judi. This isn't merely a blood substitute or a genetic engineering experiment."

Something was bound to go wrong. What if he created a monster—and the government decided to use it anyway? He'd be held accountable. Why couldn't he have stayed a harmless geek?

Trying not to worry, she wished she'd laced her soymilk with rum. "What if something goes terribly wrong and he turns out to be a monster?"

"He won't. I plan to give him a personality—well, qualities, at least. I'm programming him so he'll be the epitome of nobility with heroic traits such as courage, honor, and integrity, a regular space-age Boy Scout. He's representing mankind but for a world beyond our own."

"Felix, you've just described Race, the hero of my books. That's him exactly!" She sat up straight. "I started working on my next draft after you left, and then a light switch flipped on in my brain, and it all fell together. This creation—he can be a living, breathing Race." She reached out, grabbing at empty air, and grimaced in exasperation. "You can design him for me then design another one for the space program." No more runaway husband. No, this man would be programmed to stay. Her chest tightened at the memory of finding Ryan and Alyssa both gone. His note read, "I'm finally in love." But not with her.

Judi watched anxiously as Felix rested his head on the sofa back and shut his eyes, but angst crowded the air.

"It's a big world out there, Judi. Have you ever thought of trying to find a real man?"

"I've met plenty of Mr. Rights, but something was always wrong, either timing or logistics. And after the divorce, I didn't confine myself to this hemisphere. I've traveled the four corners of the Earth to research my books and never, I mean never, have I found anyone resembling Race. Jet setting to the most exotic places famous for worldly hero types—Rio, Athens, the nude beaches of Aruba—I've found anything but."

"Have you tried New York?" He opened his eyes

and looked at her.

She scowled. "It's the last place I'd look."

"That's usually where you'll find what you're looking for. In the last place you look."

"Felix, I'm imploring you to help me. I'm under contract to Spectrum for another five novels. Three of them have been optioned. I'm far from hurting financially. The only place I hurt is here." She patted her heart.

He looked away and rubbed his eyes, his temples, and his forehead. "You're jumping way ahead here. It's late, and my brain is tired. I worked a long day today, and I'm dying for some sleep. I can't consider something like this unless I've had a good night's sleep."

"That means you'll consider it?" Her pulse quickened.

He turned toward her. "I'll consider considering it."

"Oh, Felix, how can I ever thank you? We can work out compensation later. I'll pay any price you ask."

"I'm not interested in your money, Ju—"

She leaned in to him and gave him a sweet kiss on the lips. She felt his body jolt in surprise for a second, and then his arms wound round her. He didn't let go. She slid back in time, to the zenith of her youth. Felix was the nicest kid in the world— and the one time he'd tried to kiss her, she laughed in his face. Now she realized how much that must've hurt him.

Felix, don't go.

Her eyes snapped open, and she pulled away, worried for an instant that he'd picked up on her reverie. But thankfully, he looked too beat to think much of anything. He rubbed his eyes and stifled a yawn.

"Do you think this can work, Felix?" The words

rushed out of her. She knew the answer but wanted to hear it from him.

He hesitated for a heartbeat, and she detected a hint of doubt in his eyes. "If the mind be willing and the flesh not weak," he replied in a less-than-convincing tone. "But why do you want a manmade man instead of a God-made one?"

How could she explain that she wanted a living Race, her divine masterpiece? A creation unlike any flawed human she'd ever known? But more than that, he would want her and only her. She'd never again have to risk a broken heart.

"I've done enough shopping around to know what I want, Felix. I've dreamed about it for years. I've put my wishes on paper for the entire world to read, and now it's possible to make them come true." She pointed to the display case for her novels. There they stood, in chronological order, each cover sporting the jaunty Race Parsec against a backdrop of a glittering galaxy, in vivid artwork. Spectrum's illustrators seemed to possess a window to her mind.

"Hm, very prolific." He smiled, and she moistened her lips.

Anxiety always made her mouth go dry.

"I'll see what I can do. I've done you some royally harebrained favors, but making your dream come true would be a challenge, even for me."

"You can do it, Felix." She buzzed with energy and excitement.

"I probably can. That's what I'm afraid of."

"Reading my books will give you some insight on what I'm looking for," she urged.

"I'll make you a deal. Try spy thrillers or mysteries, and I promise I'll buy a ton of 'em, keep a copy in every room in the house—my office, my briefcase, and leave them in every men's room I go into."

She laughed. "I leave my books everywhere, too.

You never know who'll pick one up. I did write a few Regencies under a pen name. But Regencies aren't my thing. My thing is a glorious life with Race, which I soon will have if this works out." She sighed, picturing them strolling the promenade deck of the new *Queen Mary*...

"Well, I'm beat. I'd better bail before I drop right here." He stood and stretched.

What an un-Race Parsecian thing to say.

"So you'll get to the drawing board as soon as you can?" She got his jacket and followed him to the door.

He halted and turned to face her. "I told you I'd consider it. I can consider it just about anywhere. Trust me." He slipped into his jacket.

"Can I call you tomorrow to see how much progress you've made?"

"No way." She saw his grasp tighten on the doorknob. "The worst thing anyone can do is rush an inventor. If you know anything about us, you'll know we can't work under pressure. I told the same thing to ORBIT."

"I'm sorry. You just don't know how badly I've wanted this. Now that it's possible..." She trailed off.

He ran both hands roughly through his hair. "I cabbed over here, so I need one back. I can think some more on the way home."

"Anything for the creator of my dream hunk." She gave an adoring smile and laid a hand gently on his cheek.

He rolled his eyes. "Well, don't kiss the hem of my robe yet. Creating two of these beings won't leave me much time for my other pursuits—and might start to bore me after a while. I need at least four or five things to work on at once, on different subjects."

"Then see if *Let's Talk Polemics* would hire you as a host," she joked, heading for the phone.

He looked away. "Well, that I could do without.

But this commission for ORBIT is a once in a lifetime deal. Instead of interviewing thousands of scientists for this project, they asked me because of my reputation. So it's a very rare honor."

"Yes, it is. I realize that, and I'm very proud of you." A glimmer of hope coursed through her that her dream would finally come true.

She called the local cab company, wondering how she could ever thank Felix, besides paying him an enormous sum. Only a true friend would spend months in a lab helping a childhood bud live out her fantasy. Maybe she could find him the woman of his dreams. It didn't sound like he had her at home.

She ordered a cab to her address and hung up, turning to him. "Felix, can you please do something before you go into the lab?"

He groaned. "Oh, no. Now what?"

She formed the words in her mind before speaking, so as not to offend him. He was so sensitive about his inventions.

"I know you're going to map this out scientifically, and you've got the ORBIT creation in draft form, but my real-life Race has to be slightly different from what you have in mind. Not better, mind you—just different."

"Yes, Judi, he'll be anatomically correct." He straightened his sleeves.

"No, not that. You need to know exactly what I have in mind. We need to be compatible in every way, share the same interests, have the same values—"

"I really don't believe you," he interrupted, shaking his head. "I haven't even decided to definitely embark on this nearly impossible quest, and you're rattling off requirements like I'm match dot com."

"Then just read some of my books. You'll see what he's all about."

He raised his hands and let them fall at his sides. "Okay, give me the books. I'll see if I can sit through the blurbs on the back."

"I'll have you know that forty-eight percent of my readers are men," she called over her shoulder, heading for the bookcase. "Here's the first five. Come back in a week, and I'll give you the rest."

She loaded the books into a tote and handed it to him. He pretended to collapse under the weight. "This must be some heavy stuff."

"Of course. He visits worlds where a teaspoon of matter weighs trillions of tons, where gravity is powerful enough to crush boulders, and where the atmosphere is completely airless."

"So that's how he manages to keep his hair in place." He glanced at one of the covers.

"Out, you mad doctor!"

"See you on the drawing board."

He turned to leave, but she clasped his hand. "I'm glad we found each other again, Felix."

"We never lost each other, Pookie," he replied softly, using his favorite nickname for her. He tweaked her nose, as he always did when they were kids, but back then he did it to annoy her.

As he slipped out and into the waiting cab, she twirled around the room. Her heart leapt in anticipation of the most explosive love story the world would ever know.

A contented smile spread across her face as she pictured, in graphic detail, her lover approaching her, holding out his arms for her to embrace him, his aromatic essence filling the air, and his voice deep and velvety, incarnated out of the thousands of pages she'd written. Finally, she would have true love.

Then why couldn't she get Felix out of her mind?

****

Sitting in the cab, Felix took one of Judi's books

out and fanned his thumb over the pages. All these words came out of her head, he marveled.

But there's no chance of a future with her, he chided himself. *No, she's got the hots for a hunkoid who's unlike me in every way.* This fantasy action hero of hers had all the depth of a saucer, but it's what she wanted. And all he wanted was for her to be happy. "Let her go already, you idiot," he said out loud. "She's just not that into you."

"Huh?" The cabbie turned halfway around.

"Nothing. Just me talking to himself."

As the cab whizzed through the night, Felix sat cross-legged on the back seat, stretched his arms, and tried to do some centering.

Twenty minutes later, locked in the privacy of his lab at home, his heart quickened as he studied Judi's photo on the jacket of her latest book. Her voice went through his mind as he fell asleep on his cot, the book cradled in his arms.

Chapter Four

Waking up on the couch in her study, Judi opened her eyes to her cover-hunk poster, cut off at the head, which left the lower features to her whimsy. Last night's events took shape in her mind. "My dream is about to become reality. Even if it's only for the time span of one of Race's trips through a black hole, I'll be happy."

Closing her eyes, she envisioned her fierce, dangerous lover crushing her body to his in a six-pager of passion. She gave the fantasy an extra few minutes; it was Saturday.

"Enough!" She rose and yanked open the drapes. Sunshine flooded her study and brought her back to Earth.

Later, under the shower, she tried to descend from her nirvana, but her phantom lover pursued her, bare-chested and tantalizing in bulge-hugging briefs. Fortunately, her fantasies provided a comfortable living. "Yes, I'm one of the lucky ones," she gloated.

Turning up the cold water, she added, "Or am I?"

She often considered abandoning it all for something entirely different like raising alpacas in a life of celibacy. But Race's nebulous figure would always entice her to engage him in another quest of gallantry.

She couldn't let Race down after all he'd done for her.

Wrapped in a bath sheet, she headed for the phone. She could picture Iris panting by now.

****

Lounging in Iris's sunroom, Judi kicked off her shoes and toyed with the fern hanging over her head.

"Judi, I can't put this down," Iris cooed, her editor's eyes zipping back and forth across her laptop screen. She mouthed the words as she read with accompanying gestures, as if acting the story out.

"All you've read are the love scenes. The rest of the story is worth reading too, you know."

"Oh, I'll take your word for it that it's got a plot." She scrolled down and continued reading, her lips moving in time with her eyes, unable to conceal her delight. "I don't know how many thousands of these things I've read over the years, but your stuff rings chimes I never knew I had." She reached for her mint julep and took a gulp. "Whew, now all I need's a cold shower, and I can start on chapter one."

"To be honest, Iris, I don't feel it's my absolute best. *The Edge of the Event Horizon*—now that was a real tour de force."

"Who did Race slaughter in that one?" When Iris removed her glasses to polish them on her scarf, Judi noticed her glue-on lashes were extra long today, rimming her brilliant blue eyes. A tanning-salon glow bronzed her nipped-and-tucked face.

"He didn't slaughter, conquer, or shatter any kneecaps. In that one, he met up with Blast Adams, the space marine from Xatox who wanted to take our sun and use it for fuel. Race made him see the error of his ways, brought him back to Earth, and the president made him Secretary of Energy. I make Race see the good in everyone. His faith gets him through the adversity as much as the heroism does. A quality I always aspired to."

"Yeah, Blast. I wouldn't kick him out of bed either. After he cleaned himself up, I mean. I liked the way he busted up asteroids and did needlepoint at the same time." Iris stood and headed for the bar. "Another julep?"

"No, thanks." Judi sipped her margarita through its green plastic straw. "I've had enough of this fantasy world. I want a real man."

Iris returned with a mug the exact color of Race's eyes, sapphire blue. "You're talking real now?"

"I want the perfect fifty-fifty relationship with the antithesis of every mortal I've ever known who laughed at my career choice, lied about his marital status or lived too many continents away to get serious. An idyllic life with a man possessing the best of Race's attributes all rolled into one gorgeous hunk of flesh and bone."

"Mostly bone, huh?" Iris slid off her hostess slippers and reclined on her wicker lounge chair.

"I long to be treated the way he treats Finestra, catered to, desired, craved—sometimes I think I'm going to fantasize my way into a straight jacket. But I know, deep inside, my soul mate is somewhere waiting for me. And I won't have to fantasize because he'll be my fantasy come to life." She left it at that.

Iris knew all about her heartbreaking marriage, but Judi couldn't reveal where her fantasy-come-true was right now—a pencil sketch on a set of blueprints.

"I know you haven't found the love of your life, and I sympathize." She looked directly into Judi's eyes. "But a man like Race would drive you bananas. He should be just a tad flawed."

"I've had enough guys who've snored, left the bathroom a mess, and flung dirty clothes against the wall—that stuck."

"I said flawed, not Neanderthal. Race is fine for the realm he's in. But thrust him into the real world, and he'd be a misfit. Your standards are soaring way too high, Judi, and that's why I think you've been going dateless. He doesn't have to be an orangutan, but you can certainly put up with a guy who hogs the remote and forgets anniversaries. You'd get bored to death with a cardboard crusader out of a soap opera."

"I know I'm not going to find the exact duplicate of Race. He doesn't exist." *Yet,* she whispered to herself.

"Just be a bit more realistic," Iris advised, nipping at her drink and chewing the crushed ice. "He doesn't have to be that brave or that well built or that tall. Start with your ideal of Race, but make allowances...a bald spot here, a few inches there."

"You mean there—or—the-e-e-e-re?"

"Well, off his height, of course! What di-i-i-d you think I meant?"

Iris winked and reached for her laptop, reading Finestra's part out loud in a breathy Marilyn Monroe voice.

Judi left Iris alone with her fantasies and went back to her own.

****

Back home, Judi poured her cup of mocha into the kitchen sink. Who needed caffeine at a time like this?

The roof garden was her sanctuary on warm sunny days with her fragrant herb plants, birds twittering in the telephone wires, and the hollow bounce of a basketball in the distance. As she watered her basil plant, she inhaled its sweet aroma. Chewing on a sprig of mint, she settled in her canvas lounger and opened her laptop to Race's next storyline.

But Race didn't want to be part of this storyline or in this next book. Like a spoiled actor, he refused to play the role she now wrote for him. He didn't jump off the page and drive the plot this time; he just wouldn't conform to the plot at all. So she went with it. After all, this seemed to be what he wanted.

Not just another book, this marked the birth of her creation.

He would be her astral starmate but with his own distinct personality. She rattled off a list of attributes: supportive of her career, relationship-oriented, flexible, playful, spontaneous, stimulating, gregarious...

He was her dream and more. Someday soon he would also be her reality. She took a deep breath and began her first e-mail to Felix.

"Hi there! We'll talk in more detail next time we meet, which will be—when? We never did set up a meeting. You want to come back down here and do a little bistro? Village coffeehouses are great caves for the creative.

"You can walk in on three legs with three eyes & nobody'll look at you twice. Hey, it was so great seeing you again. I'm sorry we lost touch over the years—you were always a friend in a million. I'm so excited over this project I can't even start a new book—all I can think about is starting my new life with Race. Maybe he'll be ready to fill my stocking by Christmas? OK, I'll settle for Valentine's Day. But hey, if he can fill a Christmas stocking, I want him RIGHT NOW! ;) TTYL, Judi"

She went back and added, "Love" before her name and a few X's. She looked up at the clear sky and took in a deep breath of brisk air, letting it out in a contented sigh. To her, the entire world looked rosy, even SoHo from a rooftop in broad daylight.

Chapter Five

Judi arranged the masculine-scented toiletries on the spare bathroom vanity: woodsy cologne, spicy aftershave, and musky mousse in case the hairspray wasn't enough. She'd had a blast shopping for her creation on Fifth Avenue. The manicure kit fit perfectly in the little space between the sink and medicine cabinet. Of course "Race" would enjoy his weekly manicure—one more thing she needed to add to the list. His bath towels alternated with hand towels and washcloths of the richest Egyptian cotton. The monogramming could come later when she decided what his name would be.

This would be his own bathroom, so he wouldn't feel crowded—a place to relax in the hot tub with music and candles or unwind in the steam room. Guests also used this bathroom, but it would be his corner of the loft—his territory to leave towels on the floor.

She stopped herself there. Never would he leave towels on the floor! Compulsive neatness—number three on his list of traits. Or four? She tried to remember as the buzzer sounded.

One short buzz and one long buzz rang out as if to say, "I'm heeeeere!"

"Oh, no, Iris!" Like a tornado Judi whirled through the bathroom, removing the manly articles and sweeping them into drawers and cabinets. "Okay, I'm coming!" With a quick glance around the loft for any remnants of her intended, she threw open the door.

"Sorry, Iris, I was busy." She let out a puff of air

and collapsed onto her computer chair.

"Anything steamy brewing?" Iris peered around Judi's shoulder.

Today a fruity fragrance masked her natural scent of tobacco.

"Just cappuccino," Judi said.

"Come on. You're sitting there out of breath like you've just had a vigorous romp. This must be one steamy scene you're writing. Let's have a peek." Iris bent forward to peer at the monitor.

"Iris, sit down, will you? You know how I feel about people reading my WIPs. And I wasn't writing a sex scene. I was cleaning up and am taking a breather."

"A screamer looks more like it. Judi, this is me, remember? I'm not people. I've read enough of your WIPs to put another ring around Saturn. Why so touchy now?"

"I'm not touchy." Judi headed for the kitchen and poured the rich, piquant cappuccino into a clear mug.

"I've only let you see my first passes. I'm not even on the first pass yet. It's what I call the drift, when my mind drifts. Then I draw up the first and second passes. After that comes the theme. I build outward from there, to reach the first draft. Then I improvise with the busywork and put the fillers in at the end."

Iris's lips thinned as she shook her head. "I envy you creative minds. I don't know what the hell you're talking about, but it works. Just tell me what you're planning to do with him."

"Him whom?" Judi's gaze flew in Iris's direction. Trying not to spill the full mug, she handed it to Iris. No, she couldn't know! Had Iris hacked into her email?

"Race, in your next book, who else?" Lifting the mug to her lips, Iris flashed a grin before taking a sip.

"Unless there's someone other than the fictional man in your life," she teased, one brow disappearing under a lock of hair gelled into place.

"No, Iris, nobody new between the sheets since I saw you forty-eight hours ago." Had someone seen her walking around with Felix? She changed the subject. "Has Kaye Lee Ellis turned in her script yet? She told me she was wrapping it up."

"No, she hasn't," Iris replied distantly. She stared at Judi's computer as if Race would pop out like a genie.

"She's slowing down. Burning out, I guess. Pushing the big four-zero." She tossed Judi a knowing glance.

Judi knew she didn't mean forty books. "I don't want to be reminded of aging right now." She also didn't want to discuss her morning's work because it wasn't her next book but more character traits for Felix's and her creation.

"Judi, you're so antsy today." Iris peered into her cup and put it down with a jittery hand, her eyes averted from it. "Whatever's in this stuff, you've been drinking too much of it. Why don't you flick in a dash of melatonin to neutralize the caffeine?"

"I'm not jumpy. I'm just...you caused me a serious case of writus interruptus."

"Sorry. I understand. Just text me later." Iris flicked her silk scarf around her neck. "I can go—"

"No, don't. I needed a break anyway." Judi flopped onto her sofa and toyed with one of the tassels on the cushion next to her. "I've been at this since one o'clock Saturday morning."

"You have? Wow, this must be atomic." Iris rubbed her hands together with sensual pleasure as if washing with one of her lavender truffles. "Just let me take a peek, please? Just one lil ol' peek?"

"Absolutely not. Nobody sees my work 'til it's at

least presentable. And believe me, this is anything but... right now, anyway. You'll have to wait, Iris."

"Sure, sure. I've got about five hundred other dog-eared scripts I can paw through. If I want real entertainment, all I have to do is shuffle through the slush pile. Well, the main reason I came over is I've got these tickets..." She rummaged through her bag, a bright orange wicker basket that matched her shoes and belt. "Two tickets right here to Lincoln Center. It's a 'Three B's' program. Beethoven, Bach, and who was the other guy?"

"The other B is Brahms. I'd love to." Judi glanced at her calendar, sadly devoid of penciled-in appointments.

"When is it?"

"Tonight. Eight o'clock. We can grab a bite at Tosca's before we go."

"Tonight?" She'd already set up her first meeting with Felix. She couldn't possibly cancel. "Oh, Iris, I wish you'd asked sooner. Tonight's impossible."

"Why? Race can hang loose inside your computer 'til you get back."

"No, I...I have to...I have to visit my...my father. He's just gotten back from cruising the Nile, and he wants to show me his DVDs." She could feel her cheeks growing hot, knowing she couldn't lie to save her life. She'd never successfully pulled off even the tiniest white lie; she had turned bubble gum pink, horrendous with her light auburn hair whenever she had tried in the past.

"Come on, Judi, since when do you like to sit and watch home movies of the Nile? We've been friends for fifteen years, and you don't want to tell me about your plans for one night?" She fanned the tickets back and forth, snickering. "I saw you blushing, trying to hide what you were writing, and don't think I didn't notice that slightly ostentatious zigzag-patterned necktie hanging from that candlestick on your mantle. A Claudio Cavatelli, no less, 'cause I peeked. You said you were searching out the perfect fifty-fifty relationship, and you did it. Way before your deadline, too. You've got that stud you've been looking for stashed away, I know it."

Felix's tie! She'd hung it on her mirror in full view. Iris would notice a dozen more things around the apartment in due time—the new cookware and wok in the kitchen, the sheet music by her piano— things she'd bought for her creation. And Iris, known in publishing circles as "Tuna Spotter" for her picayune editing, would espy all of them. Good thing she'd hid all those toiletries.

"Stashed away?" Judi laughed. "Not quite, Iris. You can look everywhere, but the only studs you'll find in this place are the ones holding up the walls."

"Then he must be in his boardroom or flying his jet to lunch in Paris or planning your next rendezvous."

"You don't know the half of it," Judi murmured.

"Why don't you want me to know if there's a man in your life?" Iris made a show of sliding the tickets back into her bag.

"He's not in my life...yet."

"You mean you're working on him?" Iris persisted.

"Uh—yeah, I guess you can say that." Gulping enough cappuccino to fill three Iris-sized mouths, she sighed in relief—she'd been dying to say something about it.

"So tell me, what's the problem? Is he the 'm' word?" Iris asked.

"'M' word? Oh—no, he isn't married." That kick-started her second wedding fantasy—a white satin-clad bride standing on the Rock of Gibraltar, the ocean crashing beneath her and her ardent groom...

"He just hasn't succumbed to your obvious charms, then, is that it?" Iris probed.

"That's it. You hit it right on the head. He doesn't know I exist." Judi couldn't hide her smile. She enjoyed making this up more than she would have telling the real story.

"Oh, you poor thing." Iris reached in her bag, pulled out a gold cigarette case, and fished out one of her herbal cigarettes. Her eyes didn't leave Judi for a second. "Isn't it always that way? It is for me."

"I've had too many mismatches. This one's going to be custom made. I'm so close to getting him, I can taste him," Judi said.

"I'm not going there—not before lunch." Iris shook her head. "So tell me, what does he do? Where does he work, and where does he live?" Iris flicked her lighter and lit up. She pushed her glasses on top of her head, her eyes widening.

"Uh, well—He doesn't do much of anything."

"He's a congressman?"

"No... " Her hands fluttered. "He...he just goes on jaunts all over the place."

"Oh, Judi, a genuine card-carrying sugar daddy! How did he make his fortune?" She took a deep drag and blew out a smoke ring.

"Iris, I'm a fiction writer, not a reporter for the *National Intruder*."

"No, you're right. Wait 'til you go to bed with him first. Oh! Have you...I mean..." She stuck her neck forward like a pigeon waiting to be fed.

"No, I haven't slept with him yet. I'm waiting for the right time." *Like the night we meet.*

"You mean 'til he showers you with presents? Like a stock portfolio perhaps?"

"I'm not a gold digger, you know. And I'm certainly not going to jump into bed with him at the first pheromone whiff." *Maybe the second.*

"No, not 'til at least chapter three." Iris ground out the half-smoked cig in Judi's ashtray. "So, what's his name?"

"His...n...name?" Now she had her. Judi searched frantically for a name, a name out of her books, the paperboy, any man's name, as it suddenly dawned on her that she hadn't chosen a name for her future lover!

"Uh...it's, uh...Felix." The instant that name escaped her mouth she could have kicked herself. But it was the only name her brain could produce. How she hated thinking under pressure. And Iris's hammering could make the Spanish Inquisition look like a consumer poll for the newest flavor of protein bars.

"Felix? How exotic! Felix what?"

"Varlden," she replied, her voice weak with defeat. Too late. Oh, why not? The damage was already done. Felix would have to pose as her new squeeze until Mr. Heroid came into the world.

"Varlden, Varlden, I've heard that name somewhere. It's Swedish, isn't it? Does the 'a' have those two little dots over it?"

Oh, no, they couldn't have met before. Iris was so not Felix's type. For one thing, smokers absolutely repulsed him. So did women who asked more questions than an IRS auditor.

"We went to school together. We've known each other since childhood. Our fathers worked together, and our parents are close friends. We're practically family," Judi explained away, all fact now. "He's got a doctorate in physics, teaches grad courses at Columbia when the urge strikes him, and has a brilliant scientific mind."

"Why haven't you told me before?" Iris badgered. "You've been hiding him away all these decades?"

"It hasn't been that many decades, and I haven't been hiding him. He lived in California till a few years ago and...we just ran into each other at Three Steps Down. It was nice," she added sincerely.

"Nice? It's positively serendipitous!" Iris's voice

lilted. "Long lost friends reunited only to discover dormant love. That would make a great book, why don't you—"

"I'd rather just leave this for the real world, you know…don't mix fact with fiction."

"Sure. So he's the one you've been looking for, and it turns out you've known him forever. How utterly cosmic!" Iris clapped with delight.

An image of Felix flashed into Judi's mind, kicking her pulse up a notch. Her best friend was back in her life. Good old dependable Felix, never a cross word between them… Without even knowing it, Iris made her realize she'd never thought of Felix in a romantic way. As much as she adored him, he wasn't—and never would be—Race.

"No. He's not the one I've been looking for. He's messy, eccentric, and unconventional. And he's my height with beach-bum blond hair." The anti-Race.

"And he votes Libertarian and drives a hybrid. What more can a spinster ask for?"

"Now that's not Juno Ursa talking. Juno Ursa is on a lifelong mission to find a Race-type rogue, a tall dangerous pirate with a rakish grin and a lightning bolt scar across his craggy face. And here she is hooking up with the schoolboy next door. But it's positively darling." Iris adjusted her geometric lapel pin. "What made you settle? Was all the fantasizing too much for you?"

"I haven't settled. We're just friends. Always will be. But I still know my dream come true is in my stars." She gazed past Iris at her computer, which literally stored him right now. "I have a hunch he'll turn up as soon as he pulls himself together," she couldn't resist adding.

"I hope you're right. But meanwhile, I'd love to meet your cute little pal. What's his name? Freddie?"

"Felix."

"Of course. When can you bring him over for

dinner?"

"I don't know. He's so busy these days."

"Well, he's got to eat. How about tomorrow night?" She got up and helped herself to another cappuccino, glancing at Judi's calendar. She ran a finger across the days of next week. "I see your schedule's rather thin."

"I don't think so, Iris. I have a lot to do."

"Come on. Ask him. Duck l'orange awaits."

That was Judi's favorite. Felix went wild over it, too. And Iris cooked it like ambrosia for the gods. "You got me there. How can I refuse duck l'orange?"

"Tomorrow night then?"

"I'll check his schedule. But if he can't make it, the two of us can feast on your culinary masterpiece."

Iris shot her a wry look and twisted her mouth. "If he can't make it, it'll be two drippy gyros from Jimmy the Greek's."

"All right, Iris, I'll talk him into it. Now go catch a duck."

Chapter Six

They sat at his low Oriental table, cross-legged on the floor, finishing a Japanese dinner delivered by Akimoto's.

"Drop the embarkation of this colossal Earth-stopping undertaking for Iris's duck?" Felix picked up a pair of chopsticks and slid a morsel of iwashi into his mouth, chewed, and swallowed. "Judi, I finally got a picture in my head of what this guy is supposed to look like—not only that, but I can finally hear the nuances of his voice in my mind's ear. I can picture his cleft chin, and I've got his swagger so well choreographed, I'm starting to walk like that myself. I don't need any interruptions. I'm on a roll. If I stop now, I'll lose all my momentum. Don't you know anything about proficiency?"

"Sure, I work that way all the time. But part of being proficient is knowing when to take a breather. A few hours over a gourmet dinner won't destroy any serious momentum. You have to eat anyway."

She heard a faint rattling noise in the other room and nearly snapped her neck spinning around to look behind her. "What was that?"

"What was what? Judi, you're awfully jumpy tonight."

She jumped at every little noise, even though he swore his on-again-off-again S.O. was history.

"We broke up exactly two months and two weeks ago," he'd declared. "So relax."

She turned back around and took her chopsticks back in hand. "I feel uncomfortable here, thinking some ex could walk in any minute and go postal on us."

She didn't press him for details of his last breakup; she knew how difficult these things went for men. Race, on the other hand, wore his heart on his metallic sleeve.

"Iris can't wait to have us over for dinner."

"Why does she want to meet me anyway? Don't tell me she wants one of those hunkoids for herself." He drained the cup.

"Definitely not. I just...she saw your tie hanging on the candlestick and assumed I had a man."

"Why didn't you just tell her it makes for better writing?" He lifted a piece of shrimp to his lips. "I mean, if you go so far as to act out your love scenes under a strobe light, why can't you get away with having men's ties hanging around? And throw a pair of dirty shorts in the corner to make it even more authentic."

"Race doesn't dirty his underwear."

"No, how could he? He never wears any."

She beamed. "So you have been reading my books!" Good old Felix, always thinking of her.

He looked away. "One."

"Well, that's a start. Felix, Iris is a true blue friend. I couldn't let her down. I told her I've known you all my life, and she wants to meet you. So what could I say?"

Iris would flip over him, but she didn't say that. She knew it would make him blush to the roots. He still saw himself as the pudgy four-eyed nerd. But a healthy dose of female fawning would boost his ego to where it belonged.

"Tell her I'm a vampire."

"She'd track you down for sure, leading with her neck."

"Would a werewolf turn her off? I've got some fake body hair on file."

She reached over and squeezed his free hand.

"Please, Felix, just come with me tomorrow night. You'll like her. She's personable and animated."

"There'll be enough animation around here in the next few months." He twirled his chopsticks.

"You won't be able to resist this menu. She cooks like a dream. She's a first-rate entertainer. Everybody loves her dinner parties."

"Who's she trying to impress?" He tried to hide the smile that told her she'd almost won him over.

"Nobody. Iris knows it's my favorite dish," she urged. "She also knows you're a good friend of mine, and she wanted to make it special."

"Sounds like she wants to make it special for the duck."

She had him almost convinced, now how to seal the deal? "I promise, you won't have to make any more dinner party appearances after my creation is born…uh, created…built…whatever you call it."

"But meanwhile, I'm cast in the role of your boy toy." This time he didn't hide his smile.

She circled the table and kneeled next to him. "Being a boy toy isn't all that bad. A few thousand Miami Beach gigolos can't be wrong."

"Hm. I think I'd better make this bastard real humble," he murmured, nodding. "So are we going to go over those briefs I drew up?"

"Oh, would I love to go over those briefs!"

The more they talked of her hero, the more impatient she grew. She wanted to possess her unborn lover now, here, on the cushions, and under the table with the bouquet of sake lingering in the air.

"How long should our first session take?" she asked.

"A few hours. I want to go over personality traits first." He stood, holding out a hand to help her up. "Come on. Let's go put Mr. Centerfold together. I'll show you the lab."

He let her pass through the doorway first. They descended a dark narrow staircase right out of an old Lon Chaney movie.

He flipped a switch, and she felt as if she'd just passed through a time tunnel into another galaxy. Tubular neon lights illuminated the entire area in brilliant white. The one big square room had a white ceiling, white walls, white floors, and not a window hung in sight. A fan hummed. They walked between a row of lab tables to an alcove lined with shelves and file cabinets, each stamped with a four-digit number.

The laboratory reminded her of a hospital, but the atmosphere was not so pristine. She smelled no pungent disinfectants; instead, the entire area emitted a floral fragrance.

At the end of the alcove was a long narrow cot stood at the alcove's end. "Is that your..." Gulp. "S—slab?" she stammered, as that old association of mad scientists with marble slabs crept into her mind.

However, the "slab" looked like an ordinary mattress covered with a blue flowered sheet. A huge spotlight shone onto it.

He laughed, opening a drawer labeled "Supplies—J-Q" and retrieved a yellow legal pad. "P" for "Pad," she assumed.

"No, it's not a slab, it's an ordinary old mattress. That's where I take my catnaps. I work in spurts, catching forty winks here and there."

"Oh." Taking a few more cautious steps across the alcove, opposite his cot, she faced a low door that would've swept her hat off, if she'd worn one—barely high enough for her to pass through without crouching.

"What's behind here? You don't have to tell me if it's where you keep secret formulas and stuff, I'll understand."

"Why don't you go in and see?" He had that

"profound idea" gleam in his eye. It reminded her of the time he'd immersed his eyeglasses in a jar of cleaning solution and placed the jar on the washing machine during the spin cycle, for a sonic cleaning.

"No, I'll pass. You're entitled to your privacy."

"Don't be afraid." He pushed the door open and nudged her in.

She gasped as she stumbled into a space as tight and stuffy as an elevator. She squinted, trying to adjust to the pitch-blackness.

"Felix!" Her heart hammered. A light snapped on, and she blinked, once to adjust her eyes to the light, and twice in disbelief.

She faced a toilet and a sink.

"It's the head, Judi." He turned the tap in the sink. "See? Even us geniuses make use of these occasionally."

She turned and heaved a sigh of relief. "You understand that there are things you do that have the capacity to unnerve me."

"You and most people. But we mad doctors go potty just like all you common folk."

"Sorry, Felix, I guess I've read too many Gothics."

"And you write too much pulp, or we wouldn't be here right now."

His voice became crowded, his fingers encircling her arm to lead her from the bathroom. A warm shiver ran through her as she imagined her hero touching her this way.

"Here, take this chair." He pulled a lever in the wall, and down came a small desk. Grabbing a chair for himself, he plucked a pen from a caddy in the wall. "I read one of your books, and I believe I got the gist of what you want. I'm hoping I won't have to read any more. The book was adequately—ahem—explicit."

"You really should read all of them to

understand how Race grew and matured over the years, right along with me."

"If I had that much time to sit and read, I'd be reading the kind of stuff I like to read, no offense. Besides, our creation doesn't have a history. It's not like he started out as a self-centered jackass and matured into pure gold. I'm creating him as a mature adult, so what matters is how he is now."

"Is that the way you're planning to design the spaceman, too?"

"That's a bit different." He slid the pen behind his ear, a lifelong habit he probably didn't even know he had. "His traits will be for adaptability and survival purposes. We're not going for looks and personality. He'll have an amiable disposition, so whatever life is out there, they'll fare harmoniously.

"With all the work I have in that area, I'm sure not going to spend the next two years making him look like one of those romance cover dudes. He can be homely as sin, as long as he's environmentally controlled and can stand a decade in space without going insane. That's what I meant by perfect. Now, your guy..."

He pulled a sheet of paper tagged with a red label and placed it in front of them on the desk. He took another pen from the wall caddy and checked off Item Number One on the page, the forgotten first pen still wedged behind his ear. "Here are four basic behavioral styles, I want you to choose the one you prefer. The steady relater, the cautious thinker, the interacting socializer, and the dominant director. Somehow I don't think you'll go for that one."

"Since you can see him in your mind's eye, cleft chin and all, can't we do the physical characteristics first?" she asked. "That should be the easy part."

"Are looks that important to you?" His stare was so intense she looked away.

But it made her think hard. What did she want

in this man beyond drop-dead gorgeous features, basic niceties and gentlemanly manners? Someone who would share her triumphs instead of leaving her because he couldn't compete. Someone who wouldn't walk out on her without the decency of a real goodbye. Her throat constricted at the memory of that day. Ryan had kissed her like nothing was wrong. But it marked his kiss goodbye. Forever. Her heart still ached at the memory.

"It's all important to me, Felix. This time around, I'm in the driver's seat. So why not go for the gold? I thought Ryan was everything I'd wanted, but since he picked up and left, I want someone who won't leave me because he thinks we're competitors. This creation will be so confident, and at the same time so devoted, he'll never want to leave me. So forgive me for sounding selfish, but at least I'll never be hurt again."

He nodded and sadness darkened his eyes. "I know what you mean, Judi. I understand. I was just asking."

She bit her lip and turned away. "Looks aren't everything, but I'm going for the entire option package here."

"Well, I've seen your book covers, and the only time I've seen a face like his was on a statue in Florence, the name escapes me at the moment." He turned her to face him. His eyes twinkled. "I mean, he can get away with a cleft chin, but you don't want him to be prettier than you, do you?"

"I never thought of myself as pretty," she replied sincerely. Her cheeks grew warm, and her entire body flushed. "But look, I've got a list right here." She retrieved her notes, determined to stay on task.

"We'll do looks later. Behavior comes first." He stated it so emphatically that she didn't argue any further. Behavior did come first. She, more than anyone, knew that.

They spent the next few hours choosing personality traits, and when they finished she couldn't contain her delight. She jumped out of the chair and luxuriated in a long stretch. "I'll want to spend every waking moment with him. He sounds like so much fun to be with."

"Barrel of laughs," he muttered, scribbling notes.

So he wasn't Felix's dream date. But he would be her counterpart in every way. No more nights of pretending she was happy. He'd be everything she wanted in a man—and more. She read aloud from the list: "Tidy, supportive, political conservative, gourmet cook, poet, musician, social, flexible, playful, spontaneous, stimulating, gregarious, jumps from one activity to the next, works quickly, enthusiastic, optimistic, persuasive, emotional, friendly, charming, affable, affectionate...Felix, can we add 'stable' to this? I don't want any mood swings here."

"We don't have to. He's going to be programmed. His isn't a human mind, prone to all the unpredictabilities and quirks of the human personality. With him, what you see is what you get. Like it or not." He typed information on a laptop base. "From this, I'll draft up the blueprint, a computerized DNA molecule of sorts that'll be a map for his characteristics."

Judi grew more excited by the second. Her hero was finally taking shape before her eyes! She thought of something: "How about if I commission an artist to paint him? You can hang the portrait on the wall while you're working, like an artist's model. Then you can see what he looks like."

"I don't think so. I'll have some 'splainin to do if the ORBIT personnel happen to drop by here and see a poster of Hunk of the Month on my wall."

"Tell them it's for inspiration. After all, women

stick pictures of bikini-clad models to our fridges because we want to look that way."

"Oh, yeah, they'll buy that in a minute." He rolled his eyes. "Nah, I think I'll pass on the life-size poster of Leo the Lothario, thanks very much."

"Leo, that's the perfect name for him! I love it." She beamed at him.

"I hadn't even thought of names yet," he replied. "But if you want him to be Leo, then Leo it is." He shut the laptop down. "Had enough work for one night?"

"I don't consider this work. That's like saying conceiving a baby is work."

He chuckled, shaking his head. "I can think of a few subtle differences." He stood and yawned, glancing at his watch. "You want a nightcap?"

"No, I'd better get going. Thank you, Felix. You're making all my dreams come true." She stood and wrapped her arms around him in a warm loving hug. He hesitated at first, and then his arms circled her waist. Resting her head on his shoulder, she could feel the tension under his shirt. Why was he uncomfortable holding her?

"Hey, loosen up." She rubbed her hands up and down his back. "It's only me, remember?"

He pulled away at that moment. "We'd better call it a night."

She could have taken that nightcap, after all but didn't want to overstay her welcome. They had many more nights like this ahead of them.

He called her a cab and walked her to the door. She wanted to twirl him around, dance across the floor, climb to the roof, and tell the world her dream had come true.

But he looked beat, with his eyes half shut, and his hair and shirt rumpled. With a peck on the cheek, she said good night and pranced down to the waiting taxi.

****

Felix allowed himself a long luxurious yawn. "Damn, I'm beat." He glanced at his watch. As the taxi pulled away, he muttered, "How did I let her talk me into this?" It was a hell of a lot of work. And it would take her away from him forever.

But he knew they couldn't realistically make it together. They'd grown too far apart. "This dream boat is so opposite of me. I couldn't win her if I rebuilt myself from scratch," he muttered. Six-two, dark and gorgeous as opposed to five-seven, blond and "adorable"—yuk! Political conservative?

Felix got arrested for being a Trotskyite student agitator. Writing poetry and cooking gourmet meals? He once managed to rhyme moon with June, but when it came to cooking, he couldn't even boil popcorn. Neat and tidy, and cleaning up messes? He had more clothes on the floor than in the closet.

No, Felix was not who she wanted.

But that didn't stop him from caring. "I want her, I want her—" he whispered into the darkness, and added what needed to be added, "to be happy."

****

Judi knew Felix didn't want to go to Iris's dinner party; he'd protested all the way to the front door. He wanted to stay home and work. "It's just one less night you'll get to spend with your stud muffin," he warned as Judi clapped Iris's heavy brass knocker against the red lacquered door. It swung open after a few seconds.

"So this is Felix!" Iris appeared, saki cup in one hand, cigarette holder in the other as they stepped into her foyer. How she got the door open, Judi had no idea. Iris drained the cup, put it down, and extended her hand to shake Felix's, all in one sweeping gesture.

"Judi's told me so much about you!" Iris clutched his arm with five red-taloned fingers and led him into her living room. A stream of jasmine incense smoke rose from the low black table and curled up to the fringed lantern above. Judi brought up the rear.

Felix thanked Iris as she motioned him over to a chair with a red-and-gold fringed cushion. She thrust a saki cup at him. "Judi, you sit here. Saki or champagne for you? Or are you slumming it tonight?" She turned to Felix, sweeping her glasses to the top of her head, revealing two paint-box purple smudges of shadow.

Judi stifled a giggle, knowing how Felix detested purple as it reminded him of his least favorite fruit—prunes.

"Judi doesn't drink when she's writing, and I sympathize. I know what it's like to have to bear brainchildren with a hangover. So tell me about yourself." Iris lunged for the champagne bottle in a silver bucket next to Felix. "Let me." Iris filled Felix's glass. "Our repast won't be ready for another quarter of an hour yet. Judi, did you say you wanted champagne? You may have a cocktail if you wish. I didn't hear you."

"You didn't give me a chance to say what I wanted." What's with the la-di-da act? Judi wondered. Then she remembered: she'd told Iris that Felix held a bouquet of degrees. Now Iris tried to impress him in the worst way—and it sure was the worst way.

"Do tell how you amuse that phenomenal brain of yours," Iris urged, leaning forward.

"I'm a biotechnologist, specializing in genetic engineering." His eyes danced, one brow cocked amusingly. "And inventor."

"Inventor?" The ash at the end of Iris's cigarette threatened to flutter off and slam dunk into Felix's glass. "I thought you spent all your time jetting to your private island or yachting or doing whatever you pleased."

"Jetting and yachting, huh?" His glance slid over to Judi.

Uh-oh. Judi returned a shaky smile. She should've known Iris would blabber about her made-up hero's lifestyle.

"I'm afraid the only island I've been on recently is Manhattan. And the closest I've been to yachting is the pedal boats on the Charles River. You must have me confused with one of Judi's other companions—one of the fictional ones."

Judi looked away and tapped her foot as she counted to ten.

Iris continued to machine-gun Felix with questions, reminiscent of her old journalism days when she probed people's personal lives for a living. Judi felt protective of him; although she knew he could take care of himself and keep Iris out of pouncing range.

Felix's mouth twitched like a restless caterpillar. Sooner than Judi expected, his left leg crossed over the right, and he started swinging his foot like a pendulum, another of his undying habits. He'd swung that leg in many a dull history class and sent a king and two rooks flying in the chess club.

But fortunately, Iris caught on and offered them dinner. As always, the hostess outdid herself. The duck l'orange was luscious, as was her tiramisu.

While Judi helped Iris make cappuccino in the kitchen, Iris gushed: "Oh, Judi, he's adorable! Why ever did you hide him all these years? Why didn't you introduce us before? I can just cuddle him to death."

Judi glanced through the shutters at Felix, who drummed his fingers on the table, looking so fidgety that he didn't need a cappuccino. "Thanks, Iris, I'm glad you like him. We've been through a lot together."

They returned to the living room with three

cappuccino cups on a tray. Felix shot Judi a "When's this gonna end?" glance when Iris began quizzing him again.

"So where did you say you were from, Doctor? A native New Yorker? How big is your family? Are they all geniuses like you?"

"We're from Westchester. My father ran a contracting business with Judi's father, and my mother owned a poodle parlor after a stint as an opera singer. Can't get any more diverse than that, can you?"

"Oh, what a plethora of talents!" She gestured toward the sideboard. "Would you like another helping of tiramisu or a brandy?"

He looked up at Judi and abruptly said, "No, I've had enough, thanks."

"Have you inherited your mother's singing talent?" Iris batted her lashes just once a second too often.

"Not really, but my brother sure has. He loves music, especially opera."

Judi's mouth opened in surprise, and she gobbled a handful of mints to hide her astonishment. Felix didn't have any brothers!

"Your brother? There's another genius who looks like you out there?" Iris perched at the edge of her seat.

"Well, his talents lie in other areas, don't they, Judi?" He shot her another glance and if the lights had failed at that moment, the twinkle in his eye would have glowed in the dark. Judi silently warned Felix to nix the brother baloney, watching Iris conjure up ways to wangle a meeting with the elusive sibling.

"He's six-foot-two, with blue-black hair, a mustache, azure eyes that lighten to cornflower blue in the sun, and—" He hesitated and took a sip. "—a smooth hairless chest. He used to be a male stripper."

"Don't stop there!" Her eyes wide and dreamy, Iris looked more enchanted than she'd ever been by any of Judi's novels.

Felix continued with a grin. "He's an expert sky diver, speaks fluent Greek, and composed a few movie scores. Now he just plays the piano when the mood strikes him. Oh—and he paints vivid landscapes of exotic locales."

All this sounded familiar to Judi. Skydiver, language scholar, composer, painter...he'd just described her creation!

"What's his name?" Iris asked. "I'll bet it's really suave, like Jacques."

"His name is Leo."

"As in Leonardo?"

"No, Leopold. But he prefers to be called Leo."

Iris clasped her hands together and threw her head back. "Leo!" she sang. "Oh, what a symphonic name!"

"Yes, it fits him, doesn't it, Judi?"

Judi almost fell out of her chair.

"He's a confirmed bachelor, unless, of course, the right woman comes along." Felix waved his hand casually.

"Does he—" Iris nearly lost her voice. "Does he still strip?"

"Only among friends. He's gotten modest in his old age."

"Oh, what a shame for the rest of us." Iris pouted.

"He's traveling right now, but from what I hear he's due for a visit soon. Perhaps the four of us can get together, maybe take in an evening at the theater. He's an avid theatergoer, too."

Judi cleared her throat to attract his attention. She'd planned to announce Leo's arrival, but had no intention of letting her dream hero escort Iris to the theater, even if Judi did chaperon. She wanted to drag Felix out of here, but he only glanced her way and grinned, asking innocently, "Wouldn't that be fun, Judi? You and me and Iris and…Leo?" He turned back to Iris. "Do you like the theater?"

"Oh, I just adore it!"

Judi's jaw dropped. Iris abhorred the theater! Her favorite medium was what she called "cultured" films. According to Iris, soft porn fell under this category, because it was "a quasi art form" as she put it.

"Good. We'll have to make that a definite date when he gets into town. I'll tell Judi to let you know when he arrives."

Judi got to her feet. "We'd better go. I've got a few things to take care of that can't wait."

She was finally able to herd Felix out the door and into the cool night air. "Will you tell me what the hell—" She halted as a pair of nuns strolled by, taking ages to recede out of earshot. "What the hell was that all about?" With a quick glance at her trembling hands, she couldn't remember when she'd been this annoyed at Felix. It had to be when he'd offered to repair her carburetor. Only later did she discover he'd replaced her new engine with the V-6 from his father's 1972 clunker— "just to see if the transplant would take."

"Just playing along with your friend's little fantasy. I had to do something to stay awake."

"Why are we spending all these months creating the man of my dreams if you're going to pass him off as your brother and play Cupid for Iris?"

"Elementary, my dear dreamer," he replied calmly, cupping her elbow, guiding her down the street.

"Frankly, if he's made to cater to you and only you, he'll be a wuss," Felix continued. "In order to be who you want him to be, a little flirting is essential, to make him who he is—a hero. That's part of who he is, by definition. Just like your exalted Race, who has his interstellar escapades. He never confined his love life to one galaxy. You did want more than a pretty face, didn't you?"

"Okay, Dr. Wunderkind, what if he falls in love with her? It's obvious she's already screwy about him. She's probably texting her psychic already."

"He can't possibly fall in love with her. He's yours and always will be. You won't be able to get rid of him. Unless you want to," he blurted.

"But you said he should be a flirt. She might take his playful banter as a serious come-on."

"Then it's her problem if she confuses harmless flirting with serious come-ons. But you've got nothing to worry about. The four of us will have a lovely evening at the theater."

They reached the corner and a bundle of tourists loped by. One of them escaped a speeding yellow taxi by inches.

"That event will never take place if I have anything to do with it."

"Didn't your mother ever teach you to share?" he asked.

"Doll clothes and lollipops, yes. Lovers, no."

"Come on, Judi. Don't deprive the guy of a fun night out once in a while." They crossed Fifth Avenue. "If anything, he'll put her in her place. What was with all those questions, anyway? I didn't get an interrogation like that when they interviewed me for the space project. I was waiting for her to wheel out a polygraph machine."

"That's Iris. She used to be a journalist. She's very inquisitive—okay, nosy."

"I can think of a better word for her," he murmured. "In German."

"She just wanted to meet you, that's all," she said as they turned the corner onto West Ninth. "I

65

told her we've known each other since we were kids, and she was curious to meet you."

"And since we were kids, you've always had loopy friends." He grinned at her.

"Yeah. And I still do, don't I?"

Chapter Seven

Another lonely Saturday night found her flipping between the last week's soap opera episodes she'd TiVo'd while enjoying a pint of Chocoholic Extravaganza and three cartons of moo goo gai pan. At midnight she called Felix but got his voice mail. She wondered where he could be. Probably on a date. But she hoped he had one of his midnight Pilates sessions. Why it bothered her that he'd be on a date, she didn't quite know.

Whenever she thought about him, she tried to think like a computer and delete all excess data— anything that smacked of the kind of attraction she'd never had for him before. But it grew harder and harder to deny her feelings, especially when they were together, working closely, laughing, nearly touching, and reminiscing about old times. She knew he sensed it too. She could see it in his eyes when the time came to say good night.

"Oh, God, what a mess," she sighed, scraping the bottom of the ice-cream carton with her spoon. If only it were a plot to one of her books. Then she could just do a rewrite.

****

Felix called on Monday in the middle of her dinner with *Hardball* glaring from her TV.

"Hi, Judi, just called to give you a progress report on old Boris here."

Yeah, but how are you? she wanted to ask. *And although it's none of my business, where were you Saturday night?* "Sweet! How's he doing?"

"Did you say you wanted blue eyes as a first

choice and gray as a second or vice versa?"

"Azure that lightens to cornflower in the sun, and darkens to a deep indigo at dusk."

"There seems to be a scarcity of blue eyes on the market, so I had to compromise."

"How? Don't tell me he's going to have one eye in the middle of his forehead. I'll go cross-eyed gazing at it."

"Not quite. But he'll sure grab your friend Iris's attention. My intensely handsome brother, who endeavors to capture the heart of his new mistress, will be blessed with one eye of scintillating sapphire and one eye of enthralling emerald."

"Oh, Felix, that sounds positively impressionistic!"

"Whew, I thought you'd jump down my throat on that one. I know how, er...consistent you wanted him."

"No, it's great. I don't know why I never gave any of my characters different colored eyes."

"Probably because Iris fantasizes in black and white. By the way, ORBIT finalized my contract. I've got to deliver an environmentally controlled humanoid within the next sixteen months."

"That's sooner than you'd scheduled." She gave the calendar a nervous glance. "Will that be enough time?"

"Well, once I get Son of Superman off the drawing board and into your place, and debug him, it shouldn't take as long to create another one. I'll have had your guy for practice, so to speak."

"My lifelong mate as the prototype for your space cadet!" she countered with an exaggerated air of exasperation.

"I'll straighten out any of your guy's kinks or quirks."

"He's not supposed to have any kinks or quirks. He's perfect."

"I mean—deviations from the norm," she said. "The cute kinks and quirks you told me about. Kinks can be cute, you know."

"Like his chocolate syrup fetish."

"Yeah, I guess. If you have a sweet tooth, and since libido's not a necessity in outer space, my space cadet won't have any fetishes whatsoever. All I need's for this one to be halfway to Megasus and start lusting after the air hose."

"So you're saying my creation really is trial and error," she said, only half joking.

"Not at all. You wanted the perfect fifty-fifty, and that's what you'll get. But remember," he added, with a chiding hint to his voice, "you asked for it."

"Asked for what, professor?" She pushed away a twinge of agita. This endeavor and its outcome would change her life forever, but at times she felt he didn't take her seriously enough.

"He's going to be a hero, Judi. Not merely think he is. Like some mortals."

"We'll balance each other out, that's the whole idea—to be perfectly compatible and complementary. A Lewis to my Clark, a Watson to my Crick, and a Bill to my Hillary."

"I didn't know any of those partners were romantically involved."

"You know what I mean. I've got to be at Iris's office in half an hour. Are we still on for tonight?"

He paused and so did her heart.

"I think so," he finally answered. "Depends on how long this takes. I'll get back to you."

****

Felix called from his cell phone to tell Judi he was three blocks away looking for a parking space.

"Have you had dinner?" she asked.

"Why are you always trying to feed me?"

"I'm not. I just don't want you to go hungry. Sometimes you get carried away with work and forget to eat." The truth was, she loved to feed him. She just enjoyed taking care of him. Oh, she needed a man to love!

"As a matter of fact I haven't had a meal. I just grabbed a candy bar and a Coke on my way out."

Some things never change, she mused, smiling.

"Hey, you know what I could really go for?" His voice took on a playful note. She could just see him rubbing his hands together, his eyes lighting up. "A sack of Burger Hut burgers. Mmm-mmm! I can just taste those onions now!"

"On the way down the gullet or on the way back up again?"

"Hey, Judi, you don't mind if I buy a few sacks full, do you? I'm salivating already."

"What made you think of Burger Hut?"

"You."

"Me?" She stuck out her tongue. "I haven't had one of those murder burgers in—probably since last time I went there with you."

"Exactly. Probably my last visit to the gourmet palace, too. But some things you just never forget. The nearest one's in Jersey City, not far from the Holland Tunnel entrance. I'll zip over, get a few dozen with some fries, and if you can whip a couple banana shakes, it'll be just like—"

He broke up, and the phone went dead. "Felix?"

She hung up, still smiling. Just like old times, she knew what he was about to say. Only somebody as wild and wacky as Felix would drive to Jersey for Burger Hut burgers. She wouldn't have gone farther than Bleecker Street.

Okay, he's not as wild and wacky as I am, she figured. *But he's close enough to be dangerous.*

****

He showed up with a big bag of burgers and a big grin to match. Even before he got to the door, she could smell the onions.

He placed it on the counter, and she put the burgers on a plate while he plugged his laptop in. "Felix, there are only three burgers here. I thought you were getting a dozen."

"I, uh..." His grinning lips shrank into a sheepish twist. "I ate some on the way."

"You ate nine burgers? And where are the fries?" She shook the bag. It was empty.

"Well, you can't eat burgers without fries, can you?"

"Felix, you're not fourteen anymore, and neither is your digestive tract."

"I won't get sick, and even if I do, it was worth it. Go ahead, finish 'em. I think I've had enough." He sat, placing a hand on his abs.

"Sure you don't want a hair of the dog?" They did smell delicious. She closed her eyes and let the aroma send her back to all those late-night visits with wicked munchies. They always pooled their change to get a bagful of those murder burgers, or barf burgers; every vile, unappetizing name they could think of, yet they wolfed the greasy treats down like starving stevedores.

"No, you go ahead. I've already had my fun."

She'd made two banana shakes with ice cream and chocolate syrup, and brought them over to him. "Just in case they didn't happen to settle just the right way, wash 'em down with this."

"Ooh, yummy." He stabbed at the shake with the plastic straw. "A super duper triple thick shake, complete with bendy straw. How'd you get it so impenetrable?"

"It's ice cream and bananas, Felix. With syrup to make it even more sickly sweet."

"Great, now what's for dessert?" He sucked at the straw, and getting nowhere, put the cup to his lips and slurped.

"You never could control that sweet tooth, could

you?"

"A package of Krunchy Kremes would go down just right now." He wiped his lips.

"They still make those?"

"Sure. I still buy them. I keep a box in the lab for when I need a sugar fix. It's an acquired taste, you know." He flipped open the laptop.

"I don't have anything quite that nostalgic around here. I might have some Belgian chocolate roses Iris left here."

"She's definitely the type to prefer edible roses to real ones," he commented as the screen came alive. He tapped a few keys. "Okay now. You sure these traits are consistent with the relationship you want with this dude? A risk taker?" He scrolled down. "I didn't think you'd want to sit up nights worrying if he'll survive Niagara Falls in a barrel."

She sat next to him and started on her third burger.

"Oh, that'll never happen. I'll never let him out of my sight. But he should be a risk taker. It's so romantic, the thrill of the chase, the possibility of getting caught."

"Well, he's not going to be chasing you. You've got him literally eating out of your hand. As far as getting caught, neither one of you is married—"

"I didn't mean those two examples specifically. Risk-taking will be exciting to my hero, the intrigue of the unknown." She took another bite, savoring every bit. "Look at some of the risks Race takes."

"Yeah, but he has an author to pull his chestnuts out of the fire every time to ensure future sales. It just sounded a bit flaky to me. It's much smarter to play it safe. Life's got enough risks without balancing a chip on your shoulder and challenging fate to knock it off. My God, being born was a risk. Look at the odds we beat even to get conceived. Why push it?" he asked.

"I mean calculated risks. My hero can play the stock market and will probably lose money along the way, but he won't fret about it, second guess himself, or walk in the valley of regret." *Like I've been doing since Ryan left me,* she wanted to add, but didn't want to start feeling sorry for herself. That was one risk she'd lost on. But with her hero, there would be no risks. He'd be born to love her, to never stray, the surest guarantee in life a mortal could ask for. "We could even play the stock market together."

He gave a dramatic roll of his eyes. "That's a calculated risk? Playing the market is like taking a death defying leap."

"Okay, he might occasionally exceed the speed limit in the snappy red convertible I'm going to buy him. He has to have his fun."

Felix put down his shake and looked away. "Oh. Yeah. Fun. A word that's never been used with my name in the same sentence."

The third burger gone, she wiped her mouth with a napkin. "Oh, come on, Felix. We've always had a blast together. Look at what we're doing now, eating murder burgers and slurping shakes. It's just a different kind of fun, that's all."

"I guess your idea of entertainment these days is more sophisticated than Magic Mountain." A twinge of bitterness darkened his voice.

"We did more than that. How about the senior ski trip? That was a blast!"

"For you maybe, Judi. I spent the weekend writhing in agony."

"You could've kept skiing. I never heard of anyone kept from skiing with a broken thumb before."

"Hey, it hurt!"

"You big baby." She swatted him with her heart-shaped pillow.

He pulled the cushion from behind him and

bopped her over the head. She lashed back, and it became a genuine pillow fight. Giggling with delight, she slid off the couch as he dropped to the floor and proceeded to tickle the bottoms of her feet.

"No, not that! No! Please don't tickle me!" She scrambled up and dashed across the room. He chased her through the loft until she made a sudden about-face, pushed him back down on the couch, and fell on top of him. She buried her nose in his hair. "Felix, there's something I've been dying to do to you."

"Go for it."

"I want to smooth this hair down with gel and comb it until it looks like it's been combed."

He sat up, and she slid to the floor again. She got to her knees and smoothed his hair down, trying to make a part.

"Oh, so I look sloppy now."

"Not at all! I just want to see how you'll look."

"It'll just go back to the way it was when I walked in here. And no perms!"

"It's a deal!" She ransacked her closet for her hair gel, round brush, blow dryer and sculpting lotion. She had more fun than she'd had in ages as she doused his hair with gel, blow dried it, and gave him a straight side part.

"Don't you have any girlfriends you can do this with?" He looked at himself in the bathroom mirror and turned away, scowling. "Can't you have a slumber party or something?"

"I don't like to mess with other women's hair. Iris won't let anybody but Andre of Beverly Hills go near her luscious locks, and as for other girlfriends— well, I really don't have any."

He rinsed the gel out of his hair and ruffled his fingers through it. "Does that bother you? Not having any girlfriends?"

"Not really," she shot back quickly, contrary to

how she felt. She'd lost faith in any chance of having girlfriends after what Alyssa had done to her. It wasn't all Ryan's doing. She remembered how devastated she'd been when they'd run off together. She'd suppressed the hurt. Then, after weeks of ice cream cartons as bedmates, she dragged herself to the computer and created Race. Race, who skyrocketed her into the stratosphere of fame and success. Race, who she could always depend on to be there. So, in a twisted, backhanded way, she was grateful to Ryan and Alyssa for betraying her. Without them, she never would've created her fictional hero.

"What are you thinking about?" Felix's voice broke her reverie, welcoming her to the present.

"Oh—just how my husband and best friend hurt me...but it's history now." She held up a hand as he was about to speak. "Don't feel sorry for me. I created Race out of that hurt, and now I'm creating a real Race out of what's left of that hurt. So I'm glad I never got over it."

He nodded. "I'm impressed. You're strong. In a masochistic kinda way, but strong nonetheless."

She ran her finger over the bristles of the brush.

"Not because of what Alyssa did to me, but I've always preferred the company of men. Too bad I don't know any." She gave him a sideways glance and tried to keep a straight face, but it wasn't easy, once he started tickling her around her ribs.

She turned to bat him over the head with the brush but missed and caught him on the bridge of his nose.

"Yow!" His hand flew up to his face.

"I'm sorry! Oh, my God, let me look. What did I do?"

"Nothing a raw steak and a pound of stage makeup won't fix."

His left eye was a shiner already. "Felix, I'm so

sorry." She ran to get some ice, remembering the time they'd been play-wrestling and he pulled on her arm so hard, he sprained her wrist. Her father took her picture and glued it into the family album, a ten-year-old Judi bathing her arm in a plastic tub with a look of utter misery on her face.

So now they were almost even.

****

At FF&P, Fantasy, Futuristic and Paranormal Writers of America, the biggest science fiction writers' conference of the year, Judi counted the hours until her flight home. Why they chose Kansas City, she didn't know. Probably because too many people balked at Hawaii last year, and they wanted to keep it central.

Her heart was somewhere else as she sat through the autograph party, surrounded by stacks of her books and flanked by two life-sized cutouts of her covers. With her brightest PR smile, she signed books, posed for blinding flash photos, and attended the awards banquet in an off-the-shoulder chiffon that scratched and pumps that pinched. At midnight each night she slipped away and escaped to her suite to soak in the hot tub and drink mimosas.

She passed on the restaurant roundup and ordered pizza and onion rings from room service. Then she called Felix.

"Felix, how are you feeling?" She thought about how she'd last seen him with a conspicuous shiner and white tape across his nose. The poor guy, all he went through for her. "I'm really sorry about what happened."

"Don't worry, I'm a fast healer. It's also a great attention getter. My female students all want to play nurse with me."

His tone was purely playful, but an unexpected stab hit her—and she refused to believe it was anything like jealousy. Whatever created that tingling sensation, it made her miss him all the more and wish he were at her side. "I'm the one who should be changing your dressings, Felix. I'm the one who maimed you."

"I almost broke your wrist wrestling that time. So consider us even. How's the conference going? Your hand fall off from signing autographs yet?"

"*The Cutting Edge* was here, zeroing right in on me, but that's only because I had the most gorgeous hunk on my cardboard cover cutout, Race, of course."

"Oh, come on. You're the biggest star there, I'll bet."

"Not really. I wish I could've skipped this altogether. I wish you were here. I wish it had been in Palm Springs instead. I wish—"

"What was that second wish?"

"That you were here." She cringed. She hadn't meant for that to come out of her mouth. "Well, yeah—with all the space cadets here, the place could use an actual scientist."

"Just wait till they see who you have on your arm next year."

She smiled dreamily. "I'd rather play it safe than bring him to a place with two thousand women in the same room. Do you think he'd stand a chance?"

"As long as his bodyguards are better looking than he is, he should be safe."

"Oh, can you design me a few bodyguards while you're at it?" she teased.

"Sure, but they're gonna be female. None of those cougars'll come near a pair of Amazons, will they?"

"This is a convention, Felix." She looked in the mini bar for a clean stem glass. "These cougars are two thousand miles away from home. Their old men don't know what they're up to. They'd break down the Great Wall of China to get to a gorgeous hunk."

"Then you'd better leave him home with me."

"He might drive you nuts with all his cooking and cleaning and wining and dining and singing and poetry." Cradling the phone between her ear and shoulder, she popped the cork on a new bottle of champagne.

"Oh, he'll be easy to baby-sit. I'll simply pull his plug."

"Now where did you say this plug was going to be? And how big?" She let out a torrent of giggles.

He laughed along as she filled her flute with bubbly.

"Whoops!" she exclaimed as she knocked the glass over.

"Judi, have you been drinking?"

"No. Just champagne."

"Why don't you go down and mingle?" he asked.

Her lids wearily slid shut at that suggestion. She was all mingled out and couldn't wait to get back home to the quiet of her loft and truffles. "I've been mingling for fourteen hours and barely managed to escape. I slid by a reporter trying to shove a tape recorder down my cleavage. You know what these things are like. You crave privacy like fire needs water. As soon as I peeled my dress off and chiseled my makeup off, I felt alive again. Popularity isn't all it's cracked up to be."

"It's only another, what, two days?" he asked.

"Forty-seven hours and eleven minutes 'til my flight." She kicked off her shoes and stretched out on the bed. "Felix, can you pick me up? My plane gets in at noon. I hate it when there's nobody to meet me at the airport."

"Oh, I'm sorry, Judi, I've got a class at eleven."

She pressed her hand to her eyes, moving the mouthpiece away from her lips so he wouldn't hear her sigh of disappointment. Was he putting her off? What to do now, give up or push more? Go for it, she decided. She wanted to see him. "Can you come over later, then?"

"Why don't you come to my place instead? I want to go over a few things anyway."

"More personality traits?" An ember of excitement lit up her heart. And it wasn't about her unborn hero. It was about seeing Felix. In that instant, she tried to sort through the confusion of emotions. Of course she wanted to see him; they hadn't played around together in almost twenty years. But this anticipation couldn't stack up to her younger days. Back then she'd never harbored this kind of build-up, like a girl going on a date...

She now realized that it wasn't just two old friends reuniting after a few decades but more like having a new man in her life—Felix.

"Well, that and a few other things," he replied.

"Oh, I'm dying to blab this to everybody milling around down there."

"Not a word! Maybe you'd better keep at that champagne until you pass out."

A knock sounded at her door. Probably the ice cream she ordered.

"I gotta get that. Room service. Dessert. I'll see you Monday."

"Looking forward to it, Pookie."

The way he said it, it sounded like he was counting the hours, too.

As she hung up, the familiar voice at the door told her it wasn't room service. "Juuuu-di! Open up!" So she tore into that can of barbeque chips she'd been saving.

Iris still wore her evening gown. Sling-back pumps dangled from one hand, and she held a plastic cup and a cigarette in the other. She wiggled bare toes. "Come on down to the lounge, Judi. Some of the cover models are down there, and we're all going to line dance. I'm going to change into my dancing duds first."

"I'm not in the mood for shaking my booty with cover models, Iris." She turned around, went farther back into the room, and slid a dozen more chips out of the can.

Iris followed her and sat on the edge of the bed. "What's wrong, Judi? You haven't been yourself these last few weeks. You always loved these conventions. You've never spent this much time in your room, and when you did, you always had an entourage up here. What's bothering you? You can tell me."

"Does it show that much?" She sat on the bed and started eating the chips two, then three at a time, washing them down with gulps of champagne.

"Of course. To me, anyway. You just seem— lost."

Judi needed to pour her feelings out to someone. "All right, I'll tell you. But you might miss the line dancing."

"Oh, the hell with that. You're more important."

And she knew Iris meant it. "It's Felix. I—think I'm falling for him—hard. This is the last thing I thought would happen. If you'd told me twenty years ago I'd have any kind of romantic feelings for Felix, I'd have laughed you right out of the girls' locker room."

"That's what's bothering you? Good Lord, Judi, I think that's fabulous! Oh—don't tell me he's married, or—oh, no. Not the 'G' word."

She shook her head. "He's divorced, and he's straight. But there's a complication. His brother. Leo. The, uh, the romantic hero hunk stud."

"What about him? Did he get to New York yet?"

"Not exactly—not yet. He—he made a brief appearance a few weeks ago, then he—uh, he, well— left and he's coming back again—"

"And you've fallen for him, too, and you're torn

between the two of them."

Iris could zoom in on anything Judi was trying to say, either in real life or in print. That's what made Iris such a good editor: the ability to sense what came next—or what should come next.

"Iris, I'm in love with Leo. He's the one I've been looking for even before my bras had cups, the other half of the life I've been searching for. Then Felix and I reconnected, and—I just never expected this. We grew up together." She sat Indian-style on the bed and dug into the chip can. "He was like a brother or a cousin at least. He was a nerdy little scientist with glasses. I didn't see him for years, then—we're renewing our friendship and growing closer. I enjoy his company immensely, I love him to death, but I don't know if we could ever make it together."

She fished out a couple more chips. "He's a perfectionist, driven workaholic who doesn't know the first thing about romance, and a slob to boot. Now his—his brother's on the scene, he's to die for, and we've made all these fabulous plans and—God, I just don't know what the hell I'm going to do." She chomped down on four chips at a time. "Besides eat potato chips and wonder what the hell I'm going to do."

"I can tell you at least a few thousand women in this hotel alone would kill for your problem."

"It's not as glamorous as it sounds, Iris. I love them both, equally intensely, yet they're so opposite, it makes me wonder how I can love two such opposite men. What does that say about me?"

"It says you're a warm, loving, passionate woman. You just have to decide what it is you really want, what each of these men can give you. You've always wanted the trappings of romance, so the brother provides that. With Felix you've got companionship, a history, and lots of memories. They're both great catches, but you have to go deeper than that and decide who's more able to meet your needs."

"Leo will be here—I mean he's coming back to New York soon, and I'm counting the minutes until I can be with him. But I just got off the phone with Felix, and I can't wait to see him. Oh, how did I get myself into this mess?"

"Well, it takes two to tango—or in this case, three. So don't just blame yourself. Do they know how you feel about each of them?"

"Kind of, well, not exactly. Leo doesn't know how I feel about Felix, but Felix knows all about Leo, and I don't know if Leo knows how Felix feels. He just wants me and Leo to be happy because he knows I've always wanted Leo, but I know I'm hurting Felix—"

"Whoa!" Iris held her palm up, her curly wig bouncing. "You mind writing this all down and diagramming it so I can parse it? I've edited some of the most complicated plots ever written, but what you've just spewed off would make a soap scribe take up basket weaving."

Judi simply stared into her empty chip can.

"Just see how it goes, honey. You don't have to make your mind up tonight." Iris doused her cigarette in her half-full cup. "Time will tell. Trust me on that. One of them will prove to be the right one."

"I want them both, but that's not right. It's greedy, too. I've never been greedy. All I know is that one of us will get hurt in the end. I just wonder which of us it'll be. But I know where I can lay the odds."

"Don't be so pessimistic." Iris slid into her shoes. "You're all adults. I'm sure you can work it out."

Judi nodded, feeling relived but not any less torn. She wished real life could be like her books—with one hero.

****

"Felix, you home?" The front door hung wide open. She wished Felix were a little less brilliant and a little more cautious.

She let herself in, closing and locking the door. "Felix?" She called down the steps to his lab, where the Strauss waltz blasting through the speakers would have drowned out a shuttle launch.

She knocked on his lab door. It creaked open. The music assaulted her ears. A figure lurked in the shadows. It looked like Felix, but she wasn't taking any chances.

She inched back a step, ready to turn and flee when she a voice called to her.

"Don't go, ma chérie, stay and have zees dance!" It was a phony French accent if she ever heard one, so she knew he had to be horsing around in there.

"Felix, what the—eeeeeek!" She backed into the wall, crashing into his watercolor of a DNA molecule wrapped around the Earth.

All the lights went out except a weak flashlight beam. Engulfed in complete blackness, a disembodied head appeared, open eye sockets staring straight through her.

"Hey, zaa's no way to greet zee man of your dreams!" The head nodded, emphasizing each word, still in the terribly affected French. She was finally able to breathe but shook her head in disbelief.

"Felix, you are so a candidate for Bellevue!"

He finally flipped on a light and held the head next to his own, making it nuzzle his neck. "Hey, back off, buddy, I don't go that way!" He playfully slapped the head's cheek and winked at Judi. "Hmmm—still have to iron some kinks out of him. He's supposed to go for you, not me!" He placed the head on a pile of cushions and lowered the music with a remote. "You can come in, he won't bite. I mean, nothing worse than a hickey."

She took several breaths to calm herself, placing

her purse on the desk. "Have you been playing with that head all day?"

"Nah, he's pretty to look at but with all the depth of a saucer." He gave her a self-satisfied smile. "Come here and feel the skin. Like a baby's bottom." He grabbed her hand and she snatched it away.

"N—no! I don't want to touch it—him—not yet." She shuddered as if a snake had slithered by.

"Judi, this guy is going to be your S.O. You may as well get used to touching him. I invented a skin-cell-growth serum that I call Supergrow, which multiplies the cells the way ours do. It came about in the beginnings of my cloning experiments, and at first, we grew it in a lab. But once he's functioning, he'll have to apply moisturizer every day."

"Okay, so he can work that in with his nightly beauty regime. Is he going to be bald?" She forced her eyes in that direction, where the head lay on its side, eye sockets staring at nothing.

"Of course not. You wanted blue-black hair. But I'll leave that up to you. Can you look up the number for that men's rug club?"

"Felix, is that all you have so far? The head?"

"Well, it's a start, isn't it? It's going to be the most individual part of him. The rest of his body will be pretty typical. I know—you wanted me to start at the feet and work my way up so I'd get to the good parts faster." He went over to his bar and poured himself a shot. "Care to imbibe?"

"No thanks. I was just curious. I've never seen a genius at work before, and I—" She rested her hand on the table behind her and shrieked as she touched cold flesh. She spun around to see a human hand, palm up, and fingers splayed straight out. "God, what's that?"

"His left hand, of course. Or is it his right?" Felix refilled his shot glass and walked over. He lifted the hand, scratched his face with it, and placed it on the cushions next to the head. "Left. The right one's around here somewhere. Why don't you look around my bathroom and see what grabs you?"

"Oh, you are such a wack job!" She shook her head. "You must wow 'em on campus."

"Nah, I fit right in. With the physics department, anyway. As for the rest of Flesh Gordon, the torso will be ready in a week. You can come over and inspect it."

"I'd rather wait 'til he's fully grown—er, put together, so I don't have to see any more dismembered body parts."

"I didn't realize you were that squeamish." He gathered files from a cabinet. "You were never this way about my insect kingdoms."

"They always did gross me out. I just didn't want you to think I was a wuss."

He turned to look at her. "Really? And all those years you put up with it?"

"Hell, you put up with all my shenanigans. I figured it was only fair."

"I was happy to do it, Judi." His voice softened and he looked away. "That's what—friends are for."

"Now I've really got a debt to repay here. I mean, all you've done for me before is nothing compared to the trouble you're going through now."

"I can't really say it's trouble. It'll help me work the bugs out of my astronaut. And I can't say it's any worse than the time you made me call that dork who kept hitting on you. You made me pretend to be a hit man and threaten to wrap him in cement for a cruise down the Kill Van Kull."

"Well, some people just won't take no for an answer. Your Tony Soprano imitation worked. He hired an armed bodyguard."

"Wuss." He clucked.

"I still feel like I need to repay you." She squeezed his hand, wanting to touch a warm, live one.

"There's nothing to repay. What I'm doing is its own reward. Sounds corny, but—this is quite an accomplishment for me, too, Judi, not merely a favor to satisfy your whimsy. I'll be pretty proud when this is done. Happy for you, too."

She detected mixed emotions in those last words. Looking into the sharp green eyes, she saw the dedication there. And something that looked like regret as he looked away.

Was he sorry he'd agreed to build this hero? she wondered. Then she asked herself for the first time, straight out: *Am I sorry?*

No! She was destined for her creation, the extension of her soul. She felt only half alive without him. Maybe the three of them could hang out together, until Felix found another significant other. They'd have a great time double dating; maybe even go on trips together. One big happy family.

It sounded a little fanciful, but anything was possible after this. She kept that firmly in mind. "So what's next?" she asked, back in reality.

"What's next? The small details. We go buy him some clothes."

She squealed in delight. "Fifth Avenue awaits us! I saw a few things in the spring collections I'd like to get for myself."

"I thought we were shopping for Gorgeous George."

"When did you ever go on a shopping spree with a woman who didn't buy anything for herself?" She followed him outside, and they stopped at the curb.

"So I don't know much about women. I can't be good at everything."

He hailed a cab, and they headed for Fifth Avenue.

****

They returned to her place with half of Fifth

Avenue, according to Felix.

"I want him to be an exquisite dresser," she said. "And once he's here, he can pick out his own clothes. Can you program that into him? Make him able to match colors and know what tie goes with what shirt?"

"I'm a scientist, Judi, not a magician." He helped himself to a soda and a splash of rum. "A guy who cleans up after himself is rare enough. But a guy who knows how to dress?" He gave an exaggerated shudder.

"So who dresses you?"

"I'd never admit this to anyone, and I'd cut my own head off before I'd admit this to another guy, but I have a wardrobe consultant."

"You do? I'm impressed." She noticed his clothes looked tailor-made, considering he'd gone through high school and college with the same clip-on tie—and didn't think wearing socks was essential for a job interview. "Male or female?"

"Sometimes I wonder that myself. Male, but—I never bothered to check, and I don't intend to. I meet him twice a year. We get together with this tailor who comes over from Hong Kong, and my wardrobe consultant does the rest."

"I thought you looked a bit Central Park West. I do like the way you dress these days."

"Thanks. I go to these baloney-throwing scientist functions in five star hotel grand ballrooms, so I've got to look the part. But your dude here—where will you be going that he needs a six-figure wardrobe? I thought you'd keep him confined to your bedroom in his birthday suit."

"I want to show him off, too, you know, not just make him a sex slave. We'll be going to the theater, to dinner. He'll be meeting my colleagues."

"Oh, I didn't think you'd let the world even see his face."

"Of course I will. I'm relationship-oriented, and I want him to be like that, too. He's got to put me first, but he should be gregarious, so we can go out in groups, and he'll be the life of the party. I want women to ogle him and men to admire him, even ask for advice."

Felix went over to his laptop and turned it on. "I didn't exactly have him pegged for a life-of-the-party type. But shouldn't he come on a little less like gangbusters? I mean, that's okay for the first few soirées, but we have to be careful he doesn't turn into a bore. Like me."

"You've never bored me, Felix."

"No?" His bright eyes narrowed. "How about that time I tried to explain the composition of Pluto's third moon, and the next sound I heard was you snoring?"

"Come on, I had two jobs and spent my leisure time studying for finals, remember?"

He tilted his head. "How about that. But now that Pluto's been demoted to a plutoid, it doesn't seem so profound any more."

"I had more earthly concerns at the time, like passing finals, something you geniuses didn't have to worry about. But don't think you're boring, Felix. You've always fascinated me."

His entire face lit up. "No kidding? Why didn't you ever tell me?"

"I thought you knew." She mixed herself a drink and refilled his.

"You never wanted to get into discussions about anything scientific."

"That doesn't mean I find you dull or boring." She sat beside him on the sofa. "I've never wanted to be an actress, but put me in a room with Zach Slater, and we'd find something to talk about."

"Who's Zach Slater?"

She shook her head. "Never mind."

"But we never found any common ground in the scientific world," he said. "The real scientific world, I mean, not the fictional one."

"I'll level with you, Felix. I always felt inadequate around you. You were so much smarter than everybody else. Being around you intimidated me. I was afraid to open my mouth sometimes. As far as asking questions—forget it; I always thought you'd laugh at me." At this point all her insecurities ganged up on her, making her feel two feet tall. Successful writers were a dime a dozen, but scientists like Felix came along maybe once in a generation, if that.

A few vivid memories returned from their school days, when she hid her report card because it wasn't as good as Felix's and when she burned her science fair project, a papier mâché model of the moon, after Felix's exhibit, a 3-D demonstration of travel through a black hole, took first place and toured the country. Of course she could never measure up to him. At least he'd made his marriage last ten years; hers barely lasted three. Even after they'd gone their separate ways, she still strove to measure up to Felix.

"Come on, Judi." He brought her back to Earth.

"You should know me better than that. I never laughed at anybody in my life. I wouldn't dare. As for being smarter, I'm no smarter than you are. We're just good at different things. I could never sit down and write a novel. I wouldn't know where to begin."

"But look at all you've accomplished. Degrees, awards, inventions..."

"And you're a best-selling author. Nobody's ever asked me for my autograph."

She was amazed he found that admirable. It sent a warm feeling through her, like his sincere praise of her dancing after her ballet recital, how he'd knocked himself down because he couldn't dance, and she was so graceful.

"That's just the media-hyped world we live in." She gave a dismissive wave. "People get famous for the wrong reasons sometimes. And the wrong people get famous."

"I don't want to get famous," he declared. "I like to hide."

"I noticed. You hid from the prom, football games, every school dance—"

"Not because I was being a snob." He crossed his arms over his chest and actually looked smaller, more vulnerable. "I'm not comfortable in a crowd, like this hero's going to be. I'll never be like that. I freeze up when people mob me. I just dress up and go to these functions because I have to." His eyes focused on a distant spot, not looking too happy.

"Felix, that's not a fault. Don't ever put yourself down just because you're shy. It's you. I like that shy streak in you. It's very appealing. And very cute." She gave his hand a squeeze, feeling warmly connected to him, but pulled away when he began to squeeze back.

"But you just said I never went to all those football games and dances and your wild parties. Unlike your social butterfly-to-be who's still in the pupa stage," he said.

"I wasn't complaining. I wouldn't expect you to be like that. You wouldn't be you. Don't ever change. You're perfect."

"Perfect?" His eyes bugged out. "No, this dude, he'll be perfect."

"In his own way," she said. "Just like you are in yours."

"Thanks. You've restored my faith in myself." But he didn't look convinced. His eyes downcast, he frowned and backed away a bit.

"Don't look for my approval."

"I'll try not to." He looked away, and she felt she'd said something wrong. Too much praise, maybe?

"Is something bothering you?" she asked.

"No. Not at all. Forget it. Let's get back to work."

"You sure? We can keep talking if you'd like." Now she knew she'd put her foot in her mouth. She didn't want him to shut her out. "Talk to me, tell me what's on your mind. Like you used to."

He wasn't the same person she'd left almost two decades ago. They were both entirely different people. But he seemed more broody at times, reluctant to share his feelings. If only she could bring it out of him.

"No, let's just keep shaping Prince Perfect's personality here. We've got a ways to go on that." He shut out any chance of opening up to her.

"Why don't we knock off for the night, Felix? Have a couple more drinks and relax." Maybe then, she'd get him talking about his hopes, his regrets. He'd heard enough of hers for a while.

"I'll fall asleep on you this time."

"I have no problem with that," she assured him.

"Okay, pour away."

They didn't share another word. But the silence between them was more comfortable than it had ever been. Just as he'd predicted, he fell asleep, and she cradled his head in her lap, that marvelous brain that accomplished so much.

****

Judi wrapped her last Christmas present and stuffed it into a shopping bag to take to her father's. She and Felix exchanged gifts the night before, and then he headed to the airport for his annual trip to Aspen. He'd asked her to join him, but skiing was not her thing. Besides, she wanted some time alone to think. She fingered the heart-shaped diamond pendant he'd given her, feeling very close to him.

91

Something he'd chosen and touched and carefully wrapped was next to her heart.

Then the thought of Leo's impending arrival got her heart thumping. But her logical side broke in to remind her she had a dilemma on her hands. Felix would always be a part of her, just like this figment of her imagination who would soon be real. She enjoyed every moment she spent with Felix. As for her new hero, she fervently hoped it would be the same. That element of risk entered her mind—he'd be programmed to adore her, to never leave her. But what if the unthinkable happened, and she didn't feel that spark, the dizzy high that came with being in love? That warm, wonderful feeling she got when Felix was near?

No! She refused to even think that could happen, that she'd be less than madly in love with her hero. And dammit, it would be love at first sight!

She wandered back to her computer after a detour around the bar to pour herself another eggnog and over to the full-length mirror to evaluate herself for the hundredth time.

"What if he doesn't love me—or even like me?" she'd asked Felix repeatedly, staring into the mirror with images of blueprints flashing in her mind like a slide show.

"Of course he'll like you, Judi. What's not to love? I mean—like?" he corrected himself, and she beamed. Felix had never flattered her like this before. She tingled from it.

Now, sitting at her computer, she realized there was no way she could produce any more work until Leo, the man of her dreams, comfortably inhabited her domain. She had to remember that. Felix's job was to create that dream. She expected an awkward beginning with Leo, just like with any new relationship, but she consoled herself by floating away in reverie over the cozy nights they'd share by the fire. Winter would give way to lazy summer afternoons at the beach, followed by elegant cuisine and romantic cruises. She snapped the computer off. "'Til next year," she chanted and walked away.

Sipping her eggnog, she wondered what Felix was doing right now out there in Aspen. *Is he thinking of me?*

****

A slight twinge of guilt tweaked Judi's relief at the New Year's arrival as she wiped away the last remnant of artificial frost from her windows. With the tree down, the last sliver of tinsel vacuumed off the floor, and all the cookies eaten and eggnog imbibed, the place looked stark. Glancing over at the computer, she walked across the study to the cold, well-rested machine and stopped to straighten a picture on the wall. It was a Chagall she'd bought when she started making serious money.

Looking around the loft, she felt confident Leo would take to the environment she'd worked hard to mold to his tastes. She'd all but redecorated the entire place: the whitewashed walls were now a pale blue. Her piano, all tuned, shone like a mirror. The bedroom now sported burgundy curtains. A velvet bedspread draped black satin sheets. His wardrobe now filled the entire hall closet: a dinner tux, sport jackets, slacks, sweaters, leather shoes, designer jeans and tantalizingly tight swimming trunks. A backgammon game and a three-dimensional chess set sat atop the coffee table. The newest cookery filled the kitchen with the widest array of spices and delicacies she could find in the gourmet shops.

He'll be happy here, she thought confidently, bending over to pick up a piece of lint off the carpet.

****

Judi sipped her wine and took one more slice of garlic toast. The only man she ever dared eat garlic with was Felix. "I don't want to argue any more about this, Felix. My mind's made up."

"But once it's made up, that's it. He's not going to change his habits. That's the only way he's like us human guys: you can't change him."

"I said I wanted someone neat, and I'm not changing my mind about that. Heroes do not leave dirty clothes lying around."

"He won't have dirty clothes." He held his fork midair. "He doesn't sweat."

"All right, then, he can clean up after me!" she announced.

Felix dropped his fork with a clatter onto the plate. She wondered if he'd chipped it. "That would be even worse. Don't you realize how nuts that will drive you? This guy following you all over the place picking up every speck of dust you leave behind?"

Judi held her wineglass to her lips. "How can that possibly drive me nuts? It'll be like having a live-in maid. One who's willing to work in the buff at that."

She took a sip.

He wiped his hands with his napkin and closed his eyes. "All right, have it your way. But don't come running to me when you can't find your wallet and discover it's been filed under P."

"What's P?"

"Portefeuille. French for wallet. If he's going to speak four languages, there's no telling which tongue his filing system will be in."

"Now you're getting too far out, Felix. Here, have another slice of garlic toast."

"No, thanks, I'm all garlicked out, but let's polish off this vino." He emptied the wine bottle into their glasses. Tonight they were at her place ironing out the details of Leo's behavior patterns.

"What was the other thing you wanted that sounded outrageous, oh, yeah, an investment advisor?" He scrolled down the computer screen as he sipped his wine. "How romantic is that? Lying before a roaring fire with soft violins in the background, and he starts rattling off P/E ratios?"

"I thought just as long as he's providing my every emotional need, he can provide for my financial needs, too. Why not make him an economic whiz? I talked about him being a risk taker with stocks, and he should know what he's doing when he's taking those risks."

Felix tapped the mouse button with an impatient index finger. "Because it's not his job. It's one thing to play the market for fun and games. But your fun and games with him should lie elsewhere."

"There would be a time and a place."

He shook his head.

"Wouldn't there?" she probed.

"He's not human." Felix tapped the keys. "He can come up with the wrong thing at the wrong time. So can some humans, but I can't guarantee he won't ruin a romantic mood if you program something like this into him. There's no way to program timing into him. When you least expect it, he might make some very politically incorrect remarks."

She was determined to win this argument. "No matter, I want him to be financially savvy. I'm not just looking for a ball of fluff here. After all, we've already made him adept at music and history, and he can have an intelligent discussion about politics, so why not finances?"

"Maybe because I find the whole subject so tedious. I just hand everything over to my accountant. I don't even know how much money I have anymore, and to tell the truth, I really don't care."

That surprised her. This brilliant mind held no interest in money? "That's not very practical, Felix. He might be making bad investments, or even ripping you off. One day you might turn up broke."

"Then I'll call my rich author friend who can take care of me," he countered with a cocked head and a lopsided grin.

She thought as she sipped. It wasn't really a joking matter. Of course she would take care of him. After all he was doing for her.

"Financial savvy, Felix."

"Okay," he sighed, shaking his head. "You got it. But don't come—"

"Yeah, I know, running to you. I won't let you in on it if he makes a killing, either, since you're so uninterested in money."

"Now, for his—what's this?" Felix's eyes ran down the list and halted at the bottom. "Ballroom dancing? How'd this get in here?"

"Being swept across a dance floor like Cinderella is the ultimate!"

"But why'd you stick it in here among talents like doing housework and balancing checkbooks?"

She dragged her finger down the list, studying it.

"No, all the romantic traits were in there first. Those other ones—financial savvy, his objective mindset—those were the afterthoughts. Now—can you teach him to dance, or is he going to have two left feet? Uh-oh, I'm hoping you took that figuratively."

He smiled, sloshing the wine in his glass. "I can program the ability into him, but I can't guarantee anything. He's already got the charisma of Valentino and the musical ability of Chopin. I don't want to overload his circuits by trying to squeeze Cody Linley into there, too."

"He doesn't have to know any fancy steps. Slow dancing would be good enough. You can show him that, right?"

"I doubt it. I've never slow-danced." He glanced down at his feet and blushed.

"Never?" Then she remembered; he'd never been to a school dance or a prom. And his gushing over her performance at the ballet recital had been genuine. He knew as much about dancing as she did about time travel through warped space.

He shook his head. "At my wedding we did the Electric Slide. And I wouldn't have done that if I wasn't half skunked."

"Oh, Felix, you don't know what you're missing. Slow dancing is so romantic."

"Show me." He stood, holding out his hand. "So I can show him."

She was quite unprepared for this. Slow dancing with Felix? She never thought she'd see the day.

He brought her to her feet, and she tried not to jump up too eagerly. She found her *Romance With Rubinstein* CD and placed Felix's arms around her waist. "Just sway to the music. Your feet don't even have to leave the floor," she advised, as her hands wound round his neck and unconsciously began stroking his hair.

"I'm going to look pretty ridiculous doing this with him," Felix remarked, as his embrace tightened.

They stayed like that a long time, swaying in each other's arms. But she didn't pull away. Neither did he. She never wanted this song or this moment to end. This was the first time they'd ever had their arms around each other for this long. The song ended, but their embrace lingered. After a silent moment, she slowed to a stop, but they stood, fused together, and neither making a move to let go. She buried her face in the curve of his shoulder, his herbal scent sending her back to the days when she teased him unmercifully about using faggy shampoo. Now she regretted ever making fun of him.

"Felix—"

"Don't stop, Judi." The music started again. This

time it was "Romance."

She felt his growing arousal. But she didn't want to let go, either.

"I think I need some more lessons," he breathed raggedly.

"Dancing, you mean?"

"Among other things. But dancing's a good start."

"Maybe I'll teach Leo how to dance myself." She inhaled his clean, woodsy scent, letting it intoxicate her and drive her heart faster. He smelled delicious. Melting into him, she took a deeper breath then another. "You have enough to do."

"Maybe you're right."

"But you're sure catching on fast," she murmured into his hair.

"With any luck, so will he."

They danced on. She felt strange in his arms, but comfortable just the same. His arousal didn't bother her; it was natural, and she would have felt disappointed if he hadn't had that response.

Finally, he stopped. "Look at me."

She lifted her head from his shoulder, struggling to open her eyes.

"Any idea what you'll do if your, uh—coupling with this guy doesn't work out?"

"Sure. I'm not in that much of a fantasy world. But I have to think positive. I've wanted this for too long, and we're working too hard for it to fail." The familiar tug pulled at her heart trying to tear it in two, between the fictional figure who hadn't arrived yet, and the living, breathing, aroused man pressed up against her body, causing hot liquid to surge through her.

"It wouldn't be a failure. It would be something you tried that didn't work out." She saw pleading in his eyes, the hope she didn't want to encourage, but couldn't bear to discourage. "Why are you

considering the possibility that it won't work out?"
she asked. "Is there something you're not telling me
about the design or something?"

"I'm a scientist." As he pulled back from her, his
voice steadied. "Not all experiments are successful.
Let's be practical here."

"I don't want to be practical. There's nothing
practical about romantic relationships. They're
capricious, illogical, and completely driven by
emotion and elements we'll never understand. So
let's not talk science, all right?" She should've pulled
away, but her arms stayed locked around him.

"I just don't want to see you disappointed. There
are no guarantees in life, and I don't want you
jumping out the window if something goes wrong
and you two don't live happily ever after."

"Wait just a minute. How irresponsible do you
think I am anyway? That's the trouble with you,
Felix. You've always been so damn pessimistic,
looking on the dark side of everything." Finally, the
last notes of the song faded, and she came back from
orbit and pulled away. She took her arms from
around his neck. "Is your entire life one big black
cloud?"

"No, I'm just being realistic."

"Well, you're too damn realistic sometimes." She
headed back for the sofa and sat at the edge. She'd
had many an argument with him in the past about
how gloomy the future looked, and how mankind is
decimating Mother Earth with the human race on
the brink of self-destruction. "Never mind me
jumping out the window over a broken romance.
Your outlook about the planet is enough to make me
want to jump off."

"It's obvious I can't hold a coherent conversation
with you right now. Go back to your little dream
world." He packed up his laptop and walked to the
door.

"You're just as impetuous as you were as a kid, storming out when you lose an argument," she called after him.

But he let himself out and closed the door.

She didn't want him to go. Not like this.

A moment later the door opened, and he stuck his head in. "All I've been trying to say all this while is that I'll always be there for you if the incredible hunk turns out to be a dud. But that's not part of your plot, is it?"

He withdrew and slammed the door shut.

She shot up and bolted for the door, flinging it open. "Felix!" His footsteps echoed down the stairs. "Felix, come on, come back, I didn't mean—" The front door's slam cut her off.

Something stopped her from calling him out the window or running into the street to catch him. She was through chasing men, begging and pleading. Another element of her equal partnership, something she'd always longed for, a man with the physical inability to walk out on her. If he proved her wrong, she'd freely apologize. But only if the bastard would sit and listen!

She tried to put Felix out of her mind by looking around the loft. Signs of her new life were everywhere—flowers, crystal, and a plush throw rug before the fireplace. But first she had to clean up Felix's mess—the last time she'd ever have to clean up after a man!

Chapter Eight

January dragged on, cold and dark. Blasts of icy wind and sleet rattled Judi's windows. The city slept under a blanket of snow. Judi moped around in her robe and fuzzy slippers with no new book ideas. No witty dialogue fragments came to her in the middle of the night, and no plot twists visited her in the shower. She spent hours at the blank screen until she closed her eyes and began yet another daydream. This time she and Leo lounged on a Caribbean beach, naked. He chased her, he caught her, and they tumbled to the sand and rolled around...

Glancing at the calendar, she wanted to yank those pages away until his arrival date. Oh, how frustrated she felt, all this waiting—struggling to not grind her teeth, she paced the floor, picked up the top book on her TBR pile, a vampire romance, read the first chapter, got up to open the fridge and slammed it shut—no, no eating!

Iris seemed to have given up on her after bugging her about starting another book. Judi didn't expect to hear from Felix. The phone remained silent and her in-box empty—except for spam.

She wanted to call Felix and tell him how restless she felt, how she couldn't slow her pulse or sit and relax. But it seemed he was trying to sabotage this dream before it became reality, because one night he mumbled, "It might not work."

Did he want it to work?

She gave up on the muse who must've gone south for the winter, shut the computer down, and studied the list of Leo's traits with a critical editor's eye. Did she really want someone that flighty, with no concept of time, wanting to play at all hours, with no regard for work? Maybe she should discuss that with Felix and make Leo a bit more responsible. But not anal, living for work, deadlines, and his next success. She'd spent her early life observing the precision and accuracy of Felix's actions and knew she didn't want that in a lover now.

Her hand hovered over the phone. *I could discuss changes with him and get a progress report.* She dialed. His friendly voice requested, "Please leave your name and number…"

Oh, how she would've loved to hear his real, non-recorded voice. Her heart was so heavy that she didn't even have the energy to stand up straight. She just sat there, the dead receiver to her ear, staring at a wine stain on the carpet. He ran to her in the past. He'd even left his girlfriend's bed and rushed over to her.

If he got ticked enough, he might scrap this project, and she'd be back to square one, alone, with no one but the fictional Race. Felix had a short fuse. Growing up, he didn't put up with much, and she doubted he'd let go of that trait. Maybe she'd pushed him too far this time…

Over the edge.

Feeling alone, unloved, and most of all, sorry she'd started that silly argument, she put her *Rubinstein Romance* CD on and had a good cry.

****

Felix set his cell to vibrate. He didn't want to be interrupted during these final stages of creation—his living, breathing being was about to hold his first conversation.

"Please don't be a himbo. Just be capable of holding your end of an intelligent dialogue," he pleaded, placing the paddles on his creation's chest.

If this mission failed, it would be his failure. As much as he wanted Judi to desire him the way she seemed to desire this mass of synthetic vinyl and wires, he wanted it to work because his sweat went into it.

With one jolt of electricity, the heart began pumping. The artificial plasma began to circulate. The chest rose and fell. An emotional surge went through Felix as the electrical surge brought his creation to life. Now he knew what it felt like to give birth. "Here, buddy, sit up and say hello." Felix eased him to a sitting position. The eyes opened, looked around, and then focused on Felix. For an intense moment, they stared at each other. The face came alive; the lips curved into a smile.

"Hey there. I'm Felix." He held out his hand, and his creation shook it. "Welcome to—well, to Earth."

"What do I look like?" were the first words from his mouth.

"It figures you'd ask that," Felix mumbled. But that's what Judi wanted—an Adonis who wanted to be reminded of it every second.

"Hold it just a minute." Felix went over to the closet, which was stuffed with designer duds, and came back to put the finishing touch on his creation, a cashmere sport coat that brought out the colors in his eyes—both of them. "Here you go."

The man slid into the jacket and buttoned it. Felix had to admit it looked a lot better on him than on the store mannequin.

He held a hand mirror up to the classically handsome face. "Not a bad picture, if I do say so myself," Felix remarked, unable to keep the pride from his voice. But another emotion crept up and slapped him upside the head, leaving him torn. It couldn't be jealousy. This being was his labor of love, his masterpiece. Leo was stunning, but looks weren't everything. Still, the feeling weighed Felix down as he told himself once again to face the truth: *This man will belong to Judi, and she won't need you any more.*

"Rather easy on the eyes, you say? I would say it's more like drop-dead gorgeous," the velvety voice replied.

"Yeah, well, don't get too cocky, sweetheart. You may be perfect, but that's about all you've got going for you."

"I'm supposed to romance a woman, is that right?" he asked.

Felix nodded. "If 'party' can be a verb, I suppose 'romance' can be one."

"How do I go about doing that, Master?"

"That's something I haven't programmed into you yet. We have to work on it."

"Good. Because I have some knowledge of what it is but don't have the ability to go about it. From what I'm aware of, it sounds like more fun than attending the opera." He flashed his piano teeth smile.

"Oh, you'll be a love machine, all right. But keep your pants on for now."

"Is that she?" Leo pointed to the glamour photo of Judi on the wall, her red hair rich and shining, diamonds glittering at her ears and throat, and her lips curved, hinting at kissability. He gave the photo a passing glance but riveted his gaze right back to his own reflection. "Is that an old photo? She looks rather girlish."

"No, in fact, it's her latest book. The years have been very kind to her. She's the one who's drop-dead gorgeous," he added, in a private aside to himself.

"She'll do," Leo replied with an ambivalent wave of his perfectly manicured hand.

"Just remember, you're programmed to take good care of her," Felix warned. "Make her the happiest woman alive. Or else you'll be answering to me. And that's just for starters."

"Your threat is duly acknowledged, Master." He swept a dutiful bow to his creator.

Felix couldn't help sneaking an admiring glance at his creation. It was a monumental achievement for him, building this specimen out of no more than a dream. So why did his heart send him mixed signals?

"I believe you're smitten with her yourself, Master." His tone was kind, accommodating.

"You can read minds?"

"No, I'm just very perceptive. Aren't I supposed to be?" He cocked his head.

"Yes, but keep your perceptions about me to yourself. Especially when we're around her. I don't need you to make a jerk out of me."

He nodded, straightening his lapels. "I wouldn't dare defy you, Master. Simply name your wish, and I'll do my utmost to make it reality."

"Just make Judi happy. There's really nothing else I want from you." He eyed his creation up and down once again. He could see why any woman would fall head over heels for him. He was everything Felix wasn't—in height, build, manners, ad infinitum. Felix squashed his envy.

Would I trade places with an animated object? No way! Why envy a guy who didn't have taste buds?

But he refused to lie to himself. He did envy the guy almost as much as he admired him for being so flawless.

"And it's my own damn fault," Felix berated himself. He couldn't blame this guy for stealing Judi's heart. But it was too late to turn back the clock. "Damn, I should've invented time travel first."

****

This had to be the lowest point in Judi's life. She glanced outside into the cold night, the buildings dark, dull blurs of light from the streetlamps dotting the blackness. She puttered around the loft day after day, not writing, not talking to anyone, watching too many soap operas, and eating too many truffles.

Finally, she couldn't stand it any longer. She picked up the phone. If Felix weren't in, she'd go to his house and stand there 'til he showed up.

He answered after the second ring.

Her heart lurched. "Felix, it's me."

"Oh. Hello." He didn't sound mad; from his tone, she couldn't detect any emotion.

"I wanted to tell you I'm sorry. It was my fault. I didn't mean to get on your case like that—"

"Never mind. It happens to the best of us. I'm sure it'll happen with you and Leo the Lionhearted too."

"I'm sorry—and I—miss you. I really missed you over the holidays."

After a momentary pause, he finally replied, "So did I. Next Christmas we—" He halted and stammered a bit. "Oh. I keep forgetting. You'll be spoken for."

"That's all right. We can still do something together."

"Let's not rush that far ahead."

"So, have you made any more progress?" Her mouth was so dry she could've grown a cactus in there. She held her breath waiting for his reply.

"He needs some more work. Programming the personality is more complicated than I planned on."

"Then how about getting together sooner? You want to make it tonight?" She trembled like a star struck kid asking a movie star for an autograph. Why, she didn't know. This was someone she'd known forever, and her heart tripped like a hammer.

"Sure, I can come over there," he replied after a slight pause.

She held the receiver away and let out her breath. "Okay, what time?"

"Say seven?"

She mentally counted off the things she had to do by then. Get a sumptuous dinner together, bathe, get her hair and nails done, choose something to wear...

"Make it eight. Bring a nice bottle of wine, will you?"

"Of course." His voice was so soft that it melted her. Oh, how she missed him!

****

Judi primped like a high school freshman dressing for her first date. Her clingy sheath looked stunning; all that holiday eating hadn't made her clothes any tighter around the tummy or hips. She put strappy sandals on then took them off and put on black ballet slippers. She didn't want to be any taller.

He arrived at eight sharp with a bottle of champagne in tow.

"Champagne? But it's only roast leg of lamb." She was so happy to see a familiar human body at her door that she wanted to do somersaults. Especially since it was him.

"Well, new year and all that. By the way, you take the mistletoe down yet?"

A rush of excitement swelled inside her. Oh, how badly she wanted to be kissed!

"I never put up mistletoe. But—" She drew him to her. "Who needs mistletoe?" They kissed warmly. It was a struggle to pull away. The bottle wedged between them like a barrier.

"Chill this, will you? I mean the champagne." He handed her the bottle.

"Sure." But neither of them moved. They stood still, eyes locked.

He took a step back but didn't break the embrace. "Your lover's coming along great, Judi. I'm sure you'll be very happy with him."

She caught a note of regret in his voice. Felix was terrible at hiding anything because he never tried. But what would she say to him at this point? She couldn't turn back now. She stopped herself when she realized how she was thinking of her hero—as a project.

With Felix's arms around her, her thoughts whirled.

"Felix, that's wonderful." She forced enthusiasm into her voice. "We actually accomplished this. Sometimes I feel like I'm dreaming."

"Yeah, I wish I were," he muttered. Was that a Freudian slip? she wondered.

"Look, we can still spend time together," she rushed to assure him. "I'm not going to turn my back on you just because I have a new man in my life. I know we drifted apart after graduation, but now—this is different.

You'll always be part of my life."

"I know," came out in a near-whisper. "I'm just burnt out, that's all. My astronaut better be easy after this."

****

After dinner, Felix set up his laptop on Judi's coffee table. They sat on the couch together. "I figured we'd reach this part of him sooner or later."

"What part is that?" she asked.

"Loverman's ability as a lover. I mean, it's not the biggest part of a relationship, but it's a big part, I suppose."

Judi smiled. "Are you embarrassed to talk about this?"

He slid a pencil behind his ear. "Somewhat. After all, we've never talked about anything like this before."

"I told you in sophomore year, Justin Rhea was a sloppy kisser and an even sloppier lover."

"But you never went into detail and left it to my

108

imagination."

"If Wham Shazam's going to be a neat freak, he'll be neat in that area, too, I hope."

Felix nodded. "I'll make sure he's very fastidious about certain things. You'll never see your toilet seat up again."

"Good. Now—does technique have to be programmed into him?"

"Of course. Just like any other habit."

"It's going to be a habit? Like brushing his teeth every morning? He's going to lunge at me the same time every day?"

"No, I didn't mean it that way. I mean habit as behavior pattern. Like neatness—that's a habit. People have different eating habits. He'll be programmed for certain techniques, any way you want it. Er—" He waved his hands around, tugged at his collar, took an exceptionally long sip of his drink, and glanced into space. Afraid to interrupt him, she went in to refill his glass.

"Felix, we can talk about this. My God, we're practically family."

"I know. It's just that I never thought we'd ever talk about anything—" He faltered.

"Anything this sexy?"

"Well, the subject just never came up. 'Til now. But, I guess it's all in a day's work," he said.

"Yeah," came out flatly. She wished he'd be more open about this. Was her oldest friend a prude? With a ten-year marriage behind him? "Let's put it as delicately as possible, then."

"All right, how do you want him to do—things?"

Judi laughed. "Perfectly! How do you think? He's the embodiment of perfection."

"You have to be a bit more specific than just perfect this time. We're not talking about cleaning toilets here."

She stared him down. He looked away. "There

are ways and there are ways, Judi. So I hear."

"Oh, come on, Felix. Somehow I don't think you're a virgin at this late date. You've read my books. Program him to do what Race does in my love scenes."

"All thirty of them? You won't be able to walk."

"Aha! Finally! He cracks a lewd joke!" She clapped her hands.

"There's nothing lewd about it. It's an anatomical reality. My wife once—er—never mind." He shoved the glass up to his lips.

"Ah, so! You gave it to your wife so good that she couldn't walk. Now you've restored my faith in you. I can't say I ever doubted your virility, but—"

"We were talking about Flash here. We need to establish how he carries out the—the act."

"I'll tell you what. I'll get my Race books with scenes that are closest to what I have in mind, and we'll work on technique. That fair enough?"

"Sure." He nodded with a relaxed smile. "And you can throw a splash of rum into this." He held up his glass.

She went to get his rum and her books. He really is uncomfortable about this, she mused. Ironically, he knew her longer than anybody; why so uptight? She hoped this drink would loosen him up—he hadn't touched the champagne.

She opened *The Edge of the Event Horizon* to Race and Finestra's very first love scene, the most romantic she'd ever written. She sat and began reading aloud: "Finally, it was their wedding night. Finestra trembled with a delightful mixture of trepidation and excitement. She dropped her hairbrush as she fanned her hair around her shoulders the way Race liked it. She tripped over her negligee as she preened in front of the bathroom mirror, squirting perfume on her pulse points. Finally she emerged. Race reclined on the bed, waiting for her. The sight of him made her melt."

"Can anybody else in the building hear this, through the vents or something?" Felix interrupted. "I don't want to get arrested here."

"This is SoHo, Felix. I'm reading from a book. People hear this stuff live all the time and don't think twice about it. Just chill." She continued reading:

"In the glow of two candles on the nightstands, his hair shone with a blue-black halo—"

"How long is this going to last?"

"How long does it usually last?" she teased as she looked up from the book. She felt more comfortable reading her love scene with Felix than she ever did with anyone, Iris included. It all seemed so natural, working on this creation together with a common goal. The element of sensuality added to the excitement of their secret collaboration.

She read on: "A mat of curly dark hair covered Race's powerful chest, one shiny spot where a scar slashed the skin. His body was so strange to her, yet the thought of him pressed up against her, hard and wanting, made her tremble with anticipation."

A sudden thought almost took her breath away. "Felix?" She peered at him over the book. He was relaxed now, enjoying his drink. "Felix, let's do some 'hands-on' work here, no pun intended. We want to make sure Leo knows what he's doing in this department. Why not let me show you how an action hero carries out certain actions?"

"How?" He took a too-big gulp of his drink and sputtered.

"Let's act it out." She got up, excitement pumping through her. "This is my favorite love scene of all the Race books, their first encounter. This is always how I imagined my real-life Race would be. I'll show you how he does it. Then you'll have a much better idea how to show him. Just like with the dancing."

"Uh, Judi, dancing's one thing—"

"Oh, Felix, for God's sake. We've come this far already, so let's get it right. Come on. It'll be fun. You want this to be realistic; you want to design him right? Let's act some of this out. Don't worry. We'll be like actors on a set."

"I'm no actor, especially in something like this." He shook his head and took another gulp of his drink.

"You never know 'til you try." She tried to make her tone extra tempting. Inching up to him, she held the book out. "He's bare-chested. You should be bare-chested."

"You want me to take my shirt off here, in the middle of your living room?"

"Why not? It's just us. I've seen you shirtless before. Come on. This is the best way to do this. Take your shirt off, and I'll read you through it."

He took a deep, tentative breath, another reassuring gulp of his drink, and his fingers trembled over the buttons of his shirt.

"Slower."

"Huh?"

"He undresses very slowly," she said. "Almost like a strip tease."

He shook his head. "If this isn't the wackiest thing I've ever done, and it figures it's with you..."

"All right. Now." She helped him off with his shirt and ran her hand over his chest. Last time she'd seen his chest, it was on a family outing to Jones Beach when they were about fifteen. At that time, he hadn't lost all his baby fat and had the sex appeal of a beach ball. Now his pecs bulged just enough, his abs flat as a washboard. A golden mat of hair covered his chest. "You've got a really nice chest. Guys with broad chests really turn me on."

"Are you reading from the script or ad libbing?"

"No, Felix, I'm telling you. You look damn good. All that weight lifting—it's paid off."

"Thanks. Now—" He gestured toward the book. "Let's get back to business."

She continued to read. "She took a step closer, and he leaned forward, caressing the soft fabric of her negligee."

"Did you say she's in a negligee?" he asked.

"Well, yes, it's their wedding night. It's her trousseau."

"Why, pray tell, am I in half my birthday suit according to the script while you're still swathed in street clothes?"

"Oh, you want me to put on a—" She entertained a delightful thought. "Don't move. I'll be right back."

She dashed into her bedroom and threw open her closet door. Digging through her dresses, blouses, slacks, and jackets— "Whew, I have a lot of clothes!" She finally found a diaphanous chiffon number she'd worn only once, in Paris with the man she thought would become her transatlantic lover. He didn't, but the lingerie had been so beautiful and so expensive that even though he'd paid for it, she couldn't bear to throw it out. So here it hung for the last ten years. Finally she was going to get some use out of it, and much more after Mr. Macho entered the scene.

When she returned to the living room, her gaze roamed over Felix reclining on the sofa. A jumble of emotions washed over her. She'd never looked at him the way a woman looks at a man. Even in their teens, when hormones raged, she had her boyfriends, and he had—everything that kept him busy. Now, physical attraction tweaked her, but she fought it. Her future lay with her new hero. Felix wasn't prepared or able to provide romance. She knew they could never take that step. What a way to ruin a beautiful, loving friendship.

"Now where were we?" she muttered as she found her place in the book. She walked around the couch and sat next to him.

He sat up at attention. "Wow. You almost took my breath away." His eyes scanned her head to toe.

"Oh, this thing's kinda old, and—" She bunched the sheer black lace in her hand and let it slide back down her leg.

"Judi, I don't know if I can go through with this reading stuff." He tore his gaze away for a second, but fixed it right back on her.

"Sure we can. We should get this right. Let's just take one step at a time, all right?" Aware of what she was doing to him, she decided if he made the first move, she'd take it from there. But she'd never asked a man for sex and would not now.

Twenty years ago, he didn't attract her. But now was now. Still, she thought he should make the first move.

"So—" She read, "Finestra took a step closer, and Race leaned forward, caressing the soft fabric of her negligee, holding his arms out to her. Now you hold your arms out to me, Felix." They embraced, and she held the book and read over his shoulder. "The satin sheet fell away and revealed his nakedness underneath. For a second she looked away out of modesty and heard him laugh. 'It's all right, my darling. I'm your husband now,' he purred. Finestra managed a laugh through her trembling. With another step, she was at the foot of the bed, and he reached forward to take her in his arms. She thought she'd faint."

Felix halted her. "Whoa, wait a minute now. I'm not going to do a complete strip and slide under a satin sheet. I'd better have a talk with the script consultant here."

"All right, we can ad lib our way around that part. Finestra was a virgin on their wedding night.

But you know Race is a ladies' man as well as an intrepid space warrior. Well, he has to be, or I wouldn't be selling books."

"Makes me wonder which of us is doing more acting here. You trembling like a virgin or me as a ladies' man."

She gave him a playful slap on the arm. "Thanks a lot! There is one subtle difference. I can fake trembling. Ha!"

"Just get on with the act."

Judi read: "Finestra sat beside him, and his mouth descended upon hers lightly, becoming more insistent, responding to her desire."

Her eyes left the book and landed on Felix's lips. Should she kiss him this way? Would he take it further?

He answered for her: "Judi, I really want this thing to work, but unlike Race, I'm human. And like I said, I'm no actor. And this scene doesn't look like it's going to end up in a game of checkers. You get my drift?"

A tinge of disappointment nudged her. So he wasn't going to whisk her off her feet and into the bedroom, or even toss the book aside and take the natural next step. No, he was still the same old Felix. "Why is this making you so uncomfortable?"

He let out a sigh, a bit ragged this time. "Maybe it's better if we just read the parts. I can get an idea of what you want and save the dress rehearsal for another time. Like broad daylight when we haven't both had a few drinks. Or maybe just wait 'til he gets here and wing it. I don't think this was such a hot idea—I mean—" he stammered.

"Come on, this is too important to wing it when he gets here. Just go along with me, please?"

"Oh, the things you make me do."

"Like I'm pulling your teeth. You're on my couch, in my arms, with your shirt off. Just lie back and enjoy it."

She continued reading: "He broke their kiss and began tracing a finger down her neck and over each breast through her satin chemise in a slow circular motion. She sighed under his touch, the dancing flames beginning to ignite deep within her." She took Felix's hand and guided it in accordance with the story. His hand was as rigid as rigor mortis. "Felix, loosen up, will you?" She held his wrist and dangled his hand. He finally flexed his fingers. "Your hand is petrified. I have electric appliances that are more lifelike than this."

"Judi, this is awkward, to say the least. Acting out a love scene in a novel. If I don't feel like a spare prick at a wedding here—"

"There are no spare pricks. It's just you and me."

"Well, I feel just as maladroit."

"Calm down." She continued to read: "She began stroking his chest lightly, her lips upon his earlobe, her tongue darting out and flicking it playfully, her breath matching his with increasing intensity." She nipped Felix's ear.

"Ow!" he yelped, nearly deafening her.

"Yow, not so loud, Felix!"

"You damn near almost bit my ear off."

"Felix, will you sit still? Now where were we? Oh, yeah...her breath matching his..." She began to pant heavily.

"Jesus, Judi, it sounds like you're having a frigging asthma attack."

"I'm just trying to breathe heavy."

"I was about to call 9-1-1."

She kept reading: "Finestra was nervous, losing her senses in a swirl of longing.

"'You're so beautiful, Finestra, how I've been longing for this moment,' Race breathed....that's your cue, Felix."

"What was it again?"

116

"'You're so beautiful, Finestra, how I've been longing for this moment,' Race breathed..."

"Oh. 'You're so beautiful—'"

"No, don't talk it, breathe it. In my ear."

"You're...so...beautiful..."

She read on: "Between kisses and the hot blasts of his breath in her ear, his body covered hers, and her legs parted, wrapping around his waist as they moved together in an exquisite tempo. Engorged with desire, he moved to enter her. She thrust her hips forward to meet him, to take him into the depths of her soul."

"Uh—" Judi closed the book, her thumb in the place she was reading. "This is where she takes Race into the depths of her soul, and they move in exquisite tempo. You want to go through the motions or what?"

He let out a low whistle. "And he boldly goes where no man's gone before? Well, Race sure had one over on me, if he didn't have her elbow jamming into his ribs of steel."

She pulled away. "Oh, I'm sorry. My God, Felix, when I wrote this, I choreographed it perfectly in my head. Acting it out, it's like a game of Twister."

"Maybe it's just the actors, Judi. Let's face it, Brangelina we ain't."

"Let's just finish here, shall we?" She read: "She writhed under him, whimpering in the heat of the intense fire burning inside her."

She tried to emulate her heroine's passionate movements, but Felix laughed.

"Now what?"

"That's supposed to be passionate writhing?" He wiggled his brows. "It looks like you're trying to wriggle into a girdle that's too tight."

"Oh, you are just so austere. Is this really a preview of what I'm going to be facing when my fantasy man and I finally consummate our passion?

Because if it is, I'll lock the two of you in a bedroom 'til you make sure he gets it right."

"Maybe I'm the wrong teacher. How 'bout engaging the services of your friend Iris?"

"I wouldn't let her within ten penis lengths of him."

"Then you'd just better wait it out and wing it. I mean, who rehearses lovemaking, for cryin' out loud?"

"I just wanted it to be perfect."

He reached for his shirt. "You won't have any complaints. Trust me."

"Hey, Felix."

He looked up from his buttoning. "What?"

"This really was fun, wasn't it?"

"Yeah." He smiled and nodded. "Painful, but fun."

Neither of them made a move to call it a night. Their eyes locked. "Felix—" She couldn't let the moment end. The time was too right. If she didn't act now, it would never happen. "I wonder what it would be like if we really—you know—"

"With or without a book?"

"Without, of course."

"Don't go reeling in shock, but I've wondered a few times myself over the years."

"Really?" Finally the truth was coming out! *Then why the hell didn't you make a play for me?* she wanted to ask.

"Jesus, Judi, I am a guy, in case you haven't noticed. I'm sure I'm not the only one walking the Earth who's ever wondered." His eyes roved up and down the length of her, too quickly to be considered undressing her, but she knew what a fast thinker he was.

She was intensely flattered, although confused. Why didn't he come on to her? Then her mind raced back to that attempted kiss, how she'd laughed at him and mocked him, and how bad that still made her feel. Oh, God, he'd had a crush on her all that time, and she'd shooed him away like a fly! No wonder he didn't want to show any interest. She was sure it still hurt.

"That time you tried to kiss me…"

"Oh, no, Judi. That's one of two things I'd rather forget. The other one is the time I showed up to teach a class and realized I'd forgotten to put pants on. To this day, I still can't decide which incident was more humiliating."

"Well, I just want you to know how sorry I am I laughed at you. I was—"

"Forget it. It was a hundred years ago."

"No! I was a self-centered, cruel, mean, thoughtless little bimbo. And I want you to know how sorry I am."

"You never dragged me to any Wham concerts. So consider us even."

"I thought we were even that night I saw you in Three Steps Down and brought you up here, and I kissed you. But I owe you over twenty years' of compounded interest. So we'll be even in a minute."

She brought his lips to hers and gave him a warm, loving, and thorough kiss.

His hands wandered, hesitantly at first, then more fluidly. Her hand slid down his trousers and began to fondle him.

He touched her breast, and she gently pushed him away. "No, let me do everything. We're not going to go all the way. I'm not even going to remove a stitch of my own clothing. I want all the pleasure to be yours. I never should have been so cruel to you, Felix."

"You don't have to—"

"Shh." She placed her finger on his lips and gently pushed him back against the cushions. "Just let me do everything."

****

Afterward, Judi pulled the afghan over him, and they relaxed on the couch. He dozed off, and she cuddled him until he woke up.

He opened his eyes, and they shared a special smile. "This is the most bizarre episode I've ever lived through, Judi. And I don't think having Leo here is going to make it any easier. For me, anyway."

She nodded, running her finger over his jaw line. "Why can't we all get along together?"

"When did you write me into your perfect plot?"

"Please, Felix. You're a very special part of my life. There's a big place in my heart for you. I just showed you how I feel about you."

"I'm a bit confused here. I thought you were madly in love with this other guy, rearranging your entire life for him. Your heart belongs to him, by all accounts, and I'm not up to playing Flesh Gordon's understudy."

"But—it's a different kind of love."

Glancing at his watch, he sat up and searched for his clothes. "I won't ask you to explain that." He pulled on his shorts. "You know what's happening here. We both know. But this whole thing is just getting too weird, even for me." He slid into his pants and shirt and walked, albeit unsteadily, to the kitchen. He drank from her faucet. She got up to get him a glass.

He glanced at his watch again. "I've gotta go. It's late."

She wanted him to stay, so she could tell him how every day grew more difficult, how her dilemma tore at her heart—but it was too late, with her dream so close to becoming reality. She had to live with her decision.

"Look, Felix. We both knew if we ever got involved romantically, it would ruin the most beautiful friendship either one of us ever had. Let's

not destroy what we've had since grammar school.
It's too precious."

"Then we'd better never get into a situation like
what just happened on your couch there again." He
laced his shoes.

"What's wrong with two close friends sharing a
special kind of affection?"

"Absolutely nothing, but there is a slight
complication for the third party, and shortly, I'm
going to be the third party." He pulled on his coat.

"What does that mean? You're going to drop him
off here, and I'll never see you again?"

"Of course not. I'll live with it. I've had enough
practice." With his hand on the knob, he said, "I
think I will design that perfect woman after all. For
myself. Then maybe the two of them will run off
together."

"You sure you don't like pulp science fiction,
Felix? Because you just rattled off a halfway decent
plot."

"I'm at my most creative after either of two
things: yoga or an Earth-shattering orgasm. I'll see
myself out."

With a wink he was out the door.

She winked back at the closed door but didn't
feel the impulse to jump up and call him back.
They'd had a beautiful time together, and she knew
they each needed some time alone now. She cleaned
up, put her book on the shelf, and sat back down on
the sofa, wrapping herself in the afghan and his
scent.

Oh, how she wished he'd stayed. But she had to
fight this tug of war—and win.

"Look to the future!" she commanded herself,
and went to the closet to gaze at her hero's new
clothes. She wondered how Felix would look in that
suit...

"The future!" She slammed the closet door shut

and put one of her hero's favorite CDs on, Chopin's Greatest Hits.

She imagined herself waltzing in Felix's arms. No, Leo's arms!

Chapter Nine

"He's ready."

Judi's heart lurched as she gripped the receiver. She swallowed hard. "You mean—ready to face the world ready?"

"I waited an extra twenty-four hours to make sure," Felix said, "and boy, am I sure. Loverboy Leo's been circling the lab like a panther in heat, gazing at your picture, saying things like 'I'm sure the photo hardly does justice to her pulchritude' and 'I anticipate satisfying this enchantress's every whim from head to toe,' or words to that effect."

Finally—the first chapter of her magnificent love story was about to begin. Her dream, in living, loving color, remained no farther away than the length of Manhattan. "When will he be here? I mean you and Leo."

"Tomorrow night around seven? Give you time to get ready."

"Felix..." What more could she say? "How can I ever thank you?"

She heard him take a breath and hesitate. "Wait 'til he's graced you with the pleasure of his presence. Then think it over." He didn't come across as a brilliant scientist who'd just invented the most groundbreaking project of his career. He sounded subdued, tired—and was that a hint of regret underneath?

They hung up, and Judi stood there, glued to the floor with her hand on the receiver. All these months, she'd expected to dance on the balcony, shout from the rooftops, and flip cartwheels. Yet she felt tears come to her eyes along with a strange sense of loss, like she had to sacrifice one thing to achieve another. She curled her hands into fists, knowing exactly what made up that trade-off. She wouldn't see much of Felix any more.

In these last few weeks, they'd reunited and rekindled their friendship as adults, on a level they'd never achieved before. She loved him as much as always, but now it was far deeper. Her heart pounded with anticipation when she knew she'd be seeing him, and when apart, his absence gnawed at her like a hunger pang. She wanted Felix around more often, to share their triumphs and rejoice over their successes with champagne and sushi dinners. But he'd said he felt like a spare prick at a wedding—and Leo wasn't even here yet.

"Oh, what have I done?" She lowered her head and stared at the floor, wondering exactly when that anticipation sprouted wings and took off.

****

Felix hung up the phone and turned to his creation. "Tomorrow."

Leo gave Felix the thumbs up sign.

Felix regarded Leo with a combination of awe and envy. He'd built this astonishingly flawless creature out of his sweat and genius. But at the same time, he resented the broad-shouldered SOB.

Resented him for his poise, his confidence, and his dark good looks.

Resented him for being a lover who would never suffer impotence or fatigue. Resented him for the life he was about to begin.

"Leo, you've been programmed to be a gentleman, a scholar, and everything in between." Felix brushed a piece of lint off the hero's cashmere jacket. "But it's not a perfect world out there. People are insincere, greedy, and will take advantage of you. Just remember what I told you about taking it all on the chin. Don't let the bastards get you down, and that includes me.

"I'll level with you, sweetheart. You're going where I want to be, and I know you don't give a damn. You've got human qualities, but you're not human. I'm as human as human can get. I exhibit jealousy and rage and all those other ugly traits. I can be a real asshole sometimes. I might get pissed at you, or I might get offensive. But remember—it's my problem, so don't take it to heart."

"Duly noted, Master." Leo nodded, and a raven lock fell over his forehead. Without thinking, Felix pushed it back.

"But if you're in love with her and want her for yourself, why didn't you program me to self-destruct at a convenient time?" Leo asked.

That display of thoughtfulness impressed Felix. It meant his design was working well. So here they were, two unselfish men involved with the same woman, each wishing her happiness with the other.

Would a winner emerge after all this?

"No. That would not be a triumph for me. It's a copout. If she ends up with me, it can't be on the rebound."

"Very well, Master. As you wish. Meanwhile, I shall do what I was meant to do, be perfect in every way."

"Right," Felix mumbled, putting on his coat. "I hope that's all it takes."

****

Judi had arranged her loft like a honeymoon cottage. Pink satin heart pillows graced the sofa, vases of red roses exuded their sweet fragrance, and a heart-shaped box of truffles sat between the backgammon set and chessboard. She peered down at herself. Her strapless dress clung to her curves. Felix's diamond pendant nestled above her cleavage. Her light makeup enhanced her features, and the nuance of Lilac Mist adorned her pulse points.

Judi knew what Leo looked like and what he'd be wearing.

She had his body memorized down to the last little mole on his hip.

She could hear the timbre of his laugh, could picture him stroking his mustache.

She could envision his double image before the bathroom mirror as he splashed aftershave on his sleek cheeks.

There was nothing about this man she didn't know. So then why did her hands refuse to stay dry, why did her stomach leap against her throbbing heart, and why did her throat contract and leave her voiceless? She paced up to the window, peered out and paced back.

But through all the nervousness, edginess and butterflies, she felt like she was losing her best friend. Felix had sounded so sad on the phone, but maybe she'd misread him. He didn't flaunt his moods and emotions very often.

After lighting one more lavender incense cone, she changed her chandelier earrings to hoops and back again. How could anticipation be so torturous?

The phone rang. She jumped, gasped, and leapt on the receiver.

Iris. Judi's shoulders fell into a slump.

"Hi, Judi! Have you written anything else yet? I have every faith you'll top yourself again."

"No, I haven't. I've had so much going on." She forced a chirping tone, trying to keep the tension out of her voice.

"Looks like the two men in your life have your time tied up."

Not to mention my stomach, she wanted to say. "Yeah, I haven't decided what to do about them yet.

We're going away for a few days. I'll try to do some writing then, but I doubt—"

"Which we? 'We' as in you and Felix 'we' or you and Leo 'we'?"

"Actually, all three of us."

Iris gasped just as the buzzer sounded. Judi's heart responded with a slamming thud. *They're here!*

"Iris, I gotta go, I'll call ya!" She dropped the receiver, not even knowing if it landed in its cradle, and dashed to the door. She smoothed her dress over her hips and gave her head a little toss, letting her hair fall in a wave over her face. Taking a deep breath, she opened the door.

There they were, the two of them, standing in her doorway, Felix and their creation, waiting to be let into Judi's home and heart.

Greeting Felix first, she fixed her gaze on the figure she'd created out of her deepest desires. At first the reality shocked her. His blue sport coat and beige trousers looked painted on. His hair shone as black as midnight. He sported a neatly trimmed mustache, and even in the hallway's dimness, she could see one green eye and one blue. She detected a lurking secret behind those emerald-sapphire jewels, a riddle whose clues would reveal themselves in due time. Her beloved Race Parsec stood before her.

He held out his hand. It was large, yet graceful and slender. The fingers, long and tapering, could compel a piano keyboard into life, glide over her body and create fire.

She held out her hand, and for the first time, she and the product of ten fantasy books touched. Warm, soft skin wrapped around her hand in a firm, confident handshake.

A tentative smile brightened his face. He nodded almost in recognition, as if he'd seen her before, but not knowing where.

He still hadn't said a word. Felix hung back, his eyes wide with hope, yet he clasped his hands, clutching a wine bottle as if holding it for dear life.

Suddenly, the piercing blare of a car alarm destroyed the splendor of the moment. She'd never live this moment again, and that insistent noise shattered her magic.

"May we come in?" Felix asked with a hint of uneasiness.

She nodded dumbly, stepped back, and motioned them in. Her hand tingled where Leo had touched it.

Leo stepped in and glanced about the loft. His gaze fell on the Chagall, and a hint of approval touched his eyes. Who was going to speak first now that they were inside?

"Judi, I'd like you to meet Leo. Leo, this is Judi Somers, a very dear friend of mine." Felix's tone was strained and formal, but the "very dear friend" part was sincere as he looked at her with a half-smile that didn't touch his eyes.

Oh, Felix, she wanted to say. *I feel it, too, but I'm a mishmash of emotions right now.*

Then, for the first time, she heard Leo's voice. "It's a pleasure to meet you, Judi. You have a lovely home."

She'd heard him speak millions of times—in her mind. But hearing it for real sounded like a new language. His smooth baritone flowed from his throat like honey.

"Thank you," she heard herself say, in that girly whisper she thought she'd left at high school dances. She wondered what he thought of her voice. She wondered what he thought of her dress. She wondered if he thought at all.

"Let's sit down and get to know each other, shall we?" Felix struggled to sound genial, even though they'd prepared for this moment.

It's going to be very awkward, he'd warned her more than once. *Although you'll feel you've known this guy forever, it'll be a shock, actually seeing him strutting his stuff in the flesh.*

Felix led the way like a theater usher. He motioned them to sit. The two strangers stood on either side of the moderator, as if the relationship depended on Felix's next suggestion. No one sat.

Judi's eyes remained transfixed on Leo. He studied the table, ran a finger over its surface, and flicked it against his thumb. A look of mild distaste furrowed his features as if he'd found a speck of dust too many.

"May I sit down?" he asked, and without waiting for an answer, he lifted his trouser legs and sat.

She situated herself opposite him, admiring Leo's healthy Mediterranean olive complexion. She stared at the mustache. *Will that tickle when he kisses me?* His lips were so exquisitely shaped, they seemed to be made for kissing.

Their eyes met again, and Leo caught her staring. He smiled, as if to say, *You have every right to stare.*

"I've told Leo all about you," Felix chirped, his voice nearing normalcy as he tried to ease the throbbing tension. Leo sat upright without a hint of a slump or slouch. His lips parted to reveal a set of perfect white teeth.

She wondered what Felix had told him at the awakening of his senses, when he was finally able to open his eyes and see, to hear music, to touch softness, to smell flowers.

Does he know who—or what he is? she wondered.

"How do you like it here, Leo?" She cringed. She'd meant "How do you like it here?"—as in this life.

"A marvelous world. A beautiful country. New York is a fascinating city. Although I prefer Geneva."

Geneva? When the hell had Felix taken him there?

"Rome's my favorite, however. A classic city. I

could gaze at the Sistine Chapel ceiling for hours and never tire of it."

Well, of course. He wasn't supposed to tire of anything.

"Oh, and when did you visit Geneva and Rome?" she prodded as Felix reached over and patted down Leo's lapel.

"I don't remember exactly when. I just remember being there."

So that's how Felix programmed him...able to recall places; although he'd never been west of the Hudson River.

"I'd love to go again someday," he added.

"I, I heard...that you're a virtuoso pianist," Judi ventured, keeping the conversation light for now.

"Of course," he nearly sang, sprang up, and strode to the piano with the confidence of a gladiator.

"What would you like to hear? Rachmaninoff? Or something simpler like a show tune, perhaps?"

He sat on the bench, threw his arms into the air, and flexed his fingers. "I'll perform one of my favorites," he announced. "It's called 'Romance' by Anton Rubinstein."

Leo placed his fingers on the keys and filled the room with delicate strains, creating a consonance only a gifted performer could deliver. He closed his eyes and his body swayed. A dreamlike expression came to his face.

"I think he'll be so busy making love to that piano, he won't have time for me," she whispered to Felix, who watched intently, as if judging a competition.

"Don't worry, he'll have plenty of time for you," he replied. "Remember, he doesn't have to practice."

As the last chords faded, she and Felix applauded. "That was simply brilliant, Leo," Felix commended his creation.

"Judi, my darling," Leo walked over to the window and ran his fingertips over her new drapes, "you need not fear my neglecting you. As long as I'm here, your pleasure will be my every command." He tilted his head, lifted his trouser knees, and sat a bit farther from her than before.

"You...you heard what I said?" She cringed.

"Let's just say I caught the gist of the conversation. I love my music, but the music of lovemaking is more worthy of my time than bringing a mere instrument to life. I much prefer to make music with a woman, creating exquisite harmony with my own."

"Wowee," she whispered as Felix beamed like a proud papa at his child's first recital. "You sure have a way with words."

"What are words? Mere vehicles manufactured to convey the essence of our mutual discourse."

Leo craned his neck to see himself in her full-length mirror as Felix spoke. "Leo, now that we've heard you play piano, how about showing us your culinary prowess? Make it easy on yourself. How about a pot of tea?"

"The pleasure is all mine, Master." He turned to Judi, flashing those teeth that could rival the Steinway keyboard. "Would you like a spot of tea, my lady?" He now sported a British accent.

"I wish you'd talk like that all the time," she sighed. Maybe he could affect a foreign accent at her whim; tomorrow he could be French!

After tea, which Leo brewed to perfection and served in her new china teacups, Felix delivered a blow that would have knocked Judi over if Leo's magnetic force hadn't been holding her up.

"We'll have to get going now, Judi." He glanced at Leo examining her CD collection.

"What?" She shook her head. "You're kidding, right?"

"I have to take Leo back home with me for a while," he stated. Then, nearing closer to her, said, "Remember what I said about striving for perfection? Although you may not realize it by looking at him and conversing with him, he's still far from perfect. I need to equip him with some protection from the environment. Excessive sunlight and pollution will erode his epidermis—his top layer of skin. Besides that, he needs a few other things—internal things, if you will. So I can't possibly risk leaving him alone here."

"Alone? What did you think I was planning to do tonight? Run out and play canasta with the girls?"

"I know you want him all to yourself, but that's impossible. There are too many things I've still got to do with him."

"Yeah, and I can think of too many things I'd like to do with him."

"Judi, be reasonable," he pleaded. "I'm the scientist. Trust me."

Who else could she trust at this point?

Leo slid a Chaucer volume from her bookshelf with a nimble forefinger and flipped through the pages, stopping to glance at his reflection in the window.

She dumped on Felix, "It's like giving a kid a lollipop—with me as the kid here—and then snatching it away just as I'm about to take my first lick. How could you do this to me?"

"Judi, he's not safe. And I don't mean from you, so don't jump on me. I mean from the environment—radiation, even particles in the air can damage his delicate system. I jumped the gun bringing him over here tonight. I should have waited until he was completely ready."

"Can't you do that here? Or don't you want me to see him turning into a pumpkin at midnight?"

"No, Judi, I've got to take him back to the lab."

Leo looked up from the book and gave Judi a wink. She nearly melted into her teacup.

"So when will he be mine permanently?"

"Soon. Now I'd like to get him home. I've got a lecture at eight tomorrow morning, and I've still got to get my notes together."

"Can I come over and visit Leo?"

"No. Just stay home and write your books."

"Okay, okay." She gazed at Leo leafing through the *Dictionary of American Slang*, a scowl on his face. "Try to work on his sense of humor."

"Yes, he's a bit dry, isn't he?" Felix grinned at the stunningly handsome man. "Come, Leo, we've got to get going now," he called to his creation, like a master summoning his pet.

Leo replaced the book and glided over to Felix, buttoning his jacket.

Judi followed. As Leo stepped into the foyer, he took her hand and touched his lips to the back of it.

"Until we meet again, my darling lady." When their eyes met, all the blood in her body surged to her head, making her knock-kneed.

"I'll see you again very soon, Leo, and you, Felix, very soon?" She shot him a glare.

"The time will fly." He slid into his coat and grasped Leo's arm.

Just then Judi realized Leo didn't have an overcoat.

"Isn't he going to be cold?" She directed the question to Felix, who knew, if anyone did, why this man wasn't properly dressed.

"I'm environmentally controlled," Leo answered for him, as if able to explain every facet of his physical makeup. "I'll be perfectly comfortable. But we must do some more clothes shopping. Perhaps Doctor Felix can join us." He flashed that dazzling smile and caressed Judi's cheek, displaying his first spontaneous gesture of affection. She could think of a few spontaneous things she wanted to do.

"Climate control, remember?" Felix reminded her as he and Leo headed out the door.

The door shut on her future—for now.

Judi rushed to the window to see Felix and Leo, her past and her future, exit her building and disappear around the corner. Shadows lengthened on the sidewalk as darkness fell, yet she remained at the window, the curtain clutched in her hand. The empty rooms and the stark silence made her feel more abandoned than ever. She hugged herself, longing for human contact. Felix could have at least invited her to join them for dinner or a game of chess or something, not just bundle Leo up and bail. Didn't he realize how empty that made her feel?

Releasing the curtain and turning away from the world, she slinked over to the sofa and plopped down. She forced herself to anticipate Leo's delightful company and their rapturous encounters ahead. Of course Felix could join them for meals, plays, and weekend drives. She couldn't leave him out. Now that he was back in her life, she wouldn't let him go again.

Chapter Ten

When Judi's grandfather clock chimed twelve times, she realized it was midnight, and she'd been agonizing over Leo's maiden voyage for three hours. One more "What if we don't click?" or "Maybe it wasn't meant to be after all" while pacing a rut in her rug would send her out into the cold for a gallon of Coco Choco Chip. She didn't realize how much the what-if's exhausted her until she massaged toothpaste into her tired neck muscles and brushed her teeth with gritty wintergreen muscle rub. She scrubbed and gargled the mess, shook her head to clear it, and called Iris.

Her insomniac friend answered on the first ring.

"Judi! I thought you were on your ménage à trois honeymoon."

"Oh, Iris, I'm afraid the whole thing is in the early stages of a major bomb. Like my attempt at the Mafia vampire novel."

"What happened?"

"Felix and Leo happened. I think they just wanted to be alone." Judi's voice cracked with fatigue and defeat.

"Oh, well, you know how brothers are. Don't take it as a slight. How long is he going to be in town?"

"Long enough," she sighed, gazing at the moonlight touching the piano, making the keys glow—a romantic winter's night she should have been spending in his arms. "I can wait."

"They'll be back. If not, get off the fainting couch and hightail it over there. I've never known you to hesitate over what you want, Judi. Or what you think you want, at least."

"You're right. I'll spend the weekend pampering myself."

And she did. She sat up all night reading her old Race books, lounging in the hot tub, conditioning her hair, and depleting her champagne supply—in between pots of cappuccino to stay awake in order to enjoy it all.

****

Felix threw yet another losing hand of cards onto the table in frustration as Leo proudly displayed his royal flush.

"Okay, Lucky Leo, so if you become famous, you can go on the world poker tour. Although, I know you'd abhor any public accolades or idolization from strange adoring women."

"What's wrong, Doctor Felix? You bestowed this talent upon me, and you resent its manifestation in my taking you for broke." With one swift sweep of his muscled arm, Leo claimed Felix's last remaining chips. "But of course I'd never play you for real stakes. Money means nothing to me. However, I would relish the ability to enjoy women's company to the fullest. I did feel rather ill at ease in Judi's presence to the extent I'm able to feel. I'll qualify that by saying if I had pores, I could have broken a sweat."

"You may have something there." Felix asked himself why pangs of jealousy niggled at him. The creature performed exactly how Felix had programmed him to. He couldn't have perfected this Adonis any further if he'd dipped him in platinum. Even then, he'd be buffing himself all the time.

Felix let a stab of guilt linger until it hurt. He shouldn't have taken Leo away from Judi, seemingly to fix kinks. But he'd taken Leo home because jealousy had gotten the best of him. Now he disliked himself and his grossly selfish, human behavior. In contrast, Leo had no capacity for jealousy. He was a vain, superficial, pompous ass, but he'd never be human.

But Leo's wanting to enjoy a smorgasbord of female company sounded like a goal worth pursuing, even if it meant putting up with his insufferable mug for another few days.

"When do we go back to my heroine, Doctor? I honestly can't see any more room for improvement here." Leo picked up Felix's teaspoon and admired his features in the handle.

"Oh, will you stop gazing at yourself in every available reflective object!" Felix knocked the spoon out of Leo's hand. "You're gorgeous, can't you take my word for it?"

"Another trait you programmed into me, Master," Leo replied smoothly. "Trust but verify."

Felix shook his head and expelled an exasperated breath. Finally, he stood and walked over to his creation, placing a hand on his shoulder. "I'm sorry, I'm just a little—just annoying my own annoying self."

"Why are you annoyed with yourself?" Leo stacked the chips in neat piles. "You can talk to me. I'd never gossip."

"I know." Felix went to the bar and mixed himself a stiff highball, but he couldn't confess how Judi's adoring gazes at Leo had driven him nearly mad with jealousy, especially knowing he might've had a chance with her years ago but was too timid to ask her on a date. He couldn't possibly start all over at this late date.

"It's just that—" He took a long pull of his drink. "I want the best for Judi, and you were—formal and polite with her. You need to loosen up."

"But I'm a gentleman. I couldn't be overly familiar at our first meeting."

"It's not the first meeting. She's written ten books in which you've starred. She's known you for years. Chill out a bit. Show some sense of humor. I did give you one, however weak."

"Ah, yes." Leo guffawed. His broad shoulders rose and fell. "Get this. What time is it when an elephant sits on your fence?"

Felix rolled his eyes and took another pull of his drink. "You need a few visits to the comedy clubs. But relax around her. You're not trying out to be one of the queen's footmen. You're her life mate." The booze helped Felix relax; he didn't hate himself as much. "Don't take this personally," he mumbled to himself, between sips. "Judi doesn't want you. She wants this specimen of post-adolescent manhood."

Felix now had a legit excuse to keep Leo here— he needed to loosen Leo up. "Hey, bro," he addressed the hunk now combing his hair in the mirror, "I need to make sure you bask in the company of women the way beach bums bask in the sun. I'll work on your ability to be more open among females. And we've got to punch up that sense of humor. Forget the elephant sitting on the fence and the chicken that crossed the road. Listen carefully: This traveling salesman stops at a farmhouse..."

****

The phone rang on Sunday night as Judi worked at the keyboard rattling her brains to produce something coherent. Once Leo arrived, she wouldn't be getting much work done. Realizing she'd left the answering machine off, she finished typing her paragraph and answered on the sixth ring.

"What took you so long?" Felix sounded mildly vexed.

"I thought you'd need as much time as possible to fix Leo up. I know how detail-oriented you are." Her harsh tone compared with the wind rattling her windows.

"Oh, you're still ticked I had to take him back? I told you it was for his safety, and I'm not going to argue about that now. When do you want us to come over?"

She leaned back in her computer chair, struggling to keep her hopes at bay. "Is it permanent this time, or is this another quickie?"

"I wouldn't say permanent. He needs a few more final touches before he's fit to go solo for any prolonged time. I can leave him with you when I'm at work during the day, but I'll have to take him back at night before he's ready to function on his own. You can't take him out until I know he's ready. We'll play it by ear, but for now I can't take any chances. You understand."

"Why do geniuses assume everything is understandable to the inferior minds of the world?" she shot back. "But in the time you'd take to explain, he could be here. So I suppose I'll have to put him in your capable hands." What choice did she have? She battled the anxiety in her voice; her heart thumped like a jackhammer. "What time?"

"Give us a few hours. He wants to bathe, blow dry his hair, buff his toenails, the usual. Make it eight o'clock."

She rapidly calculated how long it would take to make herself glamorous and alluring. For both of them. "I'll be here."

"He looks great. Right off a Milan runway. Wait till you see him."

"I don't care if he's not bathed. It's not like he sweats."

"He wants to look alluring for you," Felix said.

"He would look alluring smothered in iwashi."

"Yeah, he would," Felix answered.

That came off sounding sarcastic to her. Why?

"See you at the witching hour, Judi. Cheers."

She hung up and dashed into the shower,

mentally reviewing her wardrobe. She finally selected a satin beige hostess gown, not too provocative, not too innocent either, and just right for their second encounter.

Although she'd spread enough makeup over her vanity top to rival a cosmetic counter, she ended up applying only clear gloss. "I sure don't need blush," she told her reflection, flushed a healthy pink with anticipation.

****

Judi stood and waited, red-carpet ready, with her upswept coiffure and glittery pumps. After several more changes of hair combs, shoes, and pantyhose—sheer or taupe? Fishnets or not? Not!—she was ready within a minute of their arrival.

At eight on the dot, like a prince and his coach out of a fairy tale, Felix and Leo arrived. This time Leo's burgundy turtleneck provided a dashing accent to the black blazer and trousers. His hair had not a strand out of place. She could picture him reclining before the hearth, his features catching the fiery glow...warmth flooded her, and her face flushed. She took a deep breath and tried to cool off.

She glanced at Felix, dressed just as impeccably in a tailored blazer and turtleneck, and instantly imagined the same scene with him...

"Why do you like to entertain your guests out in the hall, Judi?" Felix broke in. She could hear the forced politeness in his voice.

"Oh, sorry. Come on in."

Leo walked in first, acknowledging her presence with a nod. "Hello, Leo," she greeted him.

Felix headed straight for the kitchen. "I need riboflavin."

Looking out into the hall, she noticed three huge suitcases. She couldn't understand it; they hadn't bought Leo that many clothes. "Felix, what's in all these suitcases?"

"Pardon?" Felix spooned protein powder into her smoothie maker. "Oh. Those are clothes, Judi."

Leo made himself at home on her sofa. "You bought him more clothes?"

She followed Felix's path into the kitchen, her eyes fixed on the well-scrubbed gentleman on her sofa, one leg crossed casually over the other, foot swinging in perfect tempo. "I thought we were going shopping together."

"No. They're mine." Felix opened her fridge door. It swung open and banged against the wall, rattling the jars.

"Yours? What—what—"

He helped himself to the milk and poured some into the blender. "This needs something crunchy. You have any pine nuts?"

"No, I don't, and what do you mean yours?" She took a step closer.

"Judi, like I explained on the phone, for the time being, if he's going to be here for prolonged amounts of time, I'm going to have to stay here with him. And I've got Dickie and Annie with me, too." He shut off the blender. "It's for your protection," he announced, sounding like a credit card company. Leo shot her a helpless little grin, one shoulder lifting in a shrug.

This would complicate things. The three of them together? Could she handle this emotionally charged setup? She doubted it, but just then her imagination went wild. She shook her head, purging the thoughts. Forcing herself back to Earth, she splashed some champagne into a glass and took a gulp. It just made her sweat. "So there's going to be five of us?"

Felix looked up. "Five?"

"Me and you and Leo and Dickie and Annie. Who are they, Leo's kids? Or yours, maybe?"

Leo looked over at Felix, raised an eyebrow and said, "You might have ruffled a few feathers,

Master."

"Butt out, Gorgeous George." He turned to Judi. "They're my parakeets."

Now he's turning my place into Audubon Park. "So what are the sleeping arrangements, Father Flanagan?"

She couldn't let Leo see her sweat. Looking like a model in a deodorant commercial, he sat there looking calm, cool, and intensely gorgeous.

"Leo and I will sleep on the cots, out here in the alcove." Felix poured his shake into a glass.

"Cots?" She took another unwanted gulp of bubbly. "What cots? I haven't got any cots."

"The cots in your entry hall downstairs. I just had them delivered here. I thought I'd get the doorman to bring them up."

She threw her arms in the air. "There's no doorman here!"

"Not a problem, Master, I'll do it." Leo popped up.

"Bring that other stuff in, too, my good man," Felix ordered.

Leo slid out of his jacket, making a show of it. He bounded out the door and into the hall.

Judi's eyes followed him out. "What other stuff?"

"Leo's a regular Bamm-Bamm. He'll lift a hundred-pound barbell as long as the person who used it before him washed his hands." Felix stuck a straw into his glass.

"What other stuff?"

"Just some of my yoga apparatus, my inversion table, and my stretching ball. I had them delivered, too."

Leo brought in a birdcage, set it on her kitchen counter, and whistled Mozart's "Eine kleine Nachtmusic" to the two birds inside, who cocked their little heads and remained silent. Next, he went and fetched a metal contraption, set it in the middle of the living room, then exited. He came back in rolling a huge purple ball.

"What the hell are you going to do with this?" Judi nudged the ball. It rolled into her plant stand nearly knocking over her basil and oregano.

"I stretch my back on it. It's for my range of motion. The inversion table's for my back too, but when I hang upside down on it, all the blood rushes to my brain. Sometimes I do my best work hanging on that thing."

The birds started to twitter and tweet.

"I'm going to count to three, then Leo is going to witness his first hanging—and I don't mean the upside-down variety." She spoke over the chirping.

"Judi, it's simple. I've got to keep an eye on him. Make sure he's safe. He hasn't got much in the way of street smarts. For God's sakes, it's his first few days on Earth. I can't very well leave him unattended. He might go out and hurt someone without realizing he's doing anything wrong."

"High values, pure virginity, and he's a street thug?"

He shrugged and sucked through his straw. "I couldn't program him with everything that's right from wrong all at once. I've got to keep a very close watch on him until he's immersed in the culture and picks up on it."

Her growing uneasiness forced her to grip the back of the sofa for support. She'd be the one moving out! "Then tell me, how long are you going to monitor his absorption into our culture?"

"'Til I feel comfortable with it. I'll still have to bring him home and do more work on him. I told you he wasn't going to be factory-ready."

The three of them—and two feathered friends.

The charge between her and Felix was inflamed enough, but now with Leo here, she almost buckled under the emotional overload. And to think, just a few short months ago she had none of this—just an adored fictional hero to keep her juices flowing.

Leo returned, carrying one cot under each arm as if they were inflatable rubber rafts. "Where shall I put these, Master?" he asked, as if it were Felix's house and Felix's decor.

"In that alcove over there. Open my suitcases and drape my clothes over these chairs here, will you, Leo? I'm glad I'll be near the living room. I always fall asleep with the TV on." She shot him a questioning glance, and he added, "Don't worry, Judi, I'll pay my share, as well as Dickie and Annie's. Just let me know where to put my laundry and birdcage liners."

****

They spent the evening sipping coffee, discussing random topics, and making plans for nights on the town.

The subject migrated from music to politics, to space travel, and back to Felix's occupation.

"What is your next project, Master?" Leo slipped out of his shoes and made himself comfortable. With two nimble fingers, he opened his top shirt button and ran his hand lovingly over his chest. She tried to focus on something else in the room, the piano, the light socket, anything, but her roving gaze always landed on the bulge at his crotch. She averted her eyes before he saw her.

"I'm in a contract with ORBIT." Felix stifled a yawn.

She guessed the project had lost its novelty for him and was now just another job. "On a team for a mission to Megasus."

"Why, that's fascinating!" Leo's voice dripped with enthusiasm, renewing Felix's interest in the subject.

"Only problem is, it's under the strictest of confidence. I'm telling you because...well, I know

144

astronomy is one of your interests, and you love to shoot the breeze about quantum physics, black holes, and the bending of space."

"I'll keep your secret if you keep mine," Leo joked.

Judi regarded the two men, so opposite, yet complementing each other so well. Leo was her dream to the tiniest detail, yet he still felt like a stranger with that awkwardness of having just met someone.

"I would love to travel in space someday." Leo gazed past Judi out the window, his hands folded across his knees. "My ultimate mission would be to walk on another planet—inhabit another world."

Judi was impressed. She'd wanted him to be ambitious, but—wow!

"Space travel's very common these days, what with the shuttles and the probes going up all the time. You just may get your wish someday." Felix nodded. His eyes shone with that laser-sharpness.

"Ah, that's but a dream." Leo turned to Judi, a smile brightening his features. "I've got all a man could ever ask for, right here on Earth."

As he and Judi exchanged smiles, she felt the air swelling with the same electric current as the night she and Felix danced together, that first spark between them. A shiver zigzagged down her spine like a bolt of lightning. Maybe it was going to be all right. After all, how many women had two desirable men under the same garden roof?

Then the conversation evolved, and they talked into the wee hours about everything that interested her: her favorite authors, operas, and famous New York landmarks. They'd made her the center of attention. She relaxed on the sofa and kicked up her feet. This might work after all!

They finally retired just before three, Felix heading for the bathroom with his travel case to prepare for bed. Leo turned to Judi, unsnapped his cufflinks, and placed them on the table next to Felix's watch. "Our first stolen moment," he whispered.

His tongue flicked across his lips, and he browsed at her features. She waltzed up to him. Her fingers touched his cleft chin. Her lips parted.

He lowered his head. Their lips touched, fitting perfectly. Her arms went around his neck and for the first time, she touched the midnight black locks, silk against her fingertips. He brought her to him. Their bodies conformed like plaster to a mold. Yes, the mustache did tickle! She struggled to breathe. Her eyes darted in all directions underneath her closed lids, sending wild splashes of color and sunbursts through her mind.

But that tease had to suffice for tonight. Felix came out of the bathroom and cleared his throat. "Time for beddy-bye, kids."

Leo pulled away. With her gaze still locked into his, she whispered good night. When she looked at Felix, she saw despair in his eyes.

But before she had a chance to say good night, he gave a resigned nod, turned on them and went to bed.

Chapter Eleven

Morning peeped through the curtains. The thought of Leo pulled Judi out of sleep. Her heart leapt. Wondering if he looked as innocent as Race while asleep, she battled the temptation to tiptoe into the living room and gaze at him. Even her rakish villains appeared virtuous babes in sleep.

But she languished in bed, daydreaming about the life that was to begin today, a day she'd never forget.

At seven, footsteps sounded in the other room. Her heart made a double somersault. Could it be Leo coming in to kiss her out of sleep? No, it was Felix getting ready for work, she realized, as the pungent aroma of coffee beans wafted through the apartment along with some lively chirping.

Tempted to rise and join him for breakfast, she needed at least an hour to make herself glamorous. She sat up, her feet hitting the hardwood floor, jolting her into full awareness. Without a peek into the living room, she headed straight for the shower.

As she blow-dried her hair, the front door clicked shut. Now with Felix out of the house, she and Leo were alone! No one in the entire world existed but the two of them.

She applied her makeup meticulously, as if preparing for her wedding. She dabbed perfume on her pulse points. Adjusting the straps on her silver house slippers, she glanced into the mirror, dressed her lips with an expectant smile, and took a deep breath. Entering the living room, expecting to see her lover aroused from slumber, she stopped short in her tracks. There he sat, in a blue shirt and knit slacks, at her computer surfing the Internet.

The early morning light feathered through his hair, making it glint with a blue-black lustre. A pot of coffee percolated in the kitchen. A fire blazed in the hearth.

He looked up, and they regarded each other—strangers, yet two beings whose souls had always been one. Greeting her with a smile, he shut the monitor off and stood.

"Bonjour. I hope I didn't wake you with all that noise." His voice was as smooth and rich as the coffee that awakened her senses.

"No, actually Felix woke me up." She rolled the purple ball out of the way. Looking into the kitchen, she noticed something sizzling in the skillet, and the toaster oven gave off a warm orange glow.

"I'm making breakfast," he offered. "I hope you like eggs Benedict, toast with marmalade, fresh strawberries, and freshly squeezed orange juice. I'll have it in front of you in two shakes of Beethoven's baton."

Eggs Benedict? Fresh strawberries? Marmalade? She'd never bought a jar of marmalade in her life, and the only strawberries she ate were freeze-dried in cereal.

"Where did you get—"

"One of those funky little gourmet delis. Felix scurried down there for me. Good man—doesn't mind doing the go-fer stuff. The strawberries look sumptuous. Ripe and juicy." He raised a brow suggestively.

I'll give you ripe and juicy, she thought.

"Now, make yourself comfy. I'll pour you a cup of coffee, and we shall break our fast in thirty seconds."

She walked to the sofa and sat as he served her black coffee, just the way she liked it, and when she took a sip, her taste buds burst in ecstasy. "This coffee is fantastic! What on Earth is it?"

"Vanilla Amaretto. I know...rather, I heard those were your favorites, so I had them blend the beans specially for you."

"This is perfect. Just perfect." She took another sip, then another, breathing in the delicious blend of sweet almond and vanilla.

He returned with a tray holding the steaming breakfast, garnished with a single red rose in a bud vase, and placed it on the table in front of her.

"Leo, you didn't have to go through all this. I could have grabbed a bowl of cereal."

He stayed seated, his eyes fixed on her face, taking in her features as if gazing at a priceless work of art. "I wouldn't hear of it. I'm here to wait on you." He added, matter-of-factly, "You know that."

Leo toasted their health as they clinked juice glasses, and she dug into her eggs. All the uneasiness of his presence vanished as she closed her eyes and let her mouth savor the ambrosia.

"You're just too much," she marveled, biting into a succulent berry. Its tartness awakened her mouth like a spring shower.

His lips curved upward.

"What shall we do today, Judi?" He carried the dishes into the kitchen. "Would you like to listen to a few symphonies and discuss their merit? Or perhaps read to each other or just talk? You recall we promised Doctor Felix we wouldn't leave the house."

"You promised him." An artful smile curled her lips. She wanted to defy Felix's wishes and scamper through the streets, singing about her two gorgeous, desirable men.

He strolled over to the CD collection, choosing Schubert's *Unfinished Symphony*. Soon the delicate strains filled the room.

"I thought you might want to hear this." He sat next to her on the sofa, his knee lightly touching hers.

"You're a dream." She breathed a sigh that rose above Schubert. "I'll gladly spend the entire day indoors. I'll read all the poetry you want."

"I'm getting vibes." His arm slid around the top of the sofa, resting on her bare shoulder, making her quiver. "Do you feel the currents of electric magnetism charging the air?" He leaned forward. She closed her eyes, knowing that his mouth would meet hers, like magnet to steel, guided by the invisible force between them.

Their lips barely brushed, and then he pulled away as if she'd bitten him.

"What's wrong?" Her breath caught in her throat.

"I don't want to smear the lip gloss."

The last thing on her mind was lip gloss. Then she remembered: "I'm not wearing any."

His tongue darted out, a cursory movement rather than a provocative one. "But I am."

****

Judi stood at the window looking out over the quiet street, empty of roaring trucks and zooming taxicabs, and absent of workers scurrying to work. Midmorning Manhattan was on siesta until the lunch crowd spilled out into the streets.

The music finally stopped. Had six symphonies played already?

Leo headed for the stereo. He put on another CD, Vivaldi this time, and returned to the sofa.

How awkward she felt, alone with him for the first time, not knowing what to say, feeling too shy to start a conversation. She knew this man better than herself, yet a stranger had just entered her life. She had to reacquaint herself with him; after all, fiction was fiction. She'd dreamed him up, but now that he was here, he'd taken on a life of his own. It reminded her of writing—she never knew which way the storyline would turn once the characters started acting.

He didn't try to kiss her again that day; he didn't even touch her. They spent a perfectly platonic afternoon, talking about their favorite topics: literature, nutrition, and Felix.

They discussed the space program while on the subject of Felix, and Leo repeated his wish to inhabit another planet.

"I doubt that will happen in our lifetime, Leo," Judi said wistfully. "Look how long it's been between the last manned moon mission and this project of Felix's."

She reached for a truffle from the box on the table and took a nibble. "Unfortunately, it's a capitalistic excursion, the wish to set up men in space. Who do you think will get to live out in space? Only the privileged few, I'll wager. You don't think the average working class family will ever have the opportunity to view the Earth from a space station or build a condo on the Sea of Tranquility's left bank, do you? No, it's just for the elite ruling classes." She took a bigger nibble of her truffle.

"This might sound like liberalism, but I'm a product of my days as a struggling writer. I may be successful now, but my beliefs never changed. And although I write about space adventures, I have more mundane ideas about the allocation of public funds." She finished off her truffle by shoving the remainder in her mouth and chomping down on it.

He cocked his head, and his brow cocked with it. "You're wrong, Judi," he stated flatly. "It's for the betterment of all mankind. Stop thinking like such a little—Earthling."

Surprised by this abruptness, she stiffened. "Wrong? It's my opinion. How would you like it if I'd declared you wrong because I didn't agree with you?"

He gave off a casual toss of his head and

151

squared his shoulders. "Anyone can see you're wrong. Humans are pioneers by nature. Humans will inhabit other planets as the intrepid voyagers came here and settled North America. You think so many things are for the elite class because you spend too much time being brainwashed by left-wing loons."

Oh, he'd ruffled her feathers now. She leaned forward, her fists clenching. "Now wait a minute. Felix is as Libertarian as you can get, and look at him—if it weren't for his genius and ability to carry out a scientific experiment, you wouldn't even be here!"

"The great Doctor Varlden put me here to satisfy his obsessive ego. But he didn't do too bad a job of it, if I do say so myself," he bragged, buffing his nails on his shirt.

"Felix has no ego," she argued. "Even though he's one of the world's leading scientists and one of the most brilliant men alive—"

"Don't I know it."

"I'm glad you agr—"

"He informed me of that the moment I opened my eyes," Leo cut in. "He also made clear the fact that I am but a nonentity with nothing more than dazzling looks and a few sundry talents to complement my magnetic charm." He fluttered his long lashes, another Race-like characteristic she couldn't resist giving him.

How dare he put Felix down. "No, you must've taken it out of context. You misjudged him. After all, you've only been here a few days. I've known him since third grade. You have to really know him—"

"All I know is what he's shown me, which is an overeducated egghead who would like to rule the world but just hasn't got the charisma." He raised his chin and looked down his nose at her.

"Felix couldn't be more unpretentious and

modest if he tried." She crossed her arms over her chest and impatiently tapped her foot.

"Hasn't grown much in thirty years, has he? Physically or emotionally." He draped one leg over the other and swung his foot, looking more amused as her temper flared.

"And you're the picture of maturity? At the ripe old age of six days?"

He laughed, a low-throated chortle. Her fists and her teeth clenched at the same time. She wanted him to make her blood boil, but not this way!

"It's in the way he comes across to me," Leo said. "Perhaps he shows another side with you. Like you, I am merely voicing my observations. I don't believe in keeping anything in."

A horrible thought entered her mind: what if she'd created a monster? "Never mind what you believe. It all comes with being socially correct. And these days, politically correct." Something they'd overlooked. She wanted a hero with the courage of his convictions, but knowing when to shut up had escaped her list of desirable traits. Even Race knew when to put a sock in it; that was one way he managed to survive ten books.

"You wanted an outspoken hero, Judi, not a mousy wuss."

"Yes, but there's a trait called tact, which I see you're sorely lacking for the time being." She had to discuss this with Felix before somebody strangled this guy...if she didn't strangle him with one of his silk neckties first.

"We all talk about people, Judi. I'm just sincere enough to talk about them openly and constructively instead of in a derogatory manner. One thing you'll never be able to call me is a gossip. I do not fabricate. I speak the truth as I see it."

Truthfulness. Another Race-like quality on her list, up there with courage and midnight black hair.

One of his custom-made qualities, only he was clueless how to rein it in.

But she couldn't let this ineptness bother her now. It could be fixed, she was sure. This was the man she'd written about, dreamed of, and fantasized about during many lonely years, and here he was, close enough to reach out and slap.

"Let's not argue about Doctor Felix, shall we?" His voice soothed her like a milk bath. "He is my creator, after all, and he does seem to possess some redeeming qualities. He amuses me, I must admit."

"Lucky him," she retorted, amazed at how this man resembled Race in his upstaging moments. Too much, though. If Race was larger than life, Leo was larger than fiction.

"Hey, come on." He finally touched her hand, and she resisted the urge, at first, to snatch it away.

So he needed to be reconfigured a bit. Just like any new computer program, he had bugs. Felix was right; he did need work. "I didn't mean to ruffle your pretty feathers," he soothed. "We won't agree on everything. As long as one of us is willing to admit when she's wrong."

Now what did he mean by that crack? Arguing with him was a waste of time. She'd never win. She grabbed a magazine from the table and fanned her burning face. "Just remember opinions can't be wrong."

"Duly noted. Now, I'd like to model some of the clothes you chose for me. How about some accompanying music?" He sauntered into the alcove.

Sighing, she rose to find Debussy, knowing they would fall into a pattern of exquisite harmony once these kinks got ironed out.

Ten minutes later, Leo reappeared. His grand exit had given her a chance to chill. And now that she'd calmed down, she could see he'd been worth the wait. When he strutted past her in swimming trunks that grabbed every tantalizing bulge, she could see her heart thumping under her blouse.

She gave a weak nod of approval as he went back to change.

He stopped and admired his reflection between each changing, holding a hand mirror up for a rear view. He combed his hair, smoothed his brows, and splashed cologne behind his knees. How cute, she thought. But later, when she caught him studying the Window Treatment Fantasies Web site and started firing off decorating tips, she began to wonder: *Good God, is he gonna pass me up and go for Felix?*

Chapter Twelve

After he announced "checkmate" in their third game of chess that he won, Leo glanced at the clock. "My word, it's four-thirty already. I must start dinner."

"No rush, Leo." This obsessive punctuality made her feel like a private in boot camp. "Felix said he'd treat us to some delightful gourmet cuisine at L'Amarante." Listening to Leo all day, she couldn't help but pick up some of his vocabulary

"Oh, he needn't do that. After all, he does deserve some fine home cooking once in his life, doesn't he?"

She wondered if he was, in his own charming way, alluding to her lack of culinary skills. "I can cook just as well as anyone," she shot back defensively.

"Anyone human perhaps," he prompted, reached for the wooden spoon, and waved it like a conductor's wand. "You did specify a gourmet, did you not?"

Of course. A gourmet lover. Every woman's dream. And here he was, in her kitchen, forbidding her to pass the threshold, lest she make an undesirable suggestion like instant rice instead of the long-cooking variety. But he'd already planned the entire menu: fruit compote, garden salad, jambon persille, and entrecote marchand de vin with a luscious flan for dessert. *Eat your heart out, L'Amarante*, she thought, as Leo hummed the second movement of Beethoven's seventh symphony while whittling away at a kiwi.

Felix's eyes lit up when he entered the loft and

inhaled the cooking aromas. "Do I detect a culinary maestro, or did I die and go to Burger Hut?" he chanted as Leo pranced out, a checkered apron covering his tailor-fit clothes, twirling the wooden spoon.

He held it out to Felix and urged him to taste. "Just a preview, Master. Now relax while I serve you some sherry—you prefer the cream variety, do you not?"

Judi, sitting on the sofa nursing a margarita, watched as Felix sipped from the spoon, angled so that just the right amount would tease his taste buds.

"Très bon!" Felix circled his thumb and forefinger, tossing his coat over a chair.

"So how was the lovebirds' first day together, and I don't mean Dickie and Annie?" he inquired with uncertainty as he slipped his shoes off and kicked them aside.

"Just ducky." Judi feigned more enthusiasm than she actually felt; although she planned to confront Felix when the master chef wandered out of earshot.

"What did you two do today?" Felix climbed onto his inversion table, securing his ankles into the clamps and lowering his body until he was upside down.

"We had a lovely day together!" Leo emerged from the kitchen and smoothed his sleeves.

Judi eyed him with a mixture of wonder and regret. He was just too perfect—and too unlike the eccentric but lovable scientist in the middle of her living room hanging upside down. Oh, how she wanted to kiss Felix when he'd walked through the door.

Leo continued, "We talked, listened to music, I gave a fashion show, we played chess, and I won—"

"You didn't leave the house, did you?" Judi

watched with amusement as Felix regarded his creation carefully, down and up, from his inverted position.

"Of course not, Master. Not without your express permission that I may do so."

Felix's gaze reached Judi, "So nothing blew up or short-circuited?"

But Leo answered for her. "It was as calm as the Dead Sea, my good Master. Now go decontaminate. Dinner will be served momentarily."

Felix righted himself, stretched, and headed for the bathroom. Judi hoped he wouldn't make the mess in there he'd made that morning.

Dinner was exquisite, rivaling that of L'Amarante's best chefs. Leo asked every few minutes if everything was all right, clearing each course and dashing into the kitchen for the next, eager to please his master and mistress.

During coffee, the *Eroica Symphony* floated out of the speakers as her buzzer rang.

"I shall get it." Heading for the door, Leo smoothed his hair and caught another mirror-glimpse.

"No!" She hadn't meant to shout so abruptly, but instinct told her he should be out of sight. She shot a glance at Felix, stretching on his exercise ball.

He rolled off it, stood and tucked his shirt in, kicking the ball into the corner. Judi looked at all the gizmos lying and rolling around her loft. *God, it looks like Romper Room in here!*

"It's okay, no harm done." Felix nodded to Leo. "He can answer the door."

"Oh, I just, well, he's not supposed to go out alone and—"

"He's not going out." Felix placed a reassuring hand on her shoulder. "He's only going to answer the door."

"But who is he supposed to be?" A small shot of

panic shot through Judi. They sure hadn't rehearsed this part of it!

Felix gave a puzzled one-shoulder shrug. "Anybody you want him to be. I thought that was the whole idea of the exercise."

"What if it's my father?"

"Depends if you want to tell him the truth."

She shook her head, wide-eyed. "Of course I don't. He'll think I'm nuts."

Felix tried to hide a laugh, but didn't do too good a job of it. The buzzer rang again, this time more impatiently. Then a little voice inside prompted her at the short buzz and the long one. She'd heard it in her sleep enough times. "Never mind, it's only Iris."

"It is?" Felix started rolling his chiming Chinese healing balls around in his hands. "Since when are you psychic?"

"I know her buzz. Besides, she said something about coming over and reviewing some work I'd given her to read." She turned to Leo. "For now, you're Felix's brother."

Leo raised his brows, obviously pleased. He shot a glance at Felix. "So I'm the tall, dark and handsome one in the family, am I? Little bro?"

Ignoring him, Felix said to Judi, "So let her in already."

"Iris?" Leo piped up from where he stood, poised, his finger on the button ready to buzz her in. "Haven't I heard you talking about her, Master?"

"She's the one."

"Didn't you say something about going out as a foursome?"

Felix answered "yes" and Judi answered "no" at the same time.

"Why? Is she a grotesquerie or something?"

"No," Judi replied. "But you're spoken for."

"Oh?" One corner of Leo's mouth curled up, the corresponding brow rising along with it. "I haven't asked you to go steady yet."

She turned to Felix, fists clenched, nails embedded in palms. "Felix—"

"Honey, I told you that night of the disastrous duck dinner that he wouldn't be able to stand her," he guaranteed with a confident grin.

"Or maybe vice versa," she muttered, as Felix nodded for Leo to buzz the caller in.

The knock came at the door seconds later. It was Iris all right, wrapped in a hooded lynx coat. Leo opened the door wider and she plowed in, not noticing who'd opened the door. "Hi..." She halted, looked at Felix on the sofa, and then at Judi, who waved a little greeting. Finally, as if afraid to look, she peered around her shoulder to see the enigmatic entity who'd admitted her. She removed her glasses with a red-gloved hand and stood in stunned silence until Leo broke the spell.

"Goodness, it must be freezing. Your lips are blue. I'm Leo, Felix's brother." He held out his hand.

Iris simply stared. "Nice to...meet you." She tore her eyes away from the vision long enough to focus a wide angle stare at Judi, who forced a genial smile.

"You didn't tell me he was here, Judi." Her voice took on a singsong quality that would've sounded better on Dickie or Annie.

"He's trying to keep a low profile," Judi replied coquettishly, as Leo held out his arms to take Iris's coat. "He heard the president was in town and didn't want to steal the limelight."

"Why don't you make yourself comfortable, my lady, and I'll serve you a cup of espresso," Leo offered in his chivalrous knight tone.

"Sounds...great." Still unable to move, she stood as Leo slid off her coat.

"We've been getting re-acquainted," Judi explained when Iris finally regained her sense of motion and floated over to the sofa. She didn't comment on the yoga equipment in the middle of the room or the big purple ball rolling across the uneven floorboards. The birds completely escaped her scrutiny.

"Oh, I'll bet you had a lot of catching up to do," Iris drawled as Leo placed a cup in front of her. "Thanks so much. Its aroma is piquantly ambrosial."

"Yecch," Judi mumbled under her breath.

Felix glanced her way and stuck a forefinger into his open mouth. A déjà vu of the dinner party, she thought, but on a less appetizing level.

"Yes, we spent nearly the entire day as you say...catching up." Leo passed her the cream, his hand lingering on hers.

She cooed, "So where have you been all my life?"

"Oh, all over. Name a country, and I'll tell you when I visited it last." He glanced at Felix. They exchanged knowing smiles, as Leo asked, "Are you a citizen of the world like yours truly or a homespun homebody?"

Here he goes, putting his foot back in the stirrup of his high horse. Judi wondered if Iris would be able to keep up with him by the time he mounted.

The sparks in Iris's eyes could've jump-started a Mac truck. Judi knew the inevitable had taken place: her friend was enchanted with her lover. And Leo didn't lift a perfect pinkie to discourage her.

At the close of the evening, with Iris finally all talked out, it was arranged—next Friday evening the foursome would go to dinner and the symphony.

****

Judi needed to get back to work the next day, and Leo promised to stay out of her way.

He spent the entire day reading and editing Chaucer.

"So what did you think of Iris?" she asked over the fresh brewed coffee he'd made her.

He put down his copy of *The Canterbury Tales*,

and his eyes took on an amused look. "She could be a lot of fun under the right circumstances."

"Meaning?"

"In a more lively atmosphere, perhaps at a party or a comedy revue. She seems the gregarious type. Do you know if she likes the amateur comedy clubs?"

"She hates them. I mean, she can't stand amateurs. Nothing less than the most polished professionals for Iris."

"Oh, I can't believe that. I think we would have a delightful evening."

"We...as in you and she? Or we as in you and me and she and Felix?"

"Any combination of the above will do." He focused those hybrid eyes on her and chuckled. "Surely you're not jealous. Aren't you and Iris BFFs?"

"BFFs, yes. Jealous, no. Besides, she's well aware you're taken."

"Doctor Felix said I should enjoy the company of other women...on a platonic level, of course."

"I know. But it's not his life he's poking around with. It's mine." She slapped the plastic cover over her keyboard. She'd had enough fiction for one day.

"There's no harm in men and women being friends. I would never forbid you and Doctor Felix to pal around."

"Just remember who put who where, Leo. And remember what I said about anything Felix told you."

"Judi, this arrangement is to be fifty-fifty, as per your orders," he replied smoothly, with a hint of condescension. "Equal all the way. I didn't think you'd get indignant about who put who where. I'm fully aware of my situation and purpose. However, I hope you don't plan to keep me locked up like a prisoner."

"But why Iris, of all women?"

"She's the only one I've met. Might you have any others in mind?"

"Of course not. But she's not your type. She's too..." She searched her mental thesaurus for a string of adjectives.

The truth was that she didn't want to share him. They needed this time alone.

"All I'm talking about is a simple evening at dinner and the symphony, and we won't exactly be alone," he said. "Several hundred people will be checking me out."

Her jumbled emotions dammed up, and the tears spilled. She wished she could rewind time, starting with that reunion in Three Steps Down, the thrill of seeing Felix for the first time in all those years. "Time travel—now I'm thinking like him," she murmured.

Leo lifted her chin with one finger. "Please don't cry, Judi. It doesn't flatter you. You'll ruin your pretty face, not to mention this lovely imitation silk shirt. I'd never hurt you. You know me better than that."

"I'm sorry, Leo. I've been on a hormonal roller coaster."

"I understand." He brought her lips up to meet his. It was poignant rather than romantic. She felt strangely comforted but couldn't help wishing Felix were here to hold her. She wanted to go into the bathroom and inhale his shampoo.

The kiss was light, sweet, and much too short. He held her by the shoulders and brushed a strand of hair off her face then snatched his hand away and adjusted his collar with a glance in the mirror. She was tempted to shatter every shiny surface in the place if he so much as snatched another glimpse of himself in a butter knife.

"All I was suggesting was a fun night out, and you've got us betrothed. Judi, you've got to stop jumping to conclusions like that. It's very unhealthy, you know. Exacerbates elevated blood pressure." Lifting his trousers at the knees, he sat back down on the sofa and slid the bookmark out from where he'd left off.

She wanted to throttle him. But what good would that do? He would only squeal to Felix.

Chapter Thirteen

The taxi dropped them off in front of Iris's brownstone after the concert. Judi stifled a yawn and rubbed her eyes to stay alert. She longed for the comfort of bed so she could get some work done in the morning. But Iris, party animal that she was, insisted that an extra half hour's socializing wouldn't be any detriment to her career; after all, the publisher still hustled to keep up with her.

But Judi knew Iris just wanted to prolong her lash-batting contest with Leo.

At dinner, he'd smiled and winked and held out her chair. He'd poured her second, third, and fourth glasses of wine. Judi's stomach churned at every chivalrous gesture. More than once she caught herself clenching her fists. However, Felix insisted that the company of other women would build Leo's character. Judi didn't think it needed any building; it needed some slapping down with a long-nailed feminine hand.

Iris took their coats and headed for the kitchen. Leo popped up and offered to help. With a proposal the happy hostess couldn't refuse, they both disappeared into the beyond, their playful banter muffled.

Judi perked up her ears. Why couldn't Iris live in a modern high rise with paper-thin walls, so she could hear every grunt?

"What could they be doing in there?" she demanded, mostly to herself, craning her neck to catch a peek between the closed kitchen doors blocking her view.

"Comparing anatomical correctness, maybe?" Felix replied calmly. "Will you relax? Leo's a gentleman, remember? He won't do anything Race wouldn't do. She's probably just making him a drink."

"What would appeal to him? Scotch and Gator Ade?"

"I think you'd best let up, Old Mother Hubbard. He's a hero, and heroes flirt. It's harmless enough. You're not a paramour. You're a damn prison warden. How many times do I have to tell you, you've got nothing to worry about?"

"Felix, now isn't the time for a debriefing, but we both can see that your engineering is a bit flawed. He gets worse every day, and now he's playing Sir Galahad to my best friend."

Felix, never one to sit and argue a point into the ground, got up and started poking around Iris's knickknacks, her figurines from China, and her photos of Hong Kong. He peeked outside between her bamboo blinds. He waved at the incense coming from a brass Buddha and coughed.

"Is this place an opium den or what?" Felix commented. "I'm afraid to see what she has planned for this little visit."

"She's a practicing Buddhist, and I'm afraid her little visit doesn't include us. She's in there shanghai-ing Leo. Felix, you have to do some tweaking on him, and I don't mean his nose. So stop changing the subject."

He turned and stared her down. "I don't know if you'll ever be satisfied, Judi. He's being friendly, and that's his way, according to who he is. Maybe you've been without a guy for so long, you forgot what we're like."

She narrowed her eyes. Her blood boiled, giving her a near-hot flash. "That was a low blow."

He sat across from her and propped his elbows

on his knees. "I didn't mean it that way. Look what we're doing, fighting over him." He jerked his thumb in the kitchen's direction. "Let him have his fun for one night, and I'll see what I can do later. I'll take him back to the lab Friday for a few days. Meanwhile, you should have a talk with your BFF and ask her why she's hanging all over the dude who's supposed to be your property."

"To be honest, she been dude-less longer than I have. It's not her I'm worried about. I don't have to live with her the rest of my life. She'll get it out of her system. It happens all the time. Just don't be shocked when she tosses him aside and starts fluttering around you."

His eyes grew wide, and he stood. "Oh, no. I'm not her next victim. I'll create her very own synthetic fool before I'll let her within a condom's length of me."

Just then, the shutter doors swung open, and they emerged, Leo carrying a silver tray on which sat four cups and the coffeepot. Iris carried the creamer and a plate of cookies.

"I made these last night," Iris boasted, as Leo set the tray on the table. "Fat free, gluten free. Try one."

Judi reached for a cookie and took a nibble. She held back a grimace. It tasted like one of her shredded first drafts.

As they had coffee, Leo commented on the evening's performance. He voiced his opinions on the woodwind section, obscured by the strings, and expressed his annoyance at Schumann's failure to add a slow movement to the piece. "The piece was originally called a 'symphonette' since it lacked a slow movement, and do you believe Schumann never made an attempt to add one. That's what happens when you get famous and rest on your laurels." He paused to brush a speck off his jacket. "But then again, Schumann's talent never approached the levels of Mozart or Haydn."

"Oh, you're so insightful," Iris gushed, her head nodding as if attached with a string.

Judi jumped into the conversation, not only to contribute her opinions about classical composers, but to remind her lifemate-elect that she was still there.

"But Judi," he finally acknowledged her. "Mozart wrote for royalty, who regarded him as a servant. He was a disciplined hack, at best."

"That's just not so, Leo," she retorted, then reined herself in. They could argue into the wee hours for the rest of her life. She'd made "lively discourse" part of his makeup and filtered through his perfectness, this was how it came out. She'd have to talk to Felix about some fine-tuning to this part of his personality, too. She'd wanted Mr. Right, but she didn't want his first name to be Always.

The evening ended with Leo's request that Iris come over to hear him play the Chopin etudes.

Iris nodded. "I identify with Chopin. He was so sensitive. Did you read Chopin's biography? Georges Sand was his great love. It was the stuff of romance novels, so rare in real life. Their story could've come right out of Judi's books."

She doesn't know the half of it, Judi mused.

"What evening would be best to come hear you play?" Iris strained her myopic eyes to get a last look at Leo.

"That's ultimately up to Judith. I'm under her jurisdiction."

"Oh, yes, of course." She looked at Judi as if she'd forgotten she was there.

This is the last thong he's going to charm off!

"Any night this week's good for me, Iris," Judi broke in, "except Friday and the weekend." That's when Felix was taking Leo back to the lab—and she felt doused with relief over that. It would be nice to sit around in her robe, eat potato chips for breakfast, and not care about the crumbs.

"How about tomorrow night?" Good old available Iris, the only single female Judi knew whose little black book was green.

"I'll call you," Judi said as Leo stood and extended his hand. "Good night, Iris. The evening was a profusion of pleasure."

As the trio walked home, Leo peered into store windows and gaped at the motley pedestrians, unlike Judi and Felix, who'd seen it all before. But they exchanged a secret grin, amused at his amazement with the big city. The lights and sounds of a New York night surrounded them, making Judi feel at home.

She didn't want to bring this up but had to voice it. "Leo, why did you suggest another social call?" She kept her voice calm, biting back her jealousy and confusion, emotions she detested, making her madder at herself for feeling this way.

"We're both classical music aficionados, and I'm sure she'd enjoy hearing me play."

"What makes you think I wouldn't?" She held back, creating some distance between them but couldn't help studying his profile. His hair shone in the darkness, catching the streetlamps' glow and casting a halo-like luster about him. She wanted to make those eyes marvel at her, not at the passing scenery. And not at Iris.

"Of course you're perfectly welcome to listen in." He turned to watch her and the array of humanity at the same time. "After all, it is your bailiwick."

"Yes, and now that I'm sharing it with you, I'd like to see more of you and less of Iris."

"Judi, we discussed this ad nauseum," Felix reproached as they stopped at the curb. "I can tone down the flirty volume, but you don't want a mope who'll never talk to anybody, making it look like he's snubbing them."

"Of course not. But even you can see he comes on too strong with someone he just met."

"I don't happen to see it's that strong, Judi. Maybe it's because I always wish I was like that," Felix replied wistfully, reaching across Judi and giving Leo a little jab in the arm. "I would've got some live dates in high school instead of with my Mac."

"I wish I'd known you then, Master. I would've given you some pointers. And I do believe I detect a green-eyed monster," Leo quipped, leaning down to nuzzle Judi's neck.

She stepped out of his way. "Not a chance. But let's not forget that four's a crowd. And I did specify gregarious but not social butterfly. So watch it, or I'll clip those wings and stuff you back into your cocoon."

"Judi," Felix offered, "I know you're upset. But you wanted him to be the life of the party. Well, the party's on."

"But we're forgetting one detail. It's supposed to be my party."

"You're right," he admitted. "Some of these things are slightly different in practice than they are in theory." She'd never been this possessive before. But that's what Leo was to her—a prized possession.

When they got back to her loft, she sent Leo into the kitchen to bake lasagna—from scratch. That'd keep him busy and bustling for a while. She wanted him out of earshot so she could talk to Felix.

****

He sat closer to her than he should, but his need to be near her was like a physical ache. "What's on your mind, Pookie?" He tried to shove aside the growing jealousy and despair he felt when he watched them together. Part of him hated to see her

170

sad, but the other part of him, the less generous side, felt a little relief that it was going so badly. Still, he had to make things right for her.

Her face held a mixture of emotions he couldn't read.

But when tears welled up in her eyes, he didn't care about restraint or keeping his feelings under control. He leaned forward and took her into his arms, running his hand over the waves in her hair, inhaling her scent, lilacs, always lilacs, all these years, he'd dreamed of lilacs.

"I do like him, Felix, but he treats me—any way he feels like, depending on his mood. Sometimes he has no regard for my feelings at all."

"I know. He can be self-centered at times." His heart ached for her—and almost as much for himself. This could be the two of them on the sofa in a warm loving embrace with no Leo in their lives, their hearts belonging only to each other. He was through telling her this was all her doing, that this was what she'd wanted because half of this outcome was the product of his ingenuity, too. If it turned out to be a disaster that ruined her life, he'd never forgive himself.

"I said I'd try to fix him, and Rome wasn't built in a day. Be patient."

She eased out of his embrace and nodded. He touched her face with his fingertips and gently brushed away her tears. "Many amazing inventions have come to fruition with more than one trip to the drawing board."

"You're right. I'm asking too much too soon." She leaned over and plucked two truffles from the box on the coffee table. "Want one?"

He shook his head as she slid a truffle in her mouth, closed her eyes and savored it. "Mmmmm. They're sinfully decadent. You should have one."

"And deprive you? No, you go ahead." But she'd

already eaten the first one and was onto the second. "Judi, how many of those things do you eat a night?"

She licked her fingers and eyed the box as if deciding whether to make it three in a row. "I usually have one box a week delivered. But lately, I've upped it to three, a variety. This one was bittersweet, and the other was semi-sweet. I take half a dozen into the hot tub with me, assorted flavors. They make me feel immortal."

"Oh," was all he could say, simply because he couldn't relate. Empty calories sustained him through his lonely youth, but he felt just as mortal and pudgy after demolishing a bag of pretzels as before. He wondered why she "lately" needed three-dozen truffles a week and then realized—the reason was in the kitchen rolling pasta dough.

He vowed to do something about Leo, or he'd never be able to live with himself. The guy irked him as much as he did Judi, not because he was pompous or arrogant or treated her badly, but simply because he was.

"I'll tell you what, I'll take him with me tonight, back to the lab, no sense waiting 'til Friday." His eyes wandered downward to marvel over how beautiful her breasts looked under her low-cut blouse, but he stopped himself short. Now was not the time for that. "The sooner the better," he added, forcing his eyes back up to look into hers. Her smile melted him.

"That's so good of you, Felix. There must be some way I can repay you for all this."

Oh, there's a way, all right, he thought. But it wasn't going to happen. Not in this lifetime.

"If you have classes or plans, it can wait until Friday. I need the floor waxed anyway." She gave him a wink, which of course meant she was joking, but he realized at that moment she'd never winked at him, ever, for any reason. It made his heart swell, and another part of his anatomy began to distend, rather painfully. He shifted and hoped her gaze wouldn't rove downward the way his had.

"I have a dinner appointment with some colleagues, but on Wednesday morning I'll come by and get him. Then we'll be out of your hair for a week or however long it takes. I'm giving a conservative estimate here because you know how, uh—conservative I am."

She gave a halfhearted nod.

"What's the matter?" He glanced toward the kitchen where he heard Leo whistling the overture from *Marriage of Figaro*. "You do want me to work on him, don't you?"

"Of course. But I'm so used to having you around..." She fluttered her hands and played with her hair then tugged at her earring.

"You enjoy having us around?" he blurted out, trying not to burst into an ecstatic grin.

"You know I do, Felix." She inched closer.

He took that as a cue, a blatant cue, to mimic that move. Never had he picked up on signals like this from her. Maybe because she'd never sent any. But at this moment he felt like he could read her mind. She sent a silent signal to him, which he caught with astonishing clarity.

"And I never realized how much I'd missed you until I ran into you at Three Steps Down that night," she continued, her arm inching over the sofa back towards him. "All those years wasted when we could've been enjoying each other's company. Like we are now." Her fingertips lingered an inch below his hair.

"Judi," he whispered, his breath ragged. He reached over to grasp her hands. "It's about time I get real with you here." He fumbled over his words, knowing whatever he said would come out sounding like gibberish. But he had to tell her. "I've been the odd man out since Leo took his first breath. I've felt like a third wheel, a fifth wheel, and every odd number to infinity. And I hate myself for feeling this way, but—I'm jealous of him. He has you. You want him. And I'm the spare. Being on the outside looking in on this budding romance is tearing away at me."

"Oh my God." She slid forward and was in his arms in an instant. "Why didn't you ever tell me?"

"Because I don't want to ruin your dream and your life. Go on like you've been. I'll work on him and make him everything you've always wanted."

"I don't know if that will make things any better." Her warm breath tickled his neck, making him tingle everywhere. Instinctively he embraced her and held her close, planting little kisses in her hair. He shifted uncomfortably once again and inched his lower body away.

"You have to give it a try." His breathing got heavier. "Don't ever give up on your dream. I won't let you."

"I want it to work with Leo, but—" Their embrace relaxed. "I don't know whether to give it a time frame or what. I work on deadlines all the time, and it's nerve-wracking. But if it goes on indefinitely like it is, and I just can't warm up to him, years will pass, and I'll be old and gray and look back with regrets. Oh, damn, I don't know what to do."

"I'll tell you what to do. Just what I just said. Don't give up. He's what you've always wanted. It'll work."

"But what about us?" She looked him straight in the eye.

He hadn't expected that. All he'd seen coming was another rejection, a polite "no, thanks, Felix, you're a nice guy, but" or a tactful suggestion that he locate his ex and give that another shot. He never expected her to refer to them as an "us."

"One thing at a time, Judi, it's all happening too

fast."

The blood started returning to his brain, and he was thankful for that. "Let's do what we've planned. I'll take him back, and when he returns to you, take it from there. You don't skip around when you write your drafts, do you?"

"I usually write the ending first and justify my way into it."

Damn, he knew she'd say something like that. "Then let's say this isn't a draft. I don't know how it will end up, and neither do you. So let's not think up any endings or even middles. Don't even turn the page yet."

She sighed, eased herself away, and sat back. All of a sudden he'd stiffened up on her, but how easily and naturally they'd melded in each other's arms! "True."

"And it's better if I get out of here tonight." He stood and started for the alcove where his stuff was.

She caught up with him and clutched his arm. "Felix, don't leave."

"I have an early class. It's better if I just go home now."

She looked like she wanted to beg him to stay but didn't. So it was almost a relief when she let him go. "All right, good night. I'll see you again—soon." He leaned over to kiss her, just as the kitchen door burst open.

"Cookies for everybody!" Leo entered, carrying a tray heaped with huge round cookies, sprinkled with chocolate chips. "I made these whilst the lasagna is baking."

But they could have been grasshoppers for all Felix cared. "Thanks, but I'm full." He shook his head to Leo's proffered tray, the moment ruined.

"I'll see myself out. Good night, you two." He grabbed his coat and felt her arm clutching his.

"Felix, you really don't have to go."

"Judi, I'm beat. Physically, mentally, and every other way. Just let me out of here, all right?" He turned and left. She didn't try to stop him.

****

The next night, Iris blew in carrying another of her homemade delights—a somewhat lopsided chocolate cheesecake with a smiley face made of cherries on top. Leo conveniently announced that he was on a strict diet as Judi tossed another empty truffle tray away. She burned with humiliation and promised herself to cancel that automatic delivery.

"You—on a diet?" Iris argued playfully. "You're perfect! What do you have to diet for?"

"To stay perfect." He straightened his sweater, smoothed his pants legs, placed Iris's cake on the kitchen counter, and sat at the piano.

Judi waltzed over to the counter, sliced off a generous portion of Iris's cake, and ate it right there with her hands. Iris sat, ears perked up, ready for the concert.

He started playing. Judi plucked one more mouthful of cake and joined Iris.

Iris whispered sotto voce, "He's very talented."

Judi nodded her agreement and complimented Iris on the cake. "It'll be gone before tomorrow, you know," she said, and they shared a giggle.

"By the way, where's Felix?" Iris asked, as Leo played on, oblivious to his audience.

"Out with colleagues."

"Oh." Iris nodded, and they politely leaned toward Leo for another few bars when Judi asked, "Have you seen the Gaetana Linetti spring collection?"

"Yeah, I did!" Iris turned to Judi and touched her shoulder. "And do you know it, I didn't like one thing, except that short bolero number—"

"The lime green one?"

"Yeah, but I wouldn't pay two grand for it."

The chat evolved into a regular hen session as Leo played on then abruptly stopped after he'd completed the last etude.

Judi and Iris hadn't even noticed the music had stopped until Leo cleared his throat, and they looked up to see him standing in front of them.

"Oh, did you finish, Leo? It was very nice," Judi assured him, and Iris applauded.

"Now I know how Mozart felt, playing background music for royalty," he quipped as he glanced at his watch. "Sorry to break up this lively party so early, but at nine, I like to engage in my nightly ritual to assure enough sleep for my early ten-mile morning jog."

Iris's jaw dropped, and her eyes widened. "You jog ten miles every morning? How do you do it?"

"Easy. Put one foot in front of the other. And make sure your laces are securely tied. But not together."

"A-ha, now that's funny." Iris let out a genuine sounding guffaw, but Judi knew it was bogus. She hardly looked amused.

Judi now wondered if Iris was still gaga over him. Or was he wearing thin on her too?

"And I use a lot of hair spray. The wind in this city is atrocious. Not to mention dirty." He smoothed back a handful of locks.

Judi stood and made a show of tapping her watch. "You're right, Leo, it is time for your bath. And I've got to get back to work now."

Iris drained her drink. "You're right, Judi. Oh, I'll send over that new hairdresser's name tomorrow, the one Cassie uses. He's just in from Paris and does a fabulous marbleizing job. It's only four hundred dollars."

"He's on West Fourth, isn't he?"

"Yeah, next to the boutique. Oh, I'm sorry, Leo." Iris jumped back when she realized she'd stepped on his foot. "I'll just see myself out. I've got to start on Exene's galleys tomorrow. She's celebrating her fiftieth. Book, that is."

"Good for her!" Judi walked Iris to the closet and grabbed her coat.

"Speaking of books—" Leo reached over for his Chaucer and opened it to the page where he'd stopped making line edits.

"Uh—Leo, Iris doesn't need a lesson in Old English." Judi gave him a look that matched her tone. He nodded and put the book down. "I'll call Iris a cab." Judi headed for the phone, relieved the evening hadn't centered on Leo this time. He really was pleasant as part of the background.

He helped Iris on with her coat and opened the door. "I'll walk you down."

Iris bade her hostess good night, and Leo sauntered out the door to walk her downstairs.

When he came back ten minutes later, he headed straight for the hall mirror.

"So, eh—what did you two talk about down there?" she asked Leo's reflection as they both faced the mirror.

"The conversation was lackluster at best. Do you know any other females you can introduce me to? After all, Doctor Felix did say mingling would build my character."

"Yes, but he meant mingle, not dive in head first. You want to consult your thesaurus to verify the definition?"

He threw his head back and let out a genuine laugh.

"Oh, that's precious, Judi. Very good one." He ran his finger over an imaginary scoreboard. "One for the lady of the house."

"Just take your bath, Leo, and leave me some hot water this time."

****

At two a.m., Judi finished the new Mona Rossi novel and the last truffle Divine Decadence would ever deliver. Tomorrow she'd cancel the order. Thinking of how she felt about Leo had kept her awake. Mixed emotions boiled inside her. But she was madder at herself than she was at him. She wanted Leo to be outgoing, gregarious, and amicable. But somehow he crossed the line into shamelessly flirty. How could that have happened? Something had gotten misinterpreted. How long would it take to iron it out? Could she wait that long?

Her phone rang, and of course it was Iris.

"I have to talk to you." Iris was almost whispering. Did she fear Leo could overhear her on the phone?

"Judi, you have to know this. I'd never betray you, would never hurt you. I know you're nuts about that man. But I'll be perfectly honest. Yes, he's gorgeous. But I've never lied to you, and I won't start now. That...person...though I hesitate to defile the human race by referring to him as a member...he's the most despicable creature I've ever encountered in my life. What does he think he is—God's gift to estrogen?"

Judi's jaw dropped as she almost fell through the floor in surprise. A jolt of relief darted through her. Iris couldn't stand Leo!

"What the hell happened, Iris?"

"I don't know how he lives with himself—or how anyone else can."

"Well, he is a bit conceited," Judi couldn't help admitting.

"A bit! Juno Ursa, the maestress of hyperbole, uttering so gross an understatement? I thought you were an expert judge of character. He's simply oppressive. You know what he did when we walked down the stairs?" She lowered her voice.

"Went first?"

"Besides that. He wrapped his handkerchief around the door handle so he wouldn't have to touch it. Then he had the nerve to tell me not to bother pursuing him because I'm not in his league. He's— and these are his words—'biologically suited to more sophisticated women.' The fact that you're nuts about him and you're supposed to be an item didn't even enter his helium-filled mind. It's all him, him, him. I'm sorry I had to tell you this, Judi, but I just had to let you know how I felt."

She munched on something. "You can do so much better than that mirror-kisser. He doesn't care a whit for you, do you understand? He's a plastic...nonentity. Tell him to stuff that in his can of mousse and squirt it, to take a good look at himself and realize he's no better than any other jock that jogs through Central Park—"

"Okay, Iris." Judi fell back onto her pillows, eyes shut, stunned. The relief of a minute ago now mixed with embarrassment. Sympathy for Iris overshadowed her annoyance. And she knew why. Because she agreed with Iris. It wasn't just her being paranoid. Another person verified it now. Good God, she'd created a monster!

"Another thing." Iris paused, and Judi could hear her lighting a cigarette. "From my observations of him: his mannerisms, his astute scholarship, his impeccable habits...he'd make a perfect mirror character for Race. If you tone him down about ninety percent so readers will find him sympathetic."

"I'm way ahead of you, Iris." She spoke more to herself than to her friend. "I'm light-years ahead of you."

"Just something I wanted to run by you. You don't have to follow through with it," Iris continued. "We both know how few of my suggestions you do take," she added in a snarky tone that Judi knew not to take seriously.

"Oh, stop it. You're a great editor. No two people agree on everything," she said, her mind wandering. If Leo behaved this badly in such a casual setting, how would he react with a real audience?

"Yeah, tell me about it," Iris said. "Arguing seems to be Leo's hobby."

Judi sat, thinking.

"Judi, are you there?"

"Yeah...look, Iris, we've been friends a long time, and I'd hate to see that end just because of him. For a while it looked like we were on shaky ground. So I'm relieved you see him for what he is. My problem is, you saw it before I did."

"Oh, don't worry. I'd never tread on your territory. Sometimes I come on too strong. Must be the frustrated actress in me."

Judi heard her blow out a stream of smoke and go back to munching. "I'll talk to you tomorrow, Iris. I've got some more thinking to do." They hung up and Judi stretched out, hugging her pillow, realizing her fantasy hadn't become reality. And she had nobody to blame but herself.

How could she undo the damage already done? Was Leo capable of changing? Maybe he enjoyed being like this.

But did she even want a reprogrammed Leo, as a "regular guy"? That was an even more horrifying thought!

She asked herself over and over: *What do I want?* Finally, before falling asleep out of exhaustion, an answer came to her: *Now I know what I don't want.*

Chapter Fourteen

Leo never mentioned Iris's name again and neither did Judi. Iris bowed out of the picture for a while, claiming a heavy workload. Felix had taken Leo back home for a week of fine-tuning, but now it was going on two weeks. She knew the real reason—Felix needed a break from the emotionally charged atmosphere as much as she did, and Judi needed a break from all the neatness, disinfectants, and piano sonatas.

She missed Felix terribly.

She also missed Leo, in a way...not only gorgeous to look at, he helped her around the house...

Don't think of too many more positive things about him.

She paced her living room floor. "You asked for it."

She considered asking Felix to take him back permanently, but how would Felix react? He'd be hurt, she knew. This was his creation, too. She didn't want him to think she was an ingrate, either. No, she had to make this work. After all, if she and Leo got along every minute of the day, how boring would that be?

She told herself that over and over. Tension makes a romance work. She, of all people, knew that. Tension, tension, tension...a man and a woman dying to tear off each other's clothes and ravish each other, but something forces them apart...some doubt, some fear, some other person...

Once Felix and Leo returned, sparks of tension

flashed and flew, all right, but waned and swelled, like the coming and going tide. Felix's morning cheek-peck made her tingle as much as Leo's lingering kiss on her hand. The two men vied for her attention yet stayed warm and cordial toward each other. But at times she could read mixed emotions on Felix's face: achievement mingled with bitterness. She longed to talk to him, but they were never alone. Leo never left them alone.

Felix rose every morning at seven to go to work, returning in the early evening. She picked up his clothes and towels and did his laundry and his ironing. Doing these things for him didn't bother her. So he was messy. But having two neat freaks would have been a lot worse.

She wrote all day, occasionally going to the gym. Leo obediently remained indoors reading, listening to his music collection, playing piano, or preparing meals. Finally, on the one-month anniversary of Leo's arrival, Felix finished his dinner, placed his napkin on his plate, and made a long-awaited announcement: "Judi, as of tomorrow, I believe it will be safe and advisable to take Leo out."

"Are you sure?" Judi's surprise and delight made her chirp, "Really?"

"Yes, from what I've seen of his adaptation, his risks of facing the outside world are minimal," Felix replied. "I have to go to ORBIT headquarters for a convention and to discuss the space mission...and the astronaut I'm designing." He glanced at the piles of clothes spilling out of his suitcases that he'd never bothered to unpack.

He dumped the contents of his gym bag onto the floor and tossed the bag onto the sofa. "I've got to pack a few things."

Disappointment stabbed at her, knowing how much she'd miss him. She tried to hide it by looking away.

"I'll be bringing my equipment with me, too," he added.

"Equipment?" She turned to face him again.

"The stretching ball and the inversion table." He tossed a glance behind him.

She looked over her shoulder at the mini-gym taking up half her living room. "How are you getting it all down there?"

"In the plane's cargo hold."

She nodded, not surprised. "That's dedication."

"No, it isn't. It's necessity. The hotel has a fitness center fit for the Sultan of Brunai but no stretching equipment." He began tossing clothes and toiletries onto the sofa next to his gym bag.

"So how is the new spaceman coming along?"

His expression gladdened for a split second. "Of course I couldn't do anything while I was designing Leo, but I'm nearly finished now. This one isn't taking half the time Leo did. It's generic compared to him. When I'm outta here, it will be your chance to bond with Leo."

She should have been thrilled but couldn't throw the heavy weight from her shoulders, wondering how she'd get through two weeks without Felix.

"You mean you're not going to take him back to your place and chain him to your stove and his blow dryer?" She forced enthusiasm into her voice.

"No. I think he's ready to face the world without having me around. It's all up to you now, Judi." He looked into her eyes, and their gazes remained locked. She almost blurted out how much she'd miss him but bit her tongue.

He finally broke their gaze and in his authoritative professor voice, said, "Now, there are a few things you should know about him first," Felix warned, sitting on the sofa next to his piles of socks and shorts. "He's not your average schmo."

"I realized that when he took the garbage out

with the pail only half full."

He flashed her one of his "get serious already" raised-brow looks. "I mean you know he's not human. I don't like to call him an android. That sounds so science fictionish, and he is more than just a robot with human form."

"Just call him a hero," she said.

"He hasn't done anything heroic yet—not for me, anyway." He fluttered his lids playfully.

"He spent three evenings with Iris. That makes anyone a hero."

"Since I'll be leaving you alone with him for extended periods of time now, and letting you out in public, there are a few functions that you will have to perform periodically." He stuffed clothes into his bag.

"Like what?" She felt a growing unease in the pit of her stomach as her hands began to sweat. Functions? She remembered the only time she'd ever visited a farm, her disastrous attempt at milking a cow... "You never mentioned any of those types of functions."

"When we worked on the behavior patterns and designed him, I told you he would be somewhat mechanical, like a car. He'd have parts that need to be replaced. He'll need to have routine things done."

"I hope a lube job isn't one of them." She forced a laugh, but it fell flat as he continued in a grave tone.

"Wait 'til you've been intimate with him first."

She widened her eyes and stared at him. "Are you joking?"

"Of course." But his expression stayed the same. Then he broke into a subdued smile. "Cheer up, Judi. I'm handing you the honeymoon of a lifetime." He stuffed a pair of shoes into the already overstuffed bag and tried to pull it shut. The stitching stretched.

"Here, let me do that." She reached over and

emptied the bag. Why couldn't guys learn to pack? "Okay. So tell me what he really needs." She rolled his socks up and placed them in the bottom of the bag, standing his shaving kit along the side.

He shrugged. "Nothing at the moment. But like the human body, which replenishes itself periodically with self-reproducing cells, parts of Leo will have to be replaced."

"What parts?" She swallowed her concern, her mouth dry. "And pray tell, where do I get these parts? Quickie Lube?"

"I'll supply the spare parts. The human body utilizes oxygen which supplies the red blood cells that circulate throughout the bloodstream."

"I passed Biology 101, Felix." She folded a few pairs of his cotton briefs, thinking he'd look so much better in silk ones.

"This isn't a biology lesson. I thought you'd want to know what makes your hero tick."

"I was wondering what that noise was every time he shook his head."

"When I designed him, I furnished him with internal works similar to the human body, so that he would take on human characteristics such as respiration and not look like a robot. Instead of human blood plasma, he's filled with a fluid very similar to the Freon in a car's air conditioner. This fluid is called plasminth, and it's the same fluid my astronaut will need for the voyage to Megasus."

"That's how he's climate controlled?" she asked.

"Exactly. But, like a car's air conditioner, and like the space suits, his fluid has to be changed every so often. The estimate, according to my calculations, is every sixty days. It's inserted into an orifice in his body."

She blanched, afraid to ask. "Do I dare ask which one?" She rolled up a T-shirt and prepared to put it in the bag when he took it from her.

"I'm wearing that," he said. "It's my good luck flying shirt."

She unrolled it and looked at the front. It said *Einstein Didn't Brush His Hair Either* in big red letters.

"So what's this orifice you speak of, Felix?"

"It's the navel."

She let out a relieved breath. "Thank goodness. What happens if his supply isn't replenished?"

"If it's too hot, he'll burn, if it's too cold, he'll shrivel up like an old balloon. He's got no internal thermostat like we do. As our temperature's about ninety-nine, his is about fifty. And believe me, he'll need a major overhaul to get him back to normal. So you'll have to remind him to replenish his supply should it slip his mind. I'll have the substance in the next few weeks. Speaking of replenishing supplies, can you please bring my suits to the cleaners?"

"Of course."

"And baby-sit the birds?"

"I'll treat them like they're my own." She managed to zip his bag shut, pleased with herself and surprised at how comfortable she'd felt performing this wifely duty for him.

"Thanks." He nodded and toyed with his jacket button.

She couldn't think of anything to say either. It was a low moment.

"So where do you think you'll spend your first day out?" he asked.

"I'd like to take him to a museum, stroll around, you know, New York things."

"Take cabs," he said. "Or rent a limo. Don't take the subway. We don't want to risk losing him. Maybe you'd better get one of those leash things parents use for their kids."

"I won't lose him, Felix." But she didn't dare voice her true thoughts. Would it be the end of the world if he lost himself in that crowd of eleven million? People did it all the time. Purposely.

She let her imagination run away for a brief, amusing moment. What if Leo did disappear? Who would find him? Would they want to keep him? Would he make the news as another runaway groom?

"All right then." He tweaked her nose. "Have a good time."

"You too."

He looked at her with a sadness that made her want to comfort him, pulling him into a bear hug.

"It'll be quiet without you here all the time," was all she could think to say, without getting too mushy.

"You'll find things to do. Come on, you're the hero and heroine now." But his voice didn't carry any of the enthusiasm the words did.

"Yeah," she sighed. "I suppose I can buy more books for him. He's already read everything on the shelves."

"Even the ones you wrote?" He smiled.

"He doesn't have to read those. They're programmed into his Goddamned DNA or whatever you call it. Besides, he doesn't like romance novels."

"Now, that's an irony. Didn't he come from one?"

She laughed, and they sat for another quiet moment. His hand clasped hers.

"You'll call me, won't you?" she uttered.

"Sure. I can e-mail you, too. But I'll be busy down there. I probably won't get back to the hotel 'til late every night."

She nodded, a sea of unspoken words between them. It was awkward after what they'd shared that night on the sofa. Neither of them was ready to bring "feelings" up again. Now, she wanted to tell him how torn she felt. But they never had another moment alone. Until now.

"Look, Judi, there's something I'm dying to tell you."

"What?" Hope welled inside her. Could it really be that he planned to confess his love? If so, she planned to return it. He cupped her face in his hands, his eyes querying hers.

Hurry! She could hear Leo in the kitchen, whistling an aria from *Madame Butterfly*.

"I know I'm not as good looking as Leo. And I'll never be as clean or cook gourmet meals for you or serenade you at the piano."

His eyes were filled with such sadness that she wanted to cover him with kisses.

"It's just that I'm nothing like Leo—oh, what's the use?" His shoulders slumped in defeat.

She ached to tell him that all he had to do was say the word, and she'd send Leo the Lothario packing, but before she could get it out, Leo called, "Chow time!"

Felix pulled away first, and they forced themselves to head for the dinner table. But his frustrated look told her they had so many unsaid words between them.

"I'm not even in the mood for dinner." Felix excused himself, leaving her alone and miserable.

She got what she wanted. She sat, and Leo placed a linen napkin on her lap. She knew all too well that adage about asking for what you want and getting it.

****

At dawn the next day Felix headed to LaGuardia. Judi had set the alarm for six, to get up with him and walk him downstairs, but he left before she could see him off.

Looking around the loft, she her heart sank. He'd cleaned up after himself before he left; no longer did his clothes dot the floor in random piles. No loose change and subway tokens lay scattered across the tables. The coffee cups and coffee rings he always left on the table were cleared away. The empty air mocked her where once his inversion table and that goofy purple ball lay. The birds even stayed chirpless, as if they, too, missed him. The loft sparkled, everything in place, and not a speck of dust floated in the air.

It dredged up the same feelings as when Ryan left her.

Oh, how she missed her Felix!

Shaking her head to snap herself out of it, she went into the kitchen to ask Leo about breakfast. But he was at the opposite end of the loft, modeling a cream velour top and black corduroy pants, his thumbs inserted into the waistband loops. He stood so close to the full-length mirror, she thought he would to start engaging it in foreplay.

"Leo?" she called softly.

He twirled around, knocking a lamp over, but caught it before it crashed to the floor. "Ye Gods, Judi, don't scare me like that. You almost broke your lamp."

"I'm sorry. I just wanted to know if you were making breakfast."

"Of course. Just let me finish getting dressed." And with that, he flicked a mascara wand over his lashes.

****

Felix peeled off a bill for the bellhop and entered his empty hotel suite. It was fit for royalty, complete with bar, hot tub for two, fireplace, massive four-poster bed—and no one to share it with. "I've got to get out of this trap and look for somebody who doesn't remind me of her," he mumbled, lighting a fire, rubbing his hands together to get warm.

He knelt before the fire, poking at the logs with the andiron. Sparks jumped. He prodded more, producing more sparks. They rose and fell like miniature fireworks.

The fire died, and he forced himself to get up. He changed into a dinner jacket and took a cab to Elan, a private club he belonged to that ORBIT paid for. He'd once met a woman there who reminded him of Judi. He half hoped she would be there again.

****

Judi and Leo sat at a table for two in L'Amarante, sipping champagne, toasting their future together. "I shall brighten it with a million sunsets," he promised as he refilled her glass. She glanced over at the table they'd shared the first night Felix took them out. She wondered what he was doing right now, in Houston with his ORBIT cronies. Probably chugging martinis and discussing the genetic future of the human race. That was all, she hoped.

He refilled her glass again and again. They'd already gone through five hundred dollars' worth of champagne. She took another sip, wondered some more about Felix, then another sip, then another. She yawned.

She had a buzz, all right. She could barely stay awake. Finally, he unwrapped her fingers from the delicate stem and placed the glass on the table. Leo murmured,

"That's enough of this." He walked her outside, and the doorman hailed them a cab. When she got home, she was out before her head hit the pillow.

****

Surprisingly, Judi didn't wake up with a hangover. Must've been the huge dinner she ate. She always overate when she was depressed. But she wasn't just depressed.

"Girl, you're lovesick," she told her reflection in the mirror.

She tried to put Felix out of her mind and concentrate on her dream, which was now reality.

She thought of peeking at Leo in the shower, but something told her not to. They'd both felt a bit shy, and she didn't want to take a chance that he'd see her. After all, the guy practically read her mind.

The day dawned bright and brisk, and they strolled across Central Park South to Columbus Circle, enjoying the aroma of the street vendors' hot pretzels and chestnuts, the variety of passersby, the beeps and roaring engines. By dusk she was starving, so they settled at a cozy table for two in a crepe house. On the way in, two teenage girls checked Leo out and burst into a chorus of giggles, ogling him from head to toe and back again.

With a twinkle in his eye, he commented to the ardent adolescents, "You should have seen me when I was your age!"

When the waitress served their dinners, he refused his salad because the dressing came in a bottle, so she ate it as well as her own spinach crepes.

"My, you can shovel it in, can't you?" he commented as they sipped herbal tea.

"I eat when I'm—" She stopped abruptly, not wanting to get into a discussion about her feelings. "—hungry." She studied his face against the dusky ambiance. Her mind reviewed the events of their first full day alone. She took his hand. Their fingers clasped, and he stroked her palm. A shiver scampered through her. She felt sorry for anyone who was alone, who had no one to touch this way. Her thoughts returned to Felix. His presence lingered as if the three of them were still together. She wished they were. Something was missing, and she knew it had to be Felix's presence, his encouragement, his humor. He was all alone on that business trip, and she longed to be there with him.

"I have an idea," Leo purred, squeezing her hand and running a finger down the length of her palm.

"Let's go back to the loft, put on some nocturnal music, and dance. Nice and slow. And close." He lifted her hand to his lips and kissed it.

She could hear the romantic strains already. Yes, that would certainly get her mind off Felix and lift her spirits, being in the arms of her hero.

But to her surprise, she wasn't in that much of a hurry to get back.

It was a pleasant evening with a promise of snow in the air, so she suggested they walk back. When he dodged a taxi in the middle of Fifty-sixth Street, the driver leaned on the horn, shouting the appropriate expletives for a New York jaywalker. As they approached the Empire State Building, she suggested they go to the top.

"What would Doctor Felix say?" he asked.

"He has no reason to worry. It's fenced in. You couldn't possibly fall—even if you were pushed." She didn't know why the thought had even entered her mind. And yet...

Chapter Fifteen

By the end of the week, the loft echoed like a tomb without Felix, especially evenings when Leo lounged on the sofa, giving ear to his musical library with the headphones. He tried to get Judi talking, but she wasn't in the mood to chat about Russian literature, Kabuki theatre, Italian opera, or Mesopotamian history.

Finally, after years of dreaming and weeks of frustration, she had him all to herself. At dinnertime, he'd wind an apron around his lean physique and hum some aria while preparing gourmet meals.

But she felt restless and antsy. Unable to write at her usual 5,000 word a day pace because of her excitement over having Leo here, she couldn't concentrate on reading or even updating her Web site or blog. So she worked off her nervous energy on the elliptical or stationary bike. She caught herself checking the clock when Felix always came in but had to remind herself he wasn't coming back tonight—or the night after that or the night after that.

Why did she have to force herself not to reach for the phone and call him, just to see how he was doing?

One afternoon, she found herself staring at Leo over her computer, her fingers silent and still. It saddened her that she wasn't feeling the excitement, the rapture, or the joy she'd always thought she'd feel. She wondered how it all went wrong—and when.

"Come sit by me for a while," he offered as she stared straight ahead, her head propped up on her palms. "Maybe I can crack your writer's block."

Eager for a recess—her production level had plunged since he'd arrived—she went over to him.

"What's impeding that prolific imagination?" He twirled a wisp of her hair around his forefinger.

"I just don't feel compelled to write fantasies anymore. It's terrible, I can't..." She faltered as his magnetism warmed her blood, drawing her even closer, almost against her will. He hadn't moved an inch; she was simply drawn to him by his invisible chemistry. She wasn't in an amorous mood. She wanted to work. But in the next instant, she found herself in his arms.

He stroked her hair and face, whispering into her ear, "You are so beautiful."

"You can write them."

He captured her chin between two fingers and brought her face to face with him. "What is keeping you from your work?"

"You know you're all I've ever dreamed of. I can't concentrate on my work when you're around. I can't concentrate on anything except..." She could have rattled off a list of euphemisms, but the way he nodded, she knew an explanation was far from necessary. "...the man of my dreams." That was true enough. But who really was the man of her dreams? Felix, or this plastic knockoff of a pulp action hero? In her books, Race never did any of the things he did—clean up every crumb, follow her around with a dustpan, or correct her grammar. Her fantasies hadn't been that vivid; they'd been hazy, as fantasies always were.

True life was more detailed and—imperfect.

"There's nothing embarrassing about it. It was meant to be, Judi, you and I, without the obstacles and restraints of a normal couple. It's what you always wanted, and it's what you got. I'll inspire you. I'll ease all your tension so words will literally erupt from that machine. I give fabulous body rubs."

"Mmmm, that sounds good," she sighed, imagining how relaxing his strong hands would feel kneading her weary back muscles. He closed the drapes, shutting out all but a slice of sunlight. He walked over to her table and snapped off the lamp. A comforting warmth began to radiate from the hearth as he lit a fire. She lay on one of the cots, and he eased her blouse off her shoulders. He massaged her tired muscles. She dozed off.

****

"Judi! I didn't expect to hear from you so soon. I thought you'd be otherwise occupied." Felix sounded surprised—again.

"I couldn't go that long without talking to you." She paced the room, too nervous to sit. Why was she so nervous? They'd known each other forever, so why were her palms sweating?

"But we just talked the other day when you called to tell me about the lunar eclipse. It's only going to be visible in the southern hemisphere, by the way."

"Oh, sorry. Well, how are you?"

"Always surrounded by ORBIT people—never a moment's peace. How are Dickie and Annie?"

"Quiet. They miss you, too—" She cut herself off.
"Too?"

"Oh, Felix—" She ached to tell him how she missed him. But not over the phone, long distance.

"Any problems with Leo?"

"Problems? No, not really. He's just as perfect as ever. He cooks perfectly, he cleans perfectly, sings perfectly—" She finished the sentence with a sigh.

"So why do you sound like you're reciting a eulogy?"

"It's just very quiet around here, that's all. We

play chess, read, and have dinner. I miss the noise."

"Can't you two find something—well—more romantic to do?" It seemed he was just too polite to add, "Well, duh!"

"It's awkward, Felix. He won't make the first move, and neither will I. So it's like a stalemate."

She heard only silence at the other end. "Felix? You still there?"

"I'm here. You wanted a gentleman, and you got one. You wanted respect, and you got it. I don't know what else I can say about that end of it." She detected an undercurrent of impatience in his voice, the kind of tone that demanded an answer.

"I don't expect you to do anything more, Felix. You've done a fabulous job. Please don't think you're at fault. It's me—mostly. I just don't have those kinds of feelings for him yet."

"I thought you've been crazy in love with him since you started writing those books."

"I was." She tried so hard to find the right words to express her feelings, this inner yearning that Leo couldn't satisfy, but her emotions were clogged like a stuck drain. "But I was in love with the fantasy, and the breathing being that came out is altogether different. Some things are better acted out in the mind than in reality. This is going down a different track than I'd ever fantasized about."

"When I warned you about that possibility, you bit my head off and spat it out."

"Please, Felix, don't preach. It's my own fault for being so unrealistic." She rubbed her throbbing temples. Glad she was on the cordless phone, she went into her bathroom and got her bottle of aspirins.

"Oh, hell..." She heard him sigh. "Don't blame yourself. We all have dreams. The loftier they are, the harder they are to attain, and it's harder to handle when they do come true. I handle it by going on to the next goal. Channeling my energy on the next endeavor keeps me from dwelling, especially when the wish fulfillment comes with all the extra hassles, hard work, and follow up.

"At least you had the guts to make your dream reality, so don't beat yourself up. Most people never bother to make their dreams come true. It's so much easier to veg on the couch and fantasize."

As he spoke, she popped two pills onto her tongue and filled a cup with water, downing it. "Yes, there's nothing sadder than wondering what might have been. But I did it—I'll have to live with it." She headed to her bed and lay down, covering her eyes with her sleeping mask. "Simple as that."

But she no longer wanted to talk about the plot she'd written herself into.

Talking about "what might have been" made her think of the woman Felix broke up with a month before the reunion in Three Steps Down. A month wasn't a long time. Some exes tended to linger.

"Felix, did you ever see your ex after you broke up?"

"No. She came by a week later to pick up a few things she'd left at my house. She texted me to tell me when she'd be by and asked me to leave the key under the mat. She didn't want me to be there, and that was fine with me."

"Does that mean she's out of your life for good?" She tried to keep the lilt out of her voice.

Felix hesitated. "Why do you want to know all this?"

Why did she? She didn't quite know; all she knew was that she tingled with hope at the thought of seeing him again. "Just wondering—I mean, once you move back into your house, I want to make sure you and the birds have enough to eat, your clothes get washed...just ordinary stuff."

Felix chuckled. "I'm a big boy now. The birds

and I won't starve, and I won't run out of clean underwear. In fact, I just ordered a steak from room service, so I'm not starving myself—as long as someone else does the cooking and cleaning up. Why the interest in my nutrition and hygiene all of a sudden?"

"Felix, it's hardly sudden. I've known you forever. A person just doesn't stop caring—" She caught herself, not wanting to get into this over the phone, especially with that radar detector in the next room. She reached for one of the homemade bonbons Leo had left on her nightstand and devoured it.

"I'll be fine. But thanks for caring," he uttered. After another pause, he asked, "What are you nibbling on now? Don't tell me his ear."

"Better," she replied as the sensuous dark chocolate melted around her tongue. "I'm eating one of Leo's hand-rolled bonbons right now. Oh, you should taste this!"

"You sound more passionate about a bonbon than you do about him. Are you sure you're not having problems? I mean serious stuff—does he walk into walls, or has his head fallen off?"

Oh, how she wanted to let off some steam. But not now. "Well, he certainly thinks a great deal of himself. Whenever I compliment him, he's the first to agree with me."

"Of course, he knows he's a living doll. But you know how to knock him on his perfect buns when he gets to be too much."

"Oh, I know I can. I know what buttons to push."

"Right." A trace of doubt crept into his voice.

"Felix, why don't I fly out there and meet you, or even better, let's meet in Santa Fe after your business trip is over—we'll have a blast."

"Actually, I'm heading out to Phoenix after this to meet a couple of skydiving buddies and to do a few jumps. It'll give you and Leo some more time alone. I've hung around you two enough." She heard a tone of regret creep into his voice.

She rested her head on the satin pillow that she'd probably never share with anyone. "Felix, you wouldn't be in the way. I miss you. Dickie and Lizzie miss you."

"Annie. But I'll be back soon enough. Just keep working on your relationship. You know what they say about meddlesome parents."

"What who says?"

"What we always said every time our parents became the Buttinski family. Just enjoy your evening, and I hope you have ten thousand more." She noticed acceptance had replaced the earlier regret.

"You, too, Felix. Enjoy your evening, too." But she couldn't bring her voice to show any enthusiasm.

****

Felix hung up, feeling instant despair and emptiness. He could quickly turn around and cancel that diving trip. Rendezvousing with Judi in Santa Fe sounded deliciously romantic, the kind of spontaneous lovers' getaway that kept passion hot and steamy. But something stopped him: a mix of common sense and fear. The same fear that made him shut up when he'd wanted so badly to tell her how much he missed her, but couldn't bear to face the answer.

If she'd said no, he'd feel like more of a fool for seeking something that didn't exist, except in his imagination. The common sense kicked in when he'd put the phone down. She had to get Sir Suave out of her system if Felix was ever going to have a chance with her. If she turned to Felix on the rebound, he'd never feel like he'd earned her love. He wanted her only if she fell in love with him.

With Leo out of the picture permanently.

But through the loneliness and finality of their conversation, brought to ugly reality by the dead phone in his hand, he felt a spark of hope. She'd sounded desperate when she'd said goodbye, like she wanted to keep talking, so maybe she really did miss him as much as she'd said. He fought the impulse to call her back, suspecting she still sat by her phone, her hand clamped to the receiver. He wanted to tell her he'd be back soon, and they'd pick up exactly where they'd left off.

But it was better left unsaid. Let them spend every waking—and sleeping—moment together. By the time Felix got back there, either the lovebirds would be over their stalemate and so drunk in love, they wouldn't even remember his name, or they'd be ready to kill each other.

It could go either way. His educated guess on the odds was 60/40 in favor of them falling in love. After all, Leo was her dream hero. Felix was the good ol' reliable Earthling.

It was out of his hands. Now the cosmos controlled their fate. "And what will be, will be," he sighed, opening his mini-bar and grabbing a palm-sized bottle of whiskey and a packet of peanuts. That would hold him until room service showed up. To make sure he didn't give into temptation, he locked his cell phone in the safe and disconnected the suite's phones.

Now Judi and Leo were probably having dinner, talking about the latest opera they'd seen, snuggling on the couch, kissing, caressing, nibbling...

He snapped on the TV and flipped around until he found a show that would captivate him and take his mind off them once and for all.

He broke out into a wide grin, blessing his luck. *The Adventures of Buckaroo Banzai Across the Eighth Dimension* was on tonight!

****

Judi entered the kitchen and watched Leo test his cream of asparagus soup. "Felix refused, Leo. He turned down my invitation to meet him in Santa Fe. He's going skydiving."

"That's very considerate of him. Here. Try this."

She sipped from the spoon he held out to her and nodded. "Perfect. Leo, do you think Felix is trying to avoid us?"

"Not at all. He's on a business trip and working on a mission to Megasus. That's an extremely trying task. I'm sure he's got quite a full plate right now. Diving will provide some needed relaxation." He wiped his hands on a tea towel and turned to face Judi, bending his knees so that he and Judi were at eye level. "Are you tiring of me already?"

She didn't dare speak the truth. "I just thought Felix was being aloof, but maybe it's my imagination."

"You writers, always making everything larger than life." He turned and went back to his cooking. "Dinner will be ready in twenty. You want to be useful and give the table the finishing bits and pieces? Choose which candles you want, etcetera...oh, and do be careful handling those water goblets. I notice there are only seven, so I see you've broken one already."

"What makes you think I was the one who broke it?"

"I just happen to recall a crash out here in the kitchen one night. I saw you sweep up the pieces and hide them under the sink."

"That's because they were a present from Felix's parents, so don't tell him," she warned.

"One thing I'm not is a tattletale."

"Well, bully for you. Now, I'll just finish the table and leave you to your culinary endeavors." She carefully grasped two goblets and headed for the dining area but stopped short when her eye happened to catch something in the garbage bin. She bent down to look more closely and blinked in disbelief when she realized what it was. There, carelessly wadded up, covered with remnants of last night's supper, was the sport jacket she'd had tailor-made for him.

"Leo, what is this?" Placing the goblets on the countertop, she turned to face him. His back was to her as he stirred another ingredient into his potion.

"What is what? I can't possibly look now, I need to watch this until it boils, or it will congeal into an unappetizing glob."

"You don't have to turn around. Just tell me why you tossed the eight-hundred-dollar jacket I had tailor made for you into the trash bin."

"Oh, that." He stopped stirring and glanced over his shoulder. "I couldn't possibly wear that, cookie. It didn't flatter me. It made me look bulky."

She walked up to him, amazed at his blatant detachment. "Leo, you don't simply trash a tailor-made jacket. Especially one that cost eight hundred dollars."

"You didn't hear me, did you? Certainly you don't expect me to wear something that doesn't flatter my physique to its fullest."

"It looked perfect on you. A potato sack wouldn't make you look bulky. What the hell's the matter with you?" Tossing a strand of hair out of her face, she turned to dig the discarded garment out of the trash. It was splattered with cheese sauce, soggy tea bags, and grape juice, and as she held it up, a chicken bone fell out from underneath the lapel. Last night's dinner had looked scrumptious on the table, but on a custom-made jacket, it appeared a little nauseating.

"You want me to look perfect, don't you? Well, so do I." He turned away from the stove and pointed the spoon at the garbage-spattered garment. "It wasn't quite my color either. I'm a summer."

She tried counting to ten but didn't come close. "You can never wear this again!"

"Ah, so glad you finally agree. Doesn't say much for the tailor, either."

"I mean it's ruined because you turned it into compost." Her voice rose to a high-pitched wail. She took a deep breath as her teeth clenched, her anger magnified by his blasé attitude. "How could you have done such a thing!" Holding the jacket between her thumb and forefinger, she let it drop back into the pail. Eight hundred dollars and several hours of a tailor's labor, now doomed to become a part of Staten Island landfill.

"Tut, tut, now, contain yourself. I wouldn't get miffed if you'd discarded something that made you look tubby."

"You would if you'd paid eight hundred dollars for it. You're absolutely decadent!"

"I'll just have to speak to the Master about that and inquire as to what he can do. Meanwhile..." His gaze softened, and the edges of those perfectly shaped lips turned down. He bowed his head and looked at her through lowered lids, ruefully fluttering his lashes. "Does that mean you don't want me anymore?" His voice cracked.

She cupped his face in her palms. "No, Leo, this is what I've always dreamed of, and now I've got it."

"You want me to be perfect, and that includes my outward appearance, of course. Consistency is my greatest virtue."

"You're consistent, all right. Oh, boy, are you consistent..."

After dinner, as Judi reviewed the few pages she'd written in the last three weeks and Leo played another Mozart piano sonata, the buzzer rang.

"Are you expecting anyone?" Leo asked over the melodic strains, his fingers not missing a single count.

"No. Are you?"

She opened the door to Siobhan Regan, Iris's assistant editor.

"Judi, how are you? It's so good to see you again! You haven't been in touch, and Iris asked me if I would..." She brought the sentence to an abrupt halt as her eyes darted across the room, landing on Leo at the piano, his body swaying with the music, eyes half closed.

"I-I-I-I'm sorry, I didn't know you had—"

"Come on in, Siobhan." Judi let the woman enter and closed the door.

Siobhan's eyes scrutinized the performer, her jaw slack with astonishment. She blinked a few times and raised her hand to smooth back a frizzy lock of hair that seemed poised for takeoff.

Just then Leo approached the finale, raised his head, and smiled as brilliantly as if before a movie camera.

"Well, hello. I didn't know Judi had such attractive friends, or I would have come to the big city a long time ago." He stood, smoothing his trouser legs, and walked over to Siobhan, holding out his hand.

She held it loosely, still staring. He bent his head and kissed Siobhan's hand just as he'd done with Iris—and with her. Another of his gentlemanly "habits."

Judi thought it appropriate to introduce them before Leo encouraged the ardent idolizer any further. "Siobhan, this is Leo..." She halted, realizing that they hadn't given him a last name. She thought rapidly and blurted out Varlden, since she was passing him off as Felix's brother. "Leo, this is Siobhan Regan, Iris's assistant editor at Spectrum."

"Charmed, I'm sure," Leo purred, as Siobhan's

head bobbed, displaying the same behavior that had befallen Iris. So what else was new?

"M—me, too," Siobhan blubbered as Leo dropped her hand, watching it fall to her side.

"Now if you ladies will excuse me, I've got a few matters to attend to." A slight bow accompanied his ravishing smile as he politely exited.

"Is he for real, or was I dreaming?" Siobhan sighed, her unfocused eyes riveting back to Judi.

"He's real, all right. I'm sure Iris told you all about him."

"She told me he was drop-dead gorgeous, but she didn't tell me I was going to nearly drop dead." Siobhan fixed her eyes on the bathroom door. "Is he coming back out?" Her voice droned, trance-like.

"Oh, yeah. He performs his toilette ritual at the same time every night."

"He's moved in?" Her eyes and mouth gaped in sync.

"We've been...roommates for a few weeks, yes." Aware that Siobhan's next step was to her BlackBerry to blast the news, she didn't want to divulge too many details.

"Forgive me for staring, Judi, but my roommates never looked anything like that. What a hottie! Where did you find him?"

"Oh, I had to look in quite a few places."

"He's right out of every hunk flick I've ever seen. And I'll throw in the screenplay I tried to write for good measure."

"What did Iris tell you about him, anyway?" Judi asked, her curiosity piqued.

"Not much—"

"Come on, Siobhan. Iris wouldn't meet a man like Leo and not issue a press release."

"Oh, Judi...hubba hubba, I guess some lucky girl had to land him."

"He is hot, isn't he?" Pride erupted from her

voice as she eyed the eleven-by-fourteen glossy of Leo on the wall behind her computer.

"I'll tell you, when they made him, they threw away the mold," Siobhan gushed.

Judi nodded. "But I'm sure they saved the lower half."

"I wish you the best of luck. He's one in a gazillion."

"At least."

"Tell you the truth, all Iris said was that he was a conceited oaf with plastic hair who didn't give a damn about anybody but himself. But you know Iris. What you see is what you get."

"So what can I help you with, Siobhan?"

"Oh!" She dug a brown envelope out of her leather sack. "I'd almost forgotten what I came over here for. These are your galleys. She also wanted to know when the next one was coming."

"Tell her I haven't done much. I've been so busy with...well, you know..." She tossed her head toward the bathroom.

"Oooh, I get it."

Why not rub it in just a little, Judi thought, annoyed at Iris for having badmouthed Leo to someone as impressionable as Siobhan.

"Tell Iris I'll get back to her when I've got more work, so she doesn't have to send messengers over here all the time."

"I didn't mind, Judi. I'm sorry if I disturbed—"

"No problem, Siobhan. You didn't disturb a thing. Just tell her I'll get back to her...when I've got time. Meanwhile, I'm sure she'll understand my taking a sabbatical."

"I'll be glad to tell her." Siobhan turned to leave, her eyes still glazed over from the entrancing vision she'd encountered. "And tell Leo I said good night. I hope we'll meet again real soon."

She flounced out the door, her hair flying after

her.

****

"It was considerate of you to disappear as soon as Siobhan arrived," Judi said when he emerged from the bathroom in silk briefs, patting his face dry with a cotton ball. "But not quite in character."

"I didn't deliberately disappear. It was time for my bath. She just arrived at the wrong time." He dried himself off, not the way regular guys drew the towel across themselves like they were sawing wood. He patted his body as gently as he would a newborn baby, which he was, she supposed.

He neatly folded the towel. She stared at him, still amazed at his exquisite physique. He certainly is a breathing work of art.

"I think I hear the phone," she murmured, watching as he applied moisturizer to his face and throat in upward strokes.

"Whoever it is will call back." He turned his back on her and preened in the mirror. "I doubt it's for me anyway, so how important can it be?"

She made a dash for the phone, her heart in her throat, hoping it would be Felix, but it was only a telemarketer selling Myrtle Beach condos. She slammed the phone down hard enough to deafen him.

Only mad love made her do things like this.

Chapter Sixteen

Purple-proselike descriptions of Leo spread through the Spectrum offices even faster than the rumor that Judi had retired. Two more assistant editors, the copyeditor, and the art director came over one afternoon to talk her out of it.

The covered keyboard and blank computer screen heightened their suspicions as Judi served coffee and Leo's tiramisu. No sooner did they ask about her "retirement" than they wanted to know where "he" was. "He" was shopping for tonight's dinner ingredients and not expected back for a while. The spellbound ladies exited the loft, muttering tart remarks, but not before ogling the full-length poster of "him" on the living room wall.

Judi made sure word got back to Spectrum, and inevitably, the trade journals, cocktail parties, and online gossip boards, that Juno Ursa was prolific as ever.

She informed Leo of the visitors he'd missed by a scant ten minutes, when he came in carrying grocery bags and a long, skinny cardboard crate.

"My fan club arrived and didn't even wait for my return?" he joked, tearing into the crate like a kid at Christmas.

"Your fan club had to get back to work," she replied, hiding the relief in her voice. She could only imagine the circus those four would've had with Leo the Ringleader. "What is that?" He turned around to face her. She gasped.

He smiled smugly over another poster of himself, framed and mounted, a blow-up of a photo she'd snapped of him draped across the piano.

Upon expressing her liking for that particular photo out of the fifty she'd taken of him with her new digicam, he'd run out and returned with two-dozen roses. Now, a week later, she stared at yet another portrait of Leo screaming to be displayed on a depraved, forlorn wall.

****

"No, a little to the side...no, a little more...up about an inch...I said an inch, not a foot! No...no, just a tiny bit more to the right...that's it...that's it...oh! Oh, yes, yes, yes! Aaaaaah...perfect!" He spread his arms, as if ready to take flight, and threw back his head in ecstasy.

"Right there!"

She leaned on the portrait, adhering it to the wall—permanently.

This replaced the Chagall, now relegated to her bedroom. Now his face on the wall would be her loft's focal point—when he wasn't present to grace it in person. "Judi, you are a master picture-hanger! Now, let me go out and walk in again to get the full impact."

A twenty-four-by-thirty-six of him already graced the far wall, being the focal point upon entering the loft. She had to admit he photographed like a dream, even more gorgeous in the flesh than in a photo. Leo seemed just as infatuated with his mirror image as his digital photos—he spent just as much time admiring them.

"Leo, now that you've officially displaced Chagall, my old screen saver, and mouse pad, I'd like to ask a favor."

"Surely, my lady, what is it? Something special you want for dinner? If veal rollitini isn't your heart's desire tonight, I could whip up—"

"No, it's not that. I'd like you to read my book."

"Read it?" He wrinkled his nose as if she'd asked

him to empty the dishwasher. The one you're working on?"

"Yes. I haven't written anything in quite a while. I've hit a stumbling block."

"Very well. How can I bring you out of it? You need some help with your hero? I should be able to tell you what he needs to be believable, in light of all we have in common."

"No, I know more than enough about what he needs to be believable. Just the storyline in general." She went to her desk and lifted a stack of loose pages. "I need a jump-start. After all, I've spent the last month and a half just—"

"You're not tiring of me, are you?" Those eyes grew round as the dark head dropped.

She skirted the question. "I'd just like to get back to my career. It does pay the rent, you know."

"Oh, pish, Judi. I know you're enjoying a very comfortable income from your royalties...you need never labor over a keyboard again."

"Income has nothing to do with it. I like to share my work with the world. And I thought it would be nice to share it with you. Do you realize you've never read anything I've ever written?" she challenged.

"I thought I was everything you've ever written."

"Maybe so, but I want you to see some of my work. Here." She held out the manuscript to him, and he reached for it with hesitant fingers, fanning the pages with his thumb.

"Now?" he uttered.

"No, after dinner. I'll do some online banking, and you can read what I've already got. Also, I've decided something else."

"To acquire a sprawling estate in a posh locale, perhaps Palm Beach? I trust you perused the 'Exclusive Homes and Estates' section I left open on your desk." He fetched it and handed it to her.

"No, I haven't perused it." She took it but set it

back down, ignoring his pout.

"I was hoping we could look at new homes together. The pollution of the city is terribly unhealthy, you know. Gives you premature wrinkles." He critically eyed her face.

"Never mind wrinkles and the Palm Beach estate. I've made a major decision, and you want to play Donald Trump!"

"What is it then?" he asked.

"I'm changing genres. I'm turning to murder mysteries."

"Seriously?" He blinked, as if stunned.

"Yes. I don't feel the need to write about Race Parsec anymore. I've written everything that's in my heart, and now I need to move on. I'm going to enter a contest sponsored by Enigma Press, under a pseudonym. I've got to get the query in by the tenth—so I'm going to start working on it now."

"I shall help you." He gave a confident nod.

"You?"

"Certainly. I may possess the capacity to conceive some plausible ideas but maybe not so much murder mysteries. They come across as contrived. Still, I'd love to help your career, Judi. I'd be more than happy to. Anything to get you out of this blue funk of yours. At times, you're rather less than pleasant to be around, you know."

Refusing to let him get to her, she counted to ten and walked out, leaving him alone with his pictures and mirrors—all six of them.

****

Judi pulled her battered memory box from the top shelf of her closet. After sifting through a few yellowed reviews of her early books, she found some old diaries. Settling down to read about days gone past, she rediscovered many things she'd long since forgotten—like how much she missed twenty-one-year-old Felix Varlden when their lives finally took their separate paths.

He's so cute, in a dorky kinda way, with the greenest eyes I've ever seen, but he's my very best friend—I can talk about anything with Felix. Our families have always been so close. We spent our childhoods like brother and sister...

She perused the final entry written in a scribbled, rushed hand:

He's married now. I didn't go to the wedding. I got the news from Dad and Carol, who called to tell me how romantic the ceremony was, how radiant the bride looked, and how much in love they are. If I were at home, I'd probably be really depressed now, but I'm on the other side of the continent, and somehow the vastness seems to mentally and physically separate matters I must avoid. Now I'm really alone. My best friend in the whole world is gone. He belongs to somebody else. Carol told me the bride looks just like me, and she wondered if he'd chosen her intentionally. Carol watches too many soaps.

She slapped the diary shut, not wanting to read any more about her confused adolescent feelings for Felix. She'd completely forgotten how alone she'd felt when she heard of his marriage.

What had happened? she wondered. Distance had happened. Separate careers, separate lives. Too many years went by, her marriage blew up, and novel after novel exploded out of her as her hero distinctly formed in her mind. Now she had him—Leo, the dream transposed into three dimensions, the picture of perfection.

She closed the old journal and returned it to the box, sliding it back onto her top shelf.

Walking into the living room, she spotted Leo sleeping on the sofa, his hair spread over the cushion like silk. Her manuscript had slid from his hand to the floor. On it were literally hundreds of corrections in red ink. She sighed. At least he kept her humble.

****

"I'm so sorry, I just couldn't stay awake." He ran his hands through his rumpled hair. "I must look frightful, my clothes all wrinkled—"

"It's late." She straightened the pages he'd dropped. "We've had a long day."

"I regret to say that it just didn't pique my interest. I'm not big on pop fiction. I'm strictly a literature aficionado."

"It's all right, Leo," she broke in a bit too harshly. But she no longer cared. She didn't even care what she looked like in the morning anymore.

"Judi, it's simply not my area of interest. But there are places I can help you. For instance, I did notice the narrative is too introspective. There are numerous structural problems as well—"

"I understand. Just get some sleep." Without saying good night, she turned and went into her bedroom, closed and locked the door.

Regardless, it was definite—her next work would be a murder mystery. She hadn't created her sleuth yet, but she certainly had the victim in mind.

Chapter Seventeen

Leo answered the phone on the first ring as Judi studied the Web site of Enigma Press, the premier publishing house of high-end mysteries. "Oh, hello, Felix," he gave a casual, semi-bored greeting. Her heart gave an excited leap. "Shhh!" she told it.

"Yes, everything's fine, couldn't be better," he continued. "Am I what? Of course, what a silly question, ha, ha...how goes your own project?...good, good, I know it will be a smashing success, like all your creations..." As he spoke, he straightened magazines on the table, picked up pens, and lined them up on her desk. "No, that's been well under control..."

Yesterday, she'd searched frantically for her latest bank statement and discovered that Leo had taken every statement from the last ten years and filed them away by date.

She stood and dashed to the phone, hovering over Leo, hopping from one foot to another with impatience.

"I need to talk to him," she mouthed silently, gesturing with open palms as he nodded and gave abrupt "yes" or "no" answers. "Come on," she whispered. But the next thing she knew, he'd hung up.

"Why did you hang up?" she nearly shrieked. "I wanted to talk to him."

"Oh, I'm sorry." He casually brushed some crumbs into the trash bin. "He didn't ask to speak with you. Oh, and Judi, please wrap the cheese more carefully hereafter. It gets hard around the edges.

It's very simple, see, you take the edges as such, and cover it diagonally." He folded the wrap with the precision of a soldier making up his barracks bed.

She stalked away and started typing furiously, her fingers tapping the keys with a mad staccato beat, drowning out his voice.

Only it wasn't a novel she was writing this time. It was an e-mail to Felix. Swiping away tears of longing for him, she poured out her heart. "Felix, I miss you more than I ever did in the years we were apart and living separate lives. The place is so empty without you here that I feel a big part of me is missing. I can't wait to see you again." She wasn't sure if she should send it. She wondered why she was even writing it. But it helped. She was much calmer now; her chest wasn't tight and her blood didn't feel hot enough to boil, as it did so often these days.

****

"Quitting time. Dinner waits without!"

The aroma of curry made her mouth water. Her blueness faded as her taste buds awaited the delicious meal.

"Coming." She exited out of the system, and the glow vanished from the screen.

He uncorked a bottle of wine as she approached the table. His black silk shirt, open at the collar, revealed a teasing glimpse of his chest. Tight jeans clung to every muscular curve.

"Everything you make is so delicious," she said sincerely, taking her place at the meticulously set table.

"Eating is one of life's great sensual pleasures." She emphasized the sensual, hoping he'd take the subtle hint and realize there were other sensual pleasures, too—pleasures she now wanted to share with Felix. But unable to have him, she turned to the object of what was once her fantasy and hoped she could recapture some of that desire she'd carried around all these years.

"I derive great pleasure watching you devour my meals. Besides," he added as he placed a plate of steaming rice on the table, "what with all my other activities and cleaning up after you, I have a minimal amount of time for leisure. Bon appétit." He took his seat across from her.

She dug into her vegetable curry just as the phone rang. "I'll get it, you keep shoveling it in." He sprinted over to the desk.

"If it's Felix, make sure you put him through to me this time!" she commanded, hesitating with her fork in midair, her stomach now churning.

"Yes, she's right here. But we're dining at the moment. Can you call back at a more opportune time?" Deciding it couldn't be Felix because of his formal tone, she slipped the first forkful into her mouth, her taste buds bursting with pleasure

"Very well, if it's that urgent..." He cupped his hand over the phone and called to her: "Judi, it's Iris. Says it's urgent. I told her that we were dining, but she insists. Says it can't wait."

Judi pondered for a moment then decided to take the call. Iris must have urgent news, or she wouldn't insist on interrupting Judi's dinner. Iris considered dinnertime the most sensual part of the day—the beginning of her nightly ritual of self-indulgent pleasures.

Leo handed her the phone, and she swallowed her mouthful. "Yes, Iris, what is it?"

"Judi, we came to a decision today, a most timely decision." Her voice sounded firm, businesslike, and Judi knew Iris had the Spectrum mucky mucks sitting around the conference table, all ears.

"I'm dining on delectable Indian cuisine here, so what's more urgent than Peshawari Naan and Shahi

Karahi Paneer?" It didn't matter much to her who was listening.

"We got a pub date for *Race to Infinity*, and I need you to come down here and discuss a tour schedule."

"Sweet." She hadn't toured since *Race Against the Clock* a year ago November.

She missed the frenzied schedule, dashing through airports, a different hotel room every night, new restaurants, and adoring crowds. Away from New York, away from the neatness, the classical music, and—she hated to admit it—Leo. The excitement slipped into her voice as she turned to him.

Beaming, he gave her the "thumbs up" signal. "I'm very glad to hear that. I'll be there first thing in the morning. Is that soon enough?"

"Of course." Iris continued in her businesslike tone, "And I trust you'll give me an approximate completion date for the latest manuscript, so we can plan our spring schedule."

"Oh, I'll have to see about that one. It may take a bit longer. I've been busy with other things. But I'll be there tomorrow morning first thing, and we'll talk about it."

"Fine. We'll be expecting you."

"Goodbye, Iris."

"And—" Iris piped up as Judi was ready to ring off.

"Yes?"

"Congratulations."

"Thanks. Thanks to all of you!" Holding the phone in her hand a bit longer to prolong the magic of the moment, she looked at Leo scanning a Web site, his eyes sparkling.

Studying the flawless facial structure, the dark locks framing the face with stylized luster, she realized she felt nothing; no rush of desire, no liquid fire coursing through her veins. She got more excited watching the ball drop in Times Square.

He flashed that brilliant smile, opened another button on his shirt, and fanned a hand over his chest. "I hear congratulations are in order."

Sitting at the table, she placed the napkin on her lap, something she'd never done before meeting Leo.

"Thank you," she stated simply.

"I'm glad Iris is happy about your triumphs, even if she is carrying the torch." He ran his fingers through his hair. "Regardless, I feel a celebration is in order. So tonight I'm taking you to see an all-Lizst program. I'd love to see someone perform Beethoven's 'Moonlight.' If Ludwig hadn't dedicated it to the Countess Giulietta Guicciardi, he'd have written it for vous." He held out his hand to take hers.

"What time does it start?" A fleeting thought held her excitement at bay. She would love to see this with Felix. It was Felix she wanted sitting next to her, clasping hands, sharing the magic of the music.

"Eight. So you've just got time to finish dinner, and I can decide what to wear." His long fingers played over the top button of his shirt and slipped it open, then slid slowly to the second button until his shirt was open, his muscular chest exposed. He ran his splayed fingers over the dark mat of chest hair in a loving caress.

She watched, amused but hardly aroused, as her stomach cried out for more nourishment.

"I need time to make myself glamorous." She slid another forkful of the curried ambrosia into her mouth.

In an instant he was at her side, planting a light kiss on the top of her head. "Nonsense. Together we're as glamorous as any movie stars immortalized on the celluloid screen."

"Aren't we just," she muttered as he fixed his eyes on his self-portrait, sighing with adoration, a lusty smile playing on his lips.

"Oh, darling, don't you just love the way we always agree!" he gushed, clasping his hands together and scrunching his nose.

She continued eating until she nearly burst and finally dropped her fork onto her plate with a clatter. She shook her head, yet again. "Where did I go wrong?"

****

The meeting crawled to a close, the crowd dispersed, and she and Iris faced each other alone in the conference room. "I'll bet you're happy this is finally coming about." Iris gathered her materials and stood. "You haven't toured in two years."

"Iris, I'm very happy about this. In fact, this is the happiest I've been in—" Now when did she run into Felix in Three Steps Down? It seemed like a lifetime ago.

Iris swept off her glasses, and her eyes connected with Judi's. "You're still trying to work through your dilemma, is that it? It must be, if this is the only thing that's made you happy in a month of Sundays."

"I should be delirious, shouldn't I? Two men vying for my attention, and one is everything the other isn't, and vice versa." She gazed out the window at the skyline, the tops of the buildings vanishing into fog.

"So it's not just a matter of choosing one over the other." She gave Judi a "you lucky bitch" cocked head look and raised brow.

Judi eyed the half-full box of doughnuts on the side table next to the coffeepot. "I know who I want this time, but I was wrong the first time. So who knows what's right anymore? Meanwhile, none of us is coming out ahead."

"So they know about each other now?" Iris adjusted her scarf.

"I haven't exactly kept it a secret."

"And no dueling at dawn?"

Judi smiled. She felt like dueling Leo. "No, they're cool about it. Leo couldn't care less. It's like he's along for the ride. I can tell it's bothering Felix. But he's not blaming Leo. I just think he disappears to his lab during odd hours when he's not on business trips or skydiving jaunts and is brainstorming methods to solve the relationship conundrum."

"Boy, they are different, aren't they? So who's the one you want?"

She sighed heavily. "My heart wants Felix, but it can never work. We'd be at each other's throats even before the honeymoon ended. We're too much alike. Yes, I'm in love with him, I finally admitted to myself." Her voice cracked with emotion, and hot tears sprang up and trickled down her face. "But that's the problem. I'm too practical to give it a try."

Iris perched her butt on the edge of the conference table. "Then, if you don't mind me poking my nose in here, I don't think your inviting Leo to move in with you was the thing to do."

So Siobhan did open her big trap.

"No, he isn't—it's not like we're—" She didn't want to get into this with Iris. It was all too complex, too damn perplexing. She couldn't even explain it in a novel. Who the hell would believe it?

Iris didn't say another word, just waited for Judi to finish stammering.

"We're not cohabitating. He hasn't moved in. I mean, not that way. We don't 'do it,' all right?"

Iris's eyes and mouth widened at the same time.

"Never?" Her mouth remained open even after she spoke. "With either of them?"

"No. It's the only thing they have in common. They're both gentlemen."

"Neither ever made a move on you yet?"

"Not that kind of move."

Her earrings dangled as she shook her head. "But a man of the world like Leo? I had him figured for the type who's so smooth, you've got your skirt up around your waist and pantyhose down around your ankles before you realize you're on your back."

"Leo is a virgin." Judi took a wicked pleasure in revealing this. "An innocent, green-behind-the-gills, cherry, pure as the driven snow. But even more than ninety-nine and forty-four hundredths pure."

Iris's jaw dropped eleven stories right there. "No way! That luscious hunk of hormones? Never been sampled?"

"Right out of the box, Iris." She broke off a piece of doughnut and stuffed it into her mouth, licking the raspberry jelly off her fingers.

"He won't let you break him?" Iris's glasses dropped to the floor, but either she didn't notice or was too engrossed in this revelation to pick them up.

"I just don't have those kinds of feelings for him. I thought I did, when I was worshiping him from afar, but now that he's here, I just don't—I mean, the biology is there, but not the chemistry."

"So all the attraction to him is from the neck down?"

"Well, he's got a great face." Without thinking, she took the other half of doughnut.

"You know what I mean. The attraction's not mental. It's all in the head, but not the one on his shoulders."

Judi nodded, chewing thoughtfully. "You got it. My heart wouldn't be in it if we slept together. It would be strictly an animal act—raw, primal lust."

"Well, then—what do you plan on doing with Vestal Virgin if you're so convinced your love for

Felix won't outlive your estrogen supply?"

"I can't think that far ahead, Iris. I can barely think past next week when Felix comes back."

"Where is he?"

"At ORBIT headquarters. Then he's going skydiving. He wanted to leave the two of us alone."

"Wow, what a guy. Handing over a prize like you to another man, with his blessing. Do me a favor—if you decide you don't want Felix, I want first dibs on him."

She looked up from her last bit of doughnut, expecting to see that wry smile. But Iris looked dead serious.

"Forget it, Iris. You're so not each other's type. Trust me."

"Okay, just thought I'd be my usual bellicose self and ask. That's how I acquire best sellers. Well, you'd better make up your mind sometime. So he's a sloppy second, but he's a sloppy second with a good reference."

"Iris, this isn't funny."

"I'm not joking. The times I've met Felix, I found him warm, personable, smart, and just plain fun to be with. All the things his unbearable sibling isn't. But, if you can't deny your hormones the pleasure of Narcissus and his reflection, go for him, tie the knot so you can consummate your primal passion, and let your single friends have a chance."

She ached to tell her single friend she didn't stand a chance in hell with Felix. A fierce jealousy began to churn inside her. At the same time, she grew angry at Iris for trying to compromise their friendship this way. They'd never clashed over men, ever; she didn't want to start now, especially over Felix.

Her Felix.

"No way, Iris. It'd never work. Your sun signs aren't compatible, not to mention your moon signs or

Pluto signs. You come from different worlds, have disparate lifestyles and interests, and he's not even a Yankees fan. That alone should be a warning that you'd never last more than an inning together. So forget it."

"Aside from those minor details, we get along great. Besides, I think he's adorable. He's—" Iris hesitated and stooped to get her glasses.

"How long have you been attracted to Felix?" Needing a good caffeine fix, Judi reached for the coffeepot.

"Who wouldn't be? Let me tell you something. You'd better poop or get off the pot, Judi, before somebody pulls it out from under you. And I know what I'm talking about—trust me." That raised left brow meant she had more to say; the last sentence was meant to dangle.

"Then spit it out, Iris." Their eyes locked. If they'd had horns, they'd have locked, too.

"I want to be the one to tell you this, Judi. I know you don't want to hear this from him. I saw Felix with another woman."

"When?"

"Three Saturday nights ago."

Judi scanned back through her mental calendar. The night he was out with his ORBIT cronies and didn't get back 'til two a.m.

"Where?"

"Seventy-Second and Fifth."

"Doing what?"

"Getting into a cab."

"Are you sure it was him?"

"Of course it was him." Iris nodded. "He said hello to me."

"Did he introduce her?" Desperate to wet her sudden cottonmouth, she took a large gulp of coffee and grimaced.

"No. It all happened in about two seconds. But

they looked awful cozy. I saw them the Wednesday night before that, too, coming out of L'Amarante. She was practically hanging all over him."

Judi's next question was "What did she look like?" but she already knew too much. "It was probably somebody he works with."

"They sure weren't working those nights," Iris assured her.

"All right, Iris, you've made your point. So he was out with another woman. The guy's not a monk." She didn't want Iris to see how much she was hurting inside. She knew Iris hadn't meant to hurt her; it was only her way of driving home a point in her in-your-face, nakedly frank way.

"Just go walk through the park and do some thinking, Judi."

She gathered up her papers and stuffed them into her briefcase. "That's all I've been doing, Iris. For the first time in my adult life."

****

Judi came home and flung the first object in her path—Leo's duck-head walking stick. "Oh, that felt good!" Most of the pain and hurt had worked itself out during the brisk trek home from midtown. She needed that long walk. Why these pangs of jealousy gnawed at her heart, she didn't know. Felix's live-in girlfriend hadn't bothered her a bit. But that was then. Maybe it was because the news had come from Iris; she blamed the messenger.

She found Leo reclining on the sofa, listening to a Brahms symphony, and wearing nothing but a pair of briefs. He looked tantalizing, all right—but so did the box of truffles on the table next to him.

"Hey, what's that all about?" He looked up, annoyed. "Why don't you fling something of your own around?"

Her blood started to boil again, but it wasn't the half naked hunk stretched out at her fingertips that she could've strangled at this moment.

She took a deep breath and recited the words like a news anchor. "Iris saw Felix with another woman." She had to get it out. He was the last one she wanted to confide in about something like this, but she was desperate.

"Good. He was getting to be a bit of a third wheel around here," he commented. "About time he got a life."

"Did he mention anything about it to you on the phone that night? That he had a girlfriend?" She tried so hard to keep her voice calm and conversational, it didn't even sound like her own.

"Not a word. What reason would Felix have for discussing his personal life with me? I'm not my master's keeper, cookie."

She had to hear his voice. "I'm calling him."

"How weak."

Ignoring him, she went into her bedroom, closed the door and made a lunge for the phone before she had the chance to change her mind.

She punched in his cell number. His voice mail answered. She hung up.

She sat quietly, feeling like he'd abandoned her. So he'd been out with a woman...but why the hell did it bother her so much?

She headed straight for her chocolate fix in the fridge.

"Come over here. I'll take your mind off it," Leo offered, stretching his arms over his head, reaching for her hand.

She let him clasp her hand, and he drew her close, his body undeniably alluring with only a tight stretch of silk covering his loins. Caressing the perfect physique with her eyes, she looked at the lips ready to part for a kiss. Oh, why the hell not? She bent over, touching her lips to his. His tongue darted out, finding hers, drinking her into a long, leisurely kiss that ended abruptly when the Brahms piece finished. But the kiss was as mechanical as the low speed on her blender. She'd never felt so empty, so dry.

"Oh, do put some more of that on," Leo breathed. "The music is so...so sensual, I think Johannes had me in mind when he wrote that symphony."

She refused to sit here and feel sorry for herself. "Sure, why not." She rose, forcing the thought of Felix and his date out of her mind, but another wave of questions hit her as she pushed the CD player's eject button...were they together right now? Had he slept with her? "Forget it, Judi!" she said out loud, between clenched teeth. "You have no business even wondering."

"You're right, Judi," Leo remarked from across the room. "If Felix has another woman, it's really none of your business. Besides, you've got me. How could you possibly want him? I'm the one you adore. I'm everything he's not. So what if he falls in love with someone else and gets married and starts a new life and you never see him again? He's entitled to be as happy as we are. We're destined to be happier than he can ever be..."

She tuned him out then fished through her collection until she found what she wanted. In an instant the harsh, clashing chords of the Sex Pistols blasted from the speakers.

Leo popped up as if Spacelab had just crashed through the wall. "What in the name of Antonio Stradivarius is that...my word!" He clapped his hands to his ears, shaking his head violently. "What's wrong with the stereo? Is it blowing up? Halt that tripe before I explode myself!"

She sauntered over to him, pulling his hands from his ears. She'd turned the volume nearly to the maximum, and the noise was deafening, but she'd had enough of Beethoven sonatas and Mozart operas and Chopin mazurkas; she wanted to hear some vintage down 'n dirty punk rock. The music gave her an energy bordering on violence. She wanted to hurt him somehow, to violate his dignity and strip him of that pompous veneer.

She stood behind him and tied a bandanna around his eyes. "What are you doing, Judi?" He sounded agitated, almost fearful. Some hero. She snickered as she told him to shut up.

"Judi, I demand to know what's going on here. I can't see a thing."

"I'll do the demanding from now on, Lover Man." She clasped one smooth unsweaty hand and led him down the stairs to the entry hall. "Stand still," she commanded. In one swift sweep, she slid his briefs off him and yanked them out from under his feet. He stood there blindfolded in all his magnificent nakedness. She opened the door and gave him a little shove onto the sidewalk. "Charm your way out of this." She slammed the door on his perfect buns.

Chapter Eighteen

Judi's tour itinerary would take her to twenty-seven cities in six weeks. She couldn't kid herself; she couldn't get any work done. Not today anyway with the stress coursing through her. Her arms rested on her kitchen table, and she leaned her head on them, sighing.

She itched to talk with Felix, but she didn't want to bug him with messages.

"Hey, I'm a professional, and a pro writes whether she feels like it or not," she muttered to herself. So she sat at her computer and wrote an outline of a murder mystery—ten pages of tripe that would've made Sherlock Holmes cringe, but at least it gave evidence of her productivity.

"You look like you need some nourishment," Leo commented as he watched her sporadic tapping of the keys in between long stretches of staring at the screen.

"You may want to knock a few pounds off your posterior, but you shouldn't starve."

At first she ignored him. She was learning to tune out the snarky comments about her weight and fashion sense, and was still seething over last night's episode when she'd kicked him out.

But he'd treated the whole thing as a joke. He'd sat in the doorway until she came down the next morning. It hadn't bothered him a bit. He'd simply tied the bandanna around his loins and gone for a stroll. In a place like SoHo, of course no one looked twice.

"I have no appetite tonight, Leo, for dinner or

anything else," she replied, not taking her eyes off the screen. "So go amuse yourself. The way you are in the self-love department, I'm sure you'll find something to play with."

Wrapped up in her fictional realm, she worked until midnight. The more she wrote, the easier it got. Leo was asleep when she turned the lights out in the bedroom, the next day's outfit laid out on his valet. The light from the hall streaked into the room.

She dropped to her knees and observed the sleeping figure, the vague shadows playing on his hair, the long spidery lashes. She studied the elegant contours of his cheekbones, the delicate silhouette, and the touches of amusement around his mouth and eyes in the form of small creases.

Through half-closed eyes, she gazed dreamily as he became Felix, the golden locks and the penetrating, intelligent eyes. With Felix's name on her lips, she leaned over and planted a kiss on Leo's mouth. Lips parting, his body stirred in response. His arms went around her, and a soft moan escaped his lips. His eyelids fluttered open. His breaths increased with the arousal she witnessed lowering her gaze to the ridge in the sheet.

Liquid fire spread through her. She edged onto the bed next to him, pressing her body against his. Just as she was about to slide on top of him and wrap her thighs around his back, he sat up, pushing her away. She caught herself on the edge of the bed, blinking in surprise.

"Judi, what are you doing?" His accusatory tone made her feel like he'd caught her snooping in his recipe file.

"What do you think? You can't be that clueless."

"I'm sorry, Judi, but now isn't the best time. I need my beauty sleep. You know that. You'll have to schedule our trysts better than this." He got out of bed and straightened the sheet perfectly, then fell right back into a perfect sleep. He didn't snore.

"Felix, where are you?" she whispered.

****

Judi quickly finished the sentence she was typing and rose to buzz her caller in. The mailman delivered a package for Leo, more CDs from the classical music club he'd joined. There were also the usual bills and a letter from Enigma Press.

Enigma, the publisher she'd written to, under a pseudonym, with the entry to the mystery novel contest. They'd acknowledged her entry at last!

She tore at the envelope and unfolded the letter, her eyes automatically scanning the print to see how long it was...and her spirit sank as those all-too-familiar words of rejection, "We regret," registered in her mind.

The letter stated in two simple sentences that they'd received her entry and her follow-up letter withdrawing the entry.

Withdrawing the entry! She never wrote them...

But maybe someone else had. The letter slipped from her fingers. She stood stunned, her feet cemented to the floor. She couldn't even hear herself breathing. It was because she wasn't.

Leo. He'd done it. He'd written to the publisher and withdrawn her entry. Her blood pounded in her veins, and her chest tightened. Her fists clenched.

How dare he! "That meddling son of a—" She stalked the room, up and down, wanting to fly out the door to the gourmet shop, grab him by the hair and drag him home, accuse him, berate him in public, and embarrass him to the point of making him cringe.

But she forced herself to stay calm. "He's not worth it," she repeated, convincing herself that this too, would pass.

But this would never happen again. He'd never have another chance to violate her privacy this way.

Never would he be allowed anywhere near her workspace, even if she had to keep it under lock and key.

Walking up and down, from one end of the loft to the other, she rehearsed and abandoned at least a dozen ways to confront him. Finally he came in. She repressed her impulse to punch him in that perfect nose, in favor of a simple, "Why did you do it?" as she shook the letter in his handsome face.

Ignoring her, he passed her by, headed for the kitchen, and began emptying the groceries onto the table: extra virgin olive oil, caviar, and pâté. "I specifically recall you telling me your plans to abandon the mystery idea and write your memoirs—my recommendation, mind you. On Thursday night, at eleven-thirty-eight, you said—"

She crumpled the letter, tore it apart, and flung it to the floor. "Never mind what I said, Leo. Do you realize you've just ruined my chances of being published by Enigma at all? They think I'm a capricious prima donna with a two-by-four on my shoulder."

He turned his back to her and took the pâté from its wrapper. "If you'd only told me you were going ahead with this project—"

She grabbed his arm and forced him to face her.

"From now on, you are not to touch that telephone or that workspace, do you understand? You've been overstepping your bounds too much lately, and this one just about cracked the egg. I'm reaching the end of my rope, Leo, and I mean that."

"Oh, really?" A crooked smirk curled his lip. "I wasn't aware of any rope, but you do seem to have a rather short fuse."

"There's more than enough rope to wrap around your perfect neck!" she shrieked, rubbing her palms on the thighs of her jeans. "And wipe that smirk off your face before I smack it off for you."

"Temper, temper..." he chanted, waltzing over to the stereo and lifting a CD out of the collection. "You creative temperaments, always throwing tantrums and blaming it on the rest of us normal folk." Don Giovanni blared from the speakers. Leo started singing along in perfect Italian, making her head throb.

She pressed her palms to her ears. "You're unbearable!" she shouted over the orchestra and the resounding vocals, then scampered into the bedroom, slamming the door behind her.

She threw herself on her bed. The flood she'd been damming up for so long, the outburst she'd held in for weeks, finally flowed. The tears poured down her cheeks, into the corners of her mouth, sweet and salty at the same time.

Mistake...the word haunted her. She gulped for breath as her body quaked with sobs. She'd created him to her every specification. But for every trait he had, she'd discovered five he lacked. The delicate balance was somehow disturbed, and in creating Leo, the laws of the universe hadn't been obeyed. How could they be? He was man-made—he was perfect, not a creation of God, but a pseudo-person, created out of her fantasy and whimsy, and aided by a scientist who used technology to bring this being to perfection.

Felix—for whom she'd poured out her yearnings in the brittle pages of leather-bound diaries.

Felix—who'd married and divorced and earned honors of the highest caliber, all without her.

And Judi—the dreamer who confined her wild fantasies to paper, longed for her fictitious hero to come to life, all wrapped up in one sexy, considerate, intelligent, perfect man, who was barely fifty feet away while she was behind a slammed door, wishing he were human, like Felix...

Felix.

What Felix had given her made her realize how much she missed him. Every time she imagined running her hands through Leo's hair, or kissed him out of sleep, or wrapped her arms around the hard muscles, it was Felix she was loving, Felix she wanted. Felix—her true hero. Not the hero of her action adventures, but who the hell wanted that anyway?

The man in the next room was not the man she'd always wanted. The man in the next room was a monster.

****

Five whole days and Felix hadn't heard from her. He'd expected Judi to call and remind him to take his vitamins, or have his laundry done, or get his hair cut. She hadn't sent any e-mail, either. He checked that along with his stock quotes three times a day.

Maybe nature had taken its course, and the lovers were enmeshed in domestic and conjugal bliss. Maybe they'd even eloped. No, he forced that crazy notion out of his mind. Judi would never want to get married again. Not after that disaster the first time. That comforted him. She'd go to her grave single.

Tomorrow he was leaving for Phoenix and his skydiving trip. But was that the best thing to do? Five days had already passed. Five long tedious days of speeches, roundtable discussions, and a banquet that went on longer than the Academy Awards. He sat at the hotel desk, his laptop glowing, and his hand on the mouse, ready to cancel that diving trip. If Judi wanted him back home, he'd never forgive himself for going forward with something so frivolous. After counting to ten once more to make sure he wasn't acting on impulse, and a quick glance at the clock, which told him he'd been counting to ten for an hour, he went online to change his

234

reservation.

His need to be with Judi, to feast his eyes on her, to inhale her fragrance, to hear her laugh, was so strong it hurt. At the same time, he dreaded what was more likely—the lovebirds wouldn't have a minute for him. But jumping out of planes wasn't the way to find out what awaited him in New York— elation or heartbreak.

And he couldn't wait another day.

But first, he grabbed his cell and called Judi. He held his breath for three, then four rings. They're not in. They're walking through the park, or in a cozy bistro, or...

As he was about to hang up, Leo answered.

"Hey, Leo. The skydiving jaunt fell through. Where's Judi?"

"Hello, Master. She's at the gym."

"Oh." His heart fell through the floor. "So how's it going with you two?"

"Not swimmingly, I'm afraid. There's trouble in paradise, as you say."

"What do you mean?" He felt a spark of hope.

"I have a feeling, figuratively speaking, that is, my mistress is beginning to find me a bit annoying."

"In what way?" A surge of hope coursed through his veins.

"The way I clean up her messes around here, the way I straighten books on the table and pictures on the wall...I don't know what her problem is. I'm only being perfect."

Felix sprang to his feet, elation surging through him. Thank you, God! A chance after all! His spirit soared. Leo wasn't what Judi really wanted; it was what she'd thought she wanted. Maybe this would have a happy ending after all. "Tell me about it." He tried to conceal the excitement in his voice. "Are you having arguments?"

"She yells at me a lot. I suppose you can say we

argue more than the average loving couple should. Milady has a temper on her that would scare Dracula away on a full moonlit night."

"Who's the one to make up afterward?"

"It's always her. But it's at longer and longer intervals each time. In fact, I can't remember if we're actually speaking right now or not."

"Thanks, I'll call her cell."

Leo expelled a long, bored sigh. "I wouldn't. I advised her to spend a few hours working out. Needs to tone up the flab, you know. I was going to keep this to myself, but quite frankly I'm rather at loose ends here. This routine is getting old. The two of us aren't as compatible as the three of us were."

Felix hesitated, needing a moment to take it all in. *Don't waste another second*, his heart told him. "Leo, your assignment may be about to end. How would you like to go somewhere that's out of this world? Literally?"

"You mean even better than the French Riviera or the Greek Isles or those exotic locales in the South Pacific that my memory banks recall having visited with colorful clarity?"

"Better than that."

"I'll go anywhere." His tone perked up. "Where did you have in mind?"

Felix brandished a sly grin. "You're an adventurous dude. I'll surprise you."

Felix could hear movement. Was Leo already packing? "Your wish is my command, Master. So how do I make my escape? You'll take me home for a tune-up and tell her I self-destructed?"

"No, just keep being your perfect self. Keep doing one perfect thing after another. It's the small things that add up." He glanced at himself in the mirror above the dresser and was surprised at how happy he looked. His eyes were bright, his grin lit up the whole room, and he was sitting up straight, his muscles straining under his T-shirt. He gave himself a mental pat on the back for hitting his home gym when creativity eluded him.

"She's very near the end of her rope, so she says. I grant her, it's been a long rope," Leo said.

"But I'm the one who's going to rescue her from all this. Then she'll realize what a mistake she made. When she's thinking straight again." He'd sit her down, clasp her hands, and convince her that he was the hero she'd always wanted. He couldn't rush her. But oh, how to contain his eagerness once he looked into her eyes again?

"Then you'll be all ready to say 'I told you so,' right, Master?"

"No, that would sound better coming from you."

"Operation Perfect is under way, Master. Have a pleasant journey." Leo put the phone down and drummed his manicured fingers on his cleft chin— now what else could he do to make her detest him? How does one improve upon perfect?

****

Judi searched long and hard for her nail clippers. She always kept them on the bathroom vanity. Now Mr. Neatoid had gone and put them away somewhere. "Why can't he stay the hell out of my—" She didn't want to ask him where they were; she wanted him out of her face for a while. She turned her bathroom inside out then glanced at her dresser at her manicure kit. There they were. Nail clippers. The most logical place. But not where she wanted them.

She went over to her nightstand to grab one of his bonbons and noticed a book placed there, on top of the book she'd been reading. "What's this?" She picked it up, scanning the cover. *Fight The Flab!* it shouted in big red letters, with its peppy subtitle, *One Hundred and One Ways to Knock Off the Jiggles, Bulges and Blubber.* The cover displayed a before and after photo of a model in a bikini. She hurled it against the wall. The piano music ceased as the resounding crash echoed through the loft.

Was that a hearty chuckle coming from the living room? No, it couldn't be. He wouldn't dare!

She missed Felix's company as desperately as she resented Frankenstein's presence in the next room. But Felix was skydiving, and she doubted he was thinking of her at 15,000 feet.

The strains of music penetrated the wall again. "He's here to stay, all right," she murmured, shaking her head.

"Just like I wanted."

But none of this had turned out the way she'd hoped, dreamed or planned. She had to talk to him. She sat in the chair next to her bedroom window and looked out over the barren courtyard. After rehearsing over and over in her mind, she was ready.

Ready for Leo's exit interview.

Judi entered the living room, anxious to get this over with. "Hello, Leo," She greeted him softly, her voice even, her attitude jovial as she sat across from him.

"Hello, Judi," he replied, his eyes fixed on the book in front of him. "Do you want to tell me the bad news?"

"What makes you so sure there's bad news?"

"You stalk off to your room, slam the door, and emerge with half a pound of pancake mix on your face, and you don't expect me to surmise that you're about to drop a bomb on my coiffed head?"

"We need to talk, Leo."

He looked up from his book, poised for a challenge. "About me, I presume, or should I not be so presumptuous this time?"

"No, Leo, this time you're right."

"Very well then." He put the book down. "That

dress exaggerates your hips—or were you going for that effect?"

She bit her tongue and took a deep breath. "Leo, I know how badly I thought I wanted you and how many hours Felix labored over you, but—"

"You left out how much you loved me."

"I did love you, and that's the problem. It's in the past tense." She sat at the edge of the sofa.

"You're saying you don't love me anymore." His voice didn't quaver. He was undeniably cool, not flinching a muscle, consistent with his custom-made character.

"I always wanted the perfect life with the man of my dreams—but he's not you."

"You realized I'm not your hero after all." He said it for her.

"No. You're not."

"And you want me out of your life, so you can be with the man you really love. Your real hero."

She looked up from her twisted hands, and stared into those confident yet plaintive eyes. He had to be hurting; how could he see his life take such an unexpected turn and not feel some inkling of remorse...even for a man as stolid as Leo?

"Yes, Leo. That's what I want."

A smile formed on his face. Her body relaxed, and her muscles loosened as the tension ebbed, giving her renewed repose with the deep breath she inhaled.

"That's what you want."

"Yes."

"You're sure of that, Judi?"

"Yes, Leo. I've done a lot of thinking. This would be best for all of us."

He rose from the sofa and stood over her, crossing his arms and tilting his head. He nodded, as if in agreement.

"Well, you haven't thought enough because you

obviously overlooked one moot point."

"What's that?"

"Whether or not I want to leave."

She shook her head and opened her mouth to protest. Inching up, she regarded the smug face, the erect posture, and the squared shoulders. No longer was he smiling in a way to ease her anguish. He was looking down at her, laughing. The nerve of this jerk!

"But you've got to leave. We put you here, and we can destroy you just as easily."

"Oh, and be charged with murder? I'm sure you and...your hero can very comfortably live with that the rest of your lives." He tossed his head with an arrogant

"Hmmph!"

"What are you talking about, murder? You're not human. You don't even exist."

"I exist, all right. I'm a living, breathing being. I'm as alive as you are, and if you or Felix or anyone else you may contract to eliminate me commits the act, it will be considered cold-plasminthed murder."

"B—but—" she stammered, searching for the next plausible argument. For the first time in her writing life, having composed some two million words, she was dumbstruck, and moreover, enraged at this creature with a microchip for a brain telling her that he'd stay as long as he jolly well pleased.

"You were put here to obey my every command," she countered. "And now that I want you to leave, you've got to leave."

"And go where, pray tell?" He cocked a brow and placed his fists on his hips in a challenging pose.

"Go meet a woman, and be a gigolo. Get a job in a department store as a mannequin...just vacate the premises."

He folded his arms across his chest and shook his head. "I don't wish to leave, ergo I don't intend to leave. You and Dr. Varlden created me. You can't just throw me under the bus when you decide you've tired of me, like a kid with a toy. You need to learn a lesson about responsibility, young lady." He turned and sauntered over to the piano, sat down and began playing "If Ever I Would Leave You."

"You're beginning to repulse me, you know that?" she shouted over the sounds of hammers and strings.

"That's your problem, isn't it, Judi?" he replied, his fingers not once leaving the keyboard or missing a beat. He closed his eyes and shut her out completely.

She fled to the quiet of her room. There had to be a way to send him out on his own or give him to someone. Donate him to a worthy cause. The city always needed volunteers.

She sat down and conjured up her muse for a hard brainstorming session.

Chapter Nineteen

Leo played the piano until darkness fell, and then as soon as the water pounded against the shower tiles, from his position in the living room, he walked over to the phone and made a call.

"Hello, Master," he said, idly adjusting his manly equipment underneath his tight pants. "It took much less time than I'd planned. I expected days. It took minutes. The rope snapped, just like you said. She can't stand the sight of my classically handsome face." He stopped just long enough to glance across the room at the full-length poster of himself in his classic pose, shirtless, in tight jeans halfway unzipped. "I expected her to drain all the plasminth from me, she's so desperate to be rid of me. But she's far too humanitarian to commit such a heinous act. Nevertheless, my time has come." He strolled over to the hall mirror.

"That was fast." Felix sounded like he couldn't wait to get there. "How'd you manage it?"

"She asked me to leave, and I told her I didn't want to." He drew close to the mirror and examined the arch of his brows. They didn't quite match in symmetrical perfection. Perhaps Felix had wanted to give him one flaw, to hint at human fallibility. But instead of interrupting this important conversation with it, he went into his bathroom and retrieved the eyebrow tweezers from his manicure kit.

"So that's all it took," Felix replied. "Hey, I made you cleverer than I thought."

"Not clever, just perfect." *At least I will be when my brows match*, he thought, using his steady dominant hand to pluck a few stray hairs under his right brow. "But she set herself up, I must admit. I told her I had no intention of leaving, 'til death do us part. She's over the edge now. So when will you be here to rescue my contrived plotline?"

"Now."

"You want me to tell her you're coming?" Finished tweezing, he lifted one brow, then the other, striking a jaunty pose.

"No, don't say anything. Don't do anything. Just sit and look pretty until I get there."

"Oh, I look pretty, all right." He dipped a finger in his Vaseline jar and smoothed down his newly shaped symmetrical brows. "I don't think I could do any more damage if I wanted to. She couldn't hate me more if she loved me."

****

Still without a sensible humane solution for the Leo problem, Judi stood under the spray, each warm droplet a comforting ebb to her anxiety.

Right now he could be out there destroying everything I own, she thought, *or plotting to kill me in the shower!* She wished she hadn't seen *Psycho* so many times.

She loathed herself for having asked Felix to make her dream a reality. How could a real Race Parsec be so different from the one who lived in her mind?

Then it hit her like a flash of light—the real Race Parsec traveled through space, to distant planets, an intergalactic hero. Leo could do the same!

Her heart pounded with excitement. This idea could work! It would be the perfect outcome. It would make everybody happy! He could be the co-pilot to the spaceman Felix was designing.

Slowly pulling the curtain aside, she emerged, peering around. He was nowhere in sight.

Drying herself off, she opened the bathroom door a crack, peering around her bedroom. No sign he'd been in here either.

She donned a low-cut black dress, preparing to march into the living room and pitch her offer: co-pilot on ORBIT's first space mission, so he could live on the planet Megasus. It would be his chance to make history, to live his dream of walking on another world.

With the words carefully arranged in her mind like a plot outline, she straightened her spine, took a deep breath, and entered the living room. But what she saw made her halt in her tracks.

Her breathing and her heart stopped.

Felix stood before her, his arms awaiting her embrace.

She blinked more than once to make sure it was really him and she wasn't fantasizing again. But it was Felix, undoubtedly and unquestionably Felix. As her gaze strayed across the room, she saw Leo with not a trace of arrogance or defiance in his expression. In fact, he looked pleased to see Judi so happy to find him waiting for her.

Yes, he was truly her real hero; he had been all along. She found her voice, but it refused to work as she mouthed his name, the sound barely escaping her throat. "Felix."

"It's me." He smiled, opening his arms to accommodate her and all the love she'd suppressed for so many years. Love that took half her lifetime to grow, love nourished by absence and loneliness, a feeling she couldn't find words to describe.

With two leaps she was in his arms, clasping him, grabbing bunches of his hair, and inhaling that scent that had lingered in her mind for years.

Leo, a hazy blur in the background, seemed to fade into vapor as she closed her eyes and felt Felix's lips on hers, warmly inviting her to join him.

She kissed him, breathed his scent, and felt his hands setting her on fire. Rockets flared behind her closed lids, and she heard music—the sweet tinkling of velvet hammers striking strings, sending strains of love into the air—it was Leo playing her favorite piece of all time, Anton Rubinstein's "Romance."

He played for them, an unspoken request. The dance floor was all theirs as they floated away together, the only song ever written, the song composed just for them.

"Our song," he whispered as the music played on and on.

****

The music stopped. Their bodies parted, and Judi looked into the eyes of the man she loved. It all came together at once, like the final piece of a jigsaw puzzle.

"Felix," she whispered, "There's something I have to tell you. I'm in love with you. Please don't ever leave again."

He gave her a reassuring hug. "I'm not going anywhere."

She buried her face in his hair, inhaling its clean spicy scent, so *him.* "I've made such a terrible mistake, and I need to—"

"Shhh." He touched his finger to her lips. "We'll work it out, I promise."

"Felix, I know what to do about..." She tossed her head toward the piano. "I have the most radical, profound idea. But it's also so simple and obvious that I don't know why it didn't clock us both over the heads before."

His eyes widened as if he'd forgotten that Leo existed. He turned to the piano player. "Leo, you know where I live, don't you?"

"I certainly do, Master."

He reached into his pocket. "Here's twenty bucks. Go hail a cab. Wait for me on my porch."

"As you wish." Leo rose, pulled the lid over the keyboard, and headed for the door. "Good night, Master." His voice softened, and a warm smile accompanied the solemn nod. "Goodbye, Judi. The pleasure was all mine."

"Goodbye, Leo." She watched as the man she thought she'd wanted for seven years and grown to despise in two months, walked out her door and out of her life.

She turned back to Felix, grasping his arm to reassure herself that it was really him. She suddenly remembered clutching Leo's arm in the exact same manner as she'd tried to convince herself that her dream had indeed come true.

Dream!

She'd never wish for another dream to come true—ever.

"Felix, I was ready to offer him an allowance so he could start a new life somewhere and—I couldn't think of anywhere in this world." She relaxed her grip on his arm but didn't let go, her need to touch him nearly as powerful as her need to purge Leo from her life. "So I thought—how about out of this world? He could be a real-life Race. Just as I created him."

He smiled, and his eyes lit up. Their gazes locked.

"How does a voyage to Megasus sound?" she said. "On the most ambitious mission known to modern mankind? As your spaceman's co-pilot?"

"It sounds like something a brilliant author would come up with. You'll never believe me, but I thought of the same thing. Not because I'm so brilliant. I just couldn't think of one damn place on Earth for him to go. So I set my sights a little farther." He lifted her chin and gave her a quick kiss. "The headlines will read, 'ORBIT sends two manmade beings to Megasus on spacecraft Infinity

Seven. Leo and Lily.'"

"Wait—" She took a second to catch her breath. "Who is Lily?"

He smiled, and for the first time she saw a hint of pride in his eyes, in his posture. "My astronaut. I just finished creating her last week. You gave me the idea when you said 'Why not create the perfect woman?' And she is perfect—for the voyage, that is. The spacecraft is due for launch in exactly ninety days' time. Its payload will be two environmentally controlled humanoids, two perfect specimens—why send Lily alone?"

She shook her head in wonder. "So you created a woman, too. I hope they'll be very happy on Megasus together. I wonder which one of us thought of it first," she joked.

"Chances are I did. I saw him getting to you, and you making a valiant effort to make it work. But it doesn't matter who thought of it first. It just shows great minds think alike." He gave her a wink, and she melted into his arms.

"Oh, Felix, I don't have a great mind like yours, just a creative one."

"But Judi, every one of your stories has a happy ending, the result of conflicts and obstacles, one worse than the next. Our main obstacle, who also brought us together, can explore a distant solar system."

She was so happy she could feel her heart smiling.

"Yes, it is stranger than any fiction I've ever dreamed up. Remember his biggest dream was to travel in space? He'll be a hero, all right...a nonhuman hero, but he'll certainly be a hit up there on Megasus. I'm sure he'll achieve some recognition here on Earth as well...he may even be the first humanoid to receive the Nobel Prize. There'll be no living with him then!"

"I don't know exactly when it happened, but I began to realize that this guy was the complete opposite of you, and I grew to despise him. So what I really wanted was the opposite of him. But I didn't realize that 'til it was too late. You'd already brought Mr. Universe here, and I was resigned to living happily ever after with him. But I just couldn't do it, Felix. I couldn't live like that. Pretending we were perfect together. Faking it."

"I'm grateful I have a chance with you I never thought I'd have." He stroked her hair. "I've always loved you, Judi. I never stopped loving you."

"Why didn't you ever tell me?" She was on the edge of breathlessness.

"I never dreamed I'd have a future with you. Our lives went in different directions, and our paths never had a reason to cross. Then when you told me you wanted a life with this guy whose traits were the exact opposite of mine, I knew I was on the bench for good."

"But if you wanted me for yourself, why did you create this perfect lover for me?"

"I wanted you to be happy. I put you before myself, just like I do with anyone I care about. When you said you wanted this relationship and told me all the requirements, which were everything I wasn't, I knew I'd never have a chance in hell. But I still wanted you to be happy."

His eyes looked into hers, their souls connecting, making her want to kiss away all his hurt. Knowing he cared this much for her brought tears to her eyes.

"Felix, no one has ever put me ahead of themselves." She wiped away tears streaming down her cheeks. "When Ryan left me—" Her words choked her. "I thought it was me. What had I done to deserve that?"

She squeezed her eyes shut as the warmth of her tears comforted her. Somehow she knew these were the last tears she'd ever shed over this, and for one final cleansing, she let her emotions take over.

"They'd both betrayed me because I'd achieved success, something out of their reach. So I realized I couldn't have both love and success. I plowed on with my career and vowed never to trust anyone again. It took years to realize there was nothing wrong with me. All I'd ever wanted was a career and a man who loved me. But Ryan wasn't able to handle that.

"He wanted Alyssa instead, who was happy to cook and clean for him and give him babies. I thought they were sad, settling for each other. I wanted more than that. So I created Race. He gave me everything I wanted. But now I realize even the breathing Race can't give me what I need. To simply love me. I'm ready to put my heart on the line again, because I'm ready to love—not revere, worship, or idolize."

He gathered her in his arms and held her close. "Then I'm glad I waited for the prize. It was a long, painful wait, but it was worth it. But—let's face it, Judi, I'd have to be way low in the self-esteem department to be too jealous of a live fiction hero."

They shared a chuckle.

"He's what I thought I always wanted, though," she said. "Perfect in every way. So perfect, he'd never break my heart. But I was taking the easy way out. Now I know that love is a risk, but without that risk, what's the alternative? A life of loneliness and lost dreams. Endless nights by the computer with no one but truffles and made-up characters to keep me company. How heartbreaking is that?"

He nodded and met her gaze. "I know exactly how heartbreaking it is because I've been doing the exact same thing all these years. Looking everywhere for substitute Judis. Women who resembled you in the slightest way. I only went for women who reminded me of you. It got to the point where I was dating my students if they reminded me of you. But it was far from fulfilling. If anything, it was more frustrating."

"Well, you don't have to do that anymore. You've got the real me now."

"It's finally come true, then." They embraced tightly. "I never felt fulfilled, Judi, even with everything I've accomplished in the world of science. That's why I kept pushing myself. Something was missing, and I didn't know what. Now I know."

Something tickled the back of her brain. "By the way, who was that woman you were getting into a cab with a few weeks ago?" She tore her gaze from him and shifted her eyes away. "I'm just curious. It's none of my business, but—"

"You saw me?"

"Iris saw you." She returned her gaze to him, knowing he'd tell her the truth.

He rolled his eyes, shook his head and frowned, looking peeved and amused at the same time. "That was only Lily. I thought the least I could do for her was take her out on the town before she blasted off. I thought it was pretty cool, her going solo, the first female nonhuman astronaut to ever travel into space. But now, we're going to launch the first nonhuman opposite-sex couple into space. And believe me when I say they're made for each other. She's even more perfect than he is."

She broke out into a huge grin, feeling like a matchmaker who'd made the perfect match. "Oh, Felix, it's all perfect!"

"Not really." He looked down and around the room. "It was meant to happen."

"Felix, hold me forever," she whispered into his hair. "Now I want my hero to make passionate love to me."

"You don't want to wait until the wedding?"

Her eyes widened and her heart leapt. "You—

want to marry me?"

"If you don't mind being stepmother to a couple of parakeets and hanging upside down with me once in a while."

"Let's try it horizontal first." She led him into the bedroom, which she and Leo never shared. "How about I light a fire and we can gaze into the flames—and at each other."

Thankfully it was a gas fire and only took the flick of a match to get a warm glow flickering. "Right after this." She wound her arms around his neck, those brilliant eyes closed, and their lips met. A soft moan escaped from deep within her throat as he stroked her cheek with feathery touches. She parted her lips to probe shyly with her tongue, and he followed her lead. Before another rational thought entered her mind, his arms encircled her, she stroked his hair, and her heart quickened.

"Oh, Judi, I've waited so long for this." He sought her lips and they kissed deeply.

Her body grew rigid and weak at the same time. Breathing heavily, she inhaled his clean scent as he warmed her with his closeness.

For an instant, she was beyond thinking as his mouth consumed hers in demanding but patient intensity. As she shifted her body to mold against his, he eased her away, studying her in the fire glow. His eyes, sparkling like rare gems, gazed at her lovingly. "May I take you to bed, or would you like to make love here in front of the fire?"

"I can't wait another minute, Felix," she whispered, wanting him badly. And, with a furtive glance, she saw that he wanted her. There wouldn't be any time for teasing—not the first time.

"I want this to be special, Judi. Come with me." He held his hand out to her and led her to her king-sized bed. She knew that even stripping the bed would ruin this intense moment. Still in each other's arms, he lowered her to the bed and slowly, torturously, began removing her clothes. She tried to help him along, but he stayed her fingers with a soft touch.

"Let me." He planted kisses on her neck, her earlobes, and the sensitive buds of her breasts. She unbuttoned his top shirt button, but before she could explore further, he pulled away. "First I want to see you. Do you know, Judi, I've always wanted to see your beautiful body naked." He opened her blouse and removed her pants, taking his time. "I've pictured you in my arms so many times, and I've wanted to make love to you in a big bed, in firelight—just like this."

"I didn't know—" How many years had they wasted?

"Just like this." He slid her bra and panties off her and tossed them aside. Now she was completely naked, her arms reaching out for him. "You're just as beautiful as I always imagined." With gentle strokes, he caressed her until she was on fire. Yet he was still fully clothed.

"May I?" She wasn't nearly as patient as he was. She tried to disrobe him without ripping his shirt or tearing off any buttons. But he lay back and let her do everything. "Felix, you're like a marble statue. You've even got a better body than—what's his name," she said when every thread of his clothing was finally off. Muscles bulged in his arms; his broad chest boasted a mat of gold hair. Fully aroused, he was simply gorgeous.

She didn't wait for any more gentle caresses or teasing kisses. He entered her, and they moved together with exquisite and matched urgency. She arched her back as her desire intensified. The fire within her blazed and leapt as their bodies eased and tensed. She closed her eyes and felt his passion pour into her.

In the aftermath of release, he clasped her hands as they caught their breaths and gazed lovingly into each other's eyes.

"When you're ready again, we'll go real slow," he promised, kissing her lightly, igniting those fires again, just when she thought she was satiated.

"We have a lot of catching up to do, Felix. Maybe in about five years, we'll start going slow." They shared a laugh and the warmth and passion only two in love could share.

****

It was the middle of the night. All was quiet. Judi lay with her head resting on Felix's chest, her fingers laced through his hair. "It's like we never parted, isn't it, Felix?" she asked as she twined her hand around his.

"No. Only I never imagined it being this good."

"Well, I did!"

His lips sought hers once again, gently. Gentleness—what a novelty.

****

Felix let himself into his house and tossed his jacket over the banister. He flipped on the basement light and scanned his lab, his gaze halting on the handsome figure reclining on the cot.

"Ready for your rendezvous with destiny, Leo?" he asked, unconsciously picking up a pencil and sliding it behind his ear.

"I certainly am, Master. Where is Lily?"

"Your lifelong companion and co-commander at this minute is in a Fifth Avenue salon getting a permanent—and I do mean permanent."

"She'll be even more ravishing," Leo said. "I'm bringing a generous supply of styling gel for us. Weightlessness will make our hair float." He combed his fingers through his locks. "I can't wait for blastoff, my place in history, my stab at immortality, my gorgeous face—and hers, of course—plastered across every television screen on Earth. And while we're up there, I may write my memoirs."

Felix gave his creation a playful cuff on the jaw. "Don't bother. Nobody would ever believe a word of it." He smiled, turning to leave.

"Master, I have one request—"

"Yes?"

"Now that I'm fated for the stars, can I perform one last earthly act?"

"What's that?"

"Can I peel off these scrotum-hugging briefs already? They're strangling me!"

Felix laughed, giving his creation a thumbs-up. "By all means, jocko."

"Oh, thank heaven." He started wriggling out of the briefs.

"But, hey—I don't have to watch." Felix flipped a switch, plunging the lab into darkness.

Chapter Twenty

The next week flew by in a whirlwind of banquets, television appearances, and adoring crowds. Dr. Felix Varlden, creator of the first beings to travel beyond Earth's solar system, was now the most famous scientist in the world.

Judi was there at his side, her heart bursting with pride, but he couldn't see what all the fuss was about.

"They're the ones who went, not me," he insisted, shucking off his tux after another black tie dinner.

****

Cape Canaveral gleamed in the sun on launch day. Felix and Judi stood at the edge of the roaring crowd as countdown commenced, the spacecraft poised, ready for the heavens. The rockets ignited, and in a blast of bright orange flame, the craft shot upward, leaving a trail of vapor in its wake. On its way to worlds unknown, it dwindled and shrank to a minute speck.

The crowd cheered wildly as Felix whispered in her ear, "Another happy ending."

****

Judi and Felix sat on their hotel balcony, gazing into the heavens. She feasted her eyes on the most beautiful sky she had ever seen. The stars were like diamonds splashed upon the blue velvet canopy above them, and her heart burst with love for the man next to her.

"I wonder how Leo and Lily are doing," she wondered out loud, nestling her head against his shoulder.

"They should be there by this time next year," he replied as they continued to gaze into the infinite vastness. "Mission Control's been keeping a close eye on them."

She laughed, remembering the anguish Leo had put her through, with his incessant criticism, his compulsive neatness, his unbearable conceit... "I'm glad I can laugh at it now." She focused on one twinkling star.

"He made me realize how much I'd always loved you."

"As long as the characters live happily ever after, isn't that the old chestnut that'll never wear out?" He reached over and wrapped his arm around her shoulders. She sought his lips and kissed him warmly.

"It's what the readers want." Her eyes followed the curve of the Big Dipper, hanging so low in the sky, she felt she could reach out and pluck each star like a diamond pin. "You gave me what I wanted. I wanted perfect, and I got it. I sure asked for it, didn't I?" It was a rhetorical question, but she knew he'd come up with an answer.

"Just be careful what you ask for in the future." Felix chuckled. "You know the saying 'When the gods want to punish us, they answer our prayers.'"

Resting her head on his chest, she mused over how Leo had brought her and Felix together. "I thought he was out of this world."

"And he always will be, my love," he said, while caressing her cheek. "He always will be."

Epilogue

Leo smoothed down his hair and gazed out the porthole of Infinity Seven. No human being had ever known such peace.

He turned to his co-pilot and space traveling companion of the last fifteen years. She was as beautiful as the moment they'd first met, when Felix opened his lab door. Leo had staggered backward at her beauty, the lush head of dark hair, bright blue eyes, smooth complexion, and full kissable lips. And of course neither of them had aged a minute. They never would.

"Planetfall is in two days, so we need to begin our final check of the systems and equipment, my dear." He smiled and held out his hand.

Lily grasped his hand and tossed a lock of raven tresses over her shoulder. "Aye-aye, Captain, but we should address each other formally while we're up here in the crew cabin. You never know who might be listening back on Earth. If only they knew about the gravity-defying acts we perform back in the living quarters!"

"Roger. I copy." He gave her a silent wink and flicked his tongue at her. Then he checked the environmental generation systems and terraforming gear. Glowing red lights on the console informed him that the two huge cylinders of Enviroplasm, used to render alien atmospheres as Earthlike as possible, were ready for deployment.

With the end of their tranquil passage finally in sight, a blinking light at the far end of the control panel caught his eye. When it flashed like this it meant one thing—crisis. "Lily—we may have a malfunction here. But don't worry. I'll save you."

Static from the emergency receiver shattered the silence of his cabin. A voice followed, controlled but strained, and unmistakably female. "Earthbase Six, this is Serenity Base. We're under attack!"

Good God, someone out here who speaks American English!

Locking onto the signal from his communications panel, he hoped she would receive his signal. "This is Infinity Seven. What's your location?"

A gasp of surprise pierced the static. "The planet Ugur. A huge ship is hovering a few hundred feet over us and just dropped some kind of—uh—" She paused, and for a second he thought he'd lost her— "canister that our environmental instruments says altered our atmosphere to hydrogen-based. We only have a few more hours of oxygen left!"

Ugur. He checked his charts. It was a mere fifty thousand miles away. He looked out the porthole. A Mercury-sized planet loomed ahead, the fourth planet out from Megasus, and the next-door neighbor of the planet he was heading for. But why the hell would anyone be down there? Without further thought, he altered Infinity's course on the console computer and headed straight for Ugur.

"We don't have any weapons aboard, but I'll help you out. This is as good a time for me to save the universe as any."

"I just got word that the aliens have landed and Omega Section is under attack now. The aliens are killing them!" The transmission ended in a heart-wrenching sob.

Leo shouldn't have felt sadness; it hadn't been programmed into him. But he experienced it the night he left Earth forever—the only home he'd ever known. He glanced over at Lily as she wiped away a tear. His heart clenched, After all these years of being confined to a fifty-foot spacecraft, light-years from Earth, they were still so much in love.

Twenty thousand miles out, he attempted contact again. "This is Infinity Seven. Do you read me?" He hoped with all his heart he'd find the woman on Ugur well and thriving. Whoever she was, wherever she'd come from—he knew what she'd been through. It was a strong, heartfelt connection—something impossible to explain to any human.

"I read you, Infinity."

He was so relieved he almost smiled. "I'm entering your atmosphere. I see the alien ship. Whereabouts are you?"

"About five miles northwest of where the ship landed."

He could see it more clearly now, a huge blimp-shaped craft that could swallow Manhattan. "Suit up, and get indoors," he told her.

"We are. Those of us who are left. Omega section is completely wiped out, but before they died, they told us how horrible these aliens are. They have putrid yellow bodies—"

"They're not in suits?"

"They don't need them. They're breathing the hydrogen they released. They've converted our atmosphere. The canister that exploded changed the atmosphere!" A renewed panic invaded her voice.

"Stay calm, I'm coming in."

He headed for an airstrip on Serenity Base. As he made his final approach, he thought how ironic it was when one species alters a planet to suit their needs; it can wreak havoc on the other species.

Then it hit him like an avalanche. *That's it!*

He released the Enviroplasm, meant for his mission to Megasus, but they needed it here more. He couldn't let any more people die.

He hovered over the base and observed the alien

craft. Horrid creatures staggered around, clutched their chests, and dropped like flies, suffocating in the oxygen-rich air. They couldn't even make it back to their ship. He did it!

He made a perfect three-point landing on the runway and peered out the window. Lily reached over, and they embraced briefly. "Sit tight, my princess." He gave her a kiss on the cheek.

A suited figure ran toward Infinity, arms waving, leaping across the tarmac in the light gravity, like a film in slow motion.

"Stay here, Lily, and watch over the controls. I'll come back for you in a few moments."

"I obey, Commander." She dug into her supply satchel and extracted a can of mousse, squirted a dollop into her palm, and smoothed it through her hair.

"Let me have some of that," Leo commanded. He arranged his own pompadour in the shiny metal control panel, opened the hatch, and climbed down the steps to touch upon the ground. Just as he turned, the woman was in his arms, sobbing.

"Oh, thank you, thank you! You saved our lives, God, you saved us!"

He returned her embrace and took a deep breath of the oxygen he'd released. "No, I'm not God. Just a visitor from Earth doing a good deed."

"You're on the mission to Megasus, aren't you? We heard about you on the news feed."

He still couldn't see her face, only his reflection in her helmet, bent and warped and looking strangely like something out of a science fiction movie. "Yes, but where did you come from? And how long have you been here?"

"We're with the United States Marine Space Corps. On a top-secret mission. Not a civilian alive knows we're here. Well—until now."

"I can safely assume that due to the nature of

my mission, I can qualify as a non-civilian. Don't worry. Your secret is safe with me."

"This is an extraterrestrial Area Fifty-One of sorts. Don't ask me to explain any more."

"I can't even ask you to explain what you look like?"

He grinned, and she shrugged, lifting the helmet off to reveal a pleasant smile, wide-set blue eyes, and a dewy complexion. She was aesthetically pleasing enough, but no beauty like Lily. Must be human. "Marine Lieutenant Nastasia West, sir." She held out her hand, and they shook. "How can I ever thank you? You're a hero."

"Just doing what I was made to do," he answered as modestly as he could manage.

"What did they name you?"

"Leo—I mean—Race Parsec, my lady. At your service."

A word about the author...

Diana has written several historicals set in England and the U.S., and two time travel romances.

Diana is a member of Romance Writers of America and the Richard III Society. In her spare time, she has been pursuing a Master's degree in archaeology and loves to visit historical sites all over the world.

Diana and her husband own CostPro, Inc., an engineering business based in Cambridge. She is Director of Marketing.

Visit Diana at www.dianarubino.com
www.DianaRubinoAuthor.blogspot.com

Thank you for purchasing
this Wild Rose Press publication.
For other wonderful stories of romance,
please visit our on-line bookstore at
www.thewildrosepress.com

For questions or more information,
contact us at
info@thewildrosepress.com

The Wild Rose Press
www.TheWildRosePress.com